MU[illegible] PEMBROKESHIRE

An absolutely gripping crime mystery full of twists

GRETTA MULROONEY

Tyrone Swift Book 8

JOFFE BOOKS

Joffe Books, London
www.joffebooks.com

First published in Great Britain in 2021

Cover design by Nick Castle

ISBN: 978-1-78931-739-8

For Eve

PROLOGUE

He'd never liked secrets. There had been too many when he was a child — adults murmuring over his head, fragments of sentences, conversations that stopped when he entered a room. Childhood had been a puzzle, an insoluble riddle, and he had never worked out the meaning.

The matron at his boarding school had been keen on riddles. But they hadn't been fun. She'd used them to tease and bully, choosing her victims at random, belittling her target in front of the others when he couldn't come up with the answer. He could still remember the one she'd set him the night he'd arrived. He'd been wearing his new pyjamas, their stiff label scratching his neck. He'd stood, lost, in the huge, chilly dormitory with its rows of beds like an army barracks.

Only one colour, but not one size,
Stuck at the bottom, but easily flies.
Present in sun, but not in rain,
Doing no harm and feeling no pain.
What is it?

He'd been ten, homesick and bewildered. He had been aware of dozens of eyes focused on him and had felt like the fox must when the hounds are circling. They were waiting for him to fail. When he did, he'd heard some sniggers. Matron had told him he was as much use as a fart in a jam-jar. The others had laughed, glad that they weren't in the spotlight. He'd never discovered the answer. Many years later, in his twenties, he'd recalled that riddle one sleepless night and had googled it. The answer was *shadow*.

Secrets were heavy. If you could touch them, they'd burn you. They could imprison you. He'd thought up a riddle with *secret* as the answer:

If you have it, you want to share it,
But when you share it, you no longer have it.

He didn't like secrets, yet he had one of his own. He could still hear those terrible screams. They had shattered a sunlit day. The blood had stained the fissures in the rocks, darkening as it dried. When he'd realised what had happened, he'd begun to shiver, as in deep winter. For months afterwards he'd been unable to get warm. Even on this benign day, the recollection gave him goose pimples.

He'd managed to keep the lid on that chapter in his history. Just. Secrets seemed to follow at his heels like the Labrador that sometimes tracked him up and down the beach. Now someone had breathed yet another unwelcome confidence in his ear. His heart had sunk. He hadn't wanted to listen but of course, he was a soft touch. Always had been. His defences had never been strong. He was a quiet man, shy and slow to give his opinion. People misread his reserve as wisdom and interpreted his silence as an invitation to speak. And this person had wanted to share the secret so badly, whispering through warm, close breath, setting out their stall, drawing him in. How could he refuse to listen and to help?

Life had been simpler once. Not entirely free of worries, but with room to breathe. He'd done some good, lent a helping hand when it was needed. It was important to heal wounds, try to make things whole when they'd splintered. You had to do your best to put things right. He'd been doing his best since the day that blood was spilled, because he could never make that broken body whole again.

He walked on, contemplating the burden of what he knew. He didn't want to intervene, although in the end he'd probably have to. But there was a chance that this meeting might bring resolution. He would speak calmly, measure his words, and present the only honourable course of action. Maybe the person waiting for him wanted a way out.

He was almost there.

He put out his hand and brushed the cow parsley that fringed the path, bringing his palm to his nose to sniff its sweetness.

And strode on to meet his death.

CHAPTER 1

Tyrone Swift went into the café, slung down his backpack, threw himself into a chair and heaved a sigh of relief. He loosened his tie. Halfway through the court hearing, he'd noticed a crust of dried chocolate on it and knew that Branna, his sticky-fingered daughter, had been rifling through his wardrobe again. She was going through a phase of wanting to try on his clothes, which was fine by him, except for the mess it caused. He kept finding his shirts inside out, his jeans crumpled and his jackets on the floor. He was no clothes horse — his cousin Mary kindly said that his frayed look was shabby chic — and he could never fathom where buttons vanished to, but he tried to achieve a reasonably tidy appearance for clients and when needed, judges. Branna's mother, an educational psychologist, had explained to him that their daughter understood that she was a girl, but she wanted to experiment. 'She's trying out being male, it's part of her development,' Ruth had told him. He wondered if that was reading too deeply into it. He reckoned it was pure mischief and wished that his daughter would try it out instead on Marcel, Ruth's partner. Marcel was always so bloody tidy and *ironed*.

A waiter hovered, smiling, iPad in hand, for his order.

'I'm waiting for a friend, but in the meantime, a large glass of merlot would be great,' Swift said. 'The sooner the wine arrives, the better I'll feel.'

It was before him in seconds, ruby red and smelling of cloves and plums. He took a deep draught and held some in his mouth for a moment. Velvety, rich, heavenly. *Here's to us, Cedric,* he murmured. He'd been in court all morning, attending a hearing about Cedric's will, of which he was sole executor. Cedric Sheridan, his dear deceased friend and tenant, had left twenty thousand pounds to his son Oliver, a hundred and fifty thousand each to Swift and Milo, one of his oldest friends, and twenty thousand to various others. Oliver had challenged the will and then appealed a court decision upholding it. He alleged that Swift had pressurised Cedric, prevented him from seeing his son and blocked phone calls. He'd also claimed that Swift had influenced Cedric into changing his previous will, which named Oliver as the main beneficiary.

The tedious and worrying business had been dragging on for months. Today the judge had ruled that there was no evidence that Cedric had been influenced or manipulated and had upheld the terms of the will. Oliver had been furious. He'd turned up to court in a khaki artist's smock, daubed with dried plaster. When he'd sneezed, he'd shaken free a haze of dust. Presumably, he'd thought that the judge might respond sympathetically to the *I'm an impoverished, hard-done-by sculptor* guise, but she'd regarded him scathingly. Her decision was final, and Oliver would have to like it or lump it. Swift was just glad it was over, and hoped he'd never have to see the obnoxious man again or have anything to do with Camilla Finley, the journalist who'd been advising and helping Oliver.

Swift stretched his long legs. His phone pinged with a text from his friend Mark Gill, saying he'd been delayed but should be there very soon. Swift scrolled to his emails. Now that Oliver Sheridan was out of his life, he could relax and attend to an invitation from his old friend Afan to visit him in West Wales. It was a good time to take a break. Branna was away in Guernsey with Ruth for the summer and when they returned, she was due to have an operation for cochlear implants. That would be a worrying time. He and Ruth had spent months weighing up the pros and cons of surgery. Branna's hearing aids and use of sign language were helping her to work around her significant impairment. Implants might boost her hearing and confidence and open up her options to make decisions about speaking or signing. The downside was that she could lose any remaining hearing if they didn't work well. Whatever happened, they would have a major impact on her life. They would change her.

He had no work lined up for now and he was jaded after the lengthy tussle with Oliver. His on/off relationship with Nora Morrow, a DI in the Met, had ground to a halt, leaving him saddened but mainly relieved. She'd moved on to Fitz Blackmore, a detective who'd been a mutual friend. Swift missed her humour and quick wit but not her prickliness and unpredictable temper. When he'd told his cousin Mary that he and Nora were no longer together, she'd said, '*I won't pretend I'm not relieved. She has a good reputation in the Met, but she's too volatile up close and personal. I'd decided to kidnap you if you ever indicated that you were going to move in with her.*' Mary believed he had bad judgement where women were concerned. She might be right. A period of solitude would be a sensible idea.

A few days in Wales, far from personal baggage, solicitors, courts and London's muggy August fumes was an attractive prospect. He found the email that Afan Griffith had sent in July. It had been unexpected — they'd worked together at Interpol in Lyon over ten years ago but hadn't been in touch since. He'd been pleased at the contact.

Hi there, Ty, long time no see or hear. I meant to keep in touch, but you know how it goes, which always sounds a feeble excuse. I have thought of you and wondered how you're doing. I see from your website that you're now working as a private investigator. I'd love to hear more about that.

I've been living in this remote place for some time. I'm back in the land of my fathers, near Holybridge, in Pembrokeshire. I live and work in Tir Melys — it means Sweet Land — a community of small-holdings, and I love it here. It's remote, peaceful and quiet. I feel that I'm doing some good. The frantic, workaday world seems wonderfully far away. It's hard graft, growing my own food, but rewarding, and I'd never go back to the 9-to-5 daily grind. I'm also into beekeeping in a big way. Like the honey, life is mainly sweet. People here have their differences but that's true of any community. There is a sour note that troubles me and plays on my mind. I'd like to run it by you, check out your perspective.

Do you fancy a couple of days in Pembrokeshire? Plenty of room here and it would be great to catch up. There's no Wi-Fi, I have to come into Holybridge for that, usually over the weekend. Although I have a phone, it's turned off here as the signal's non-existent, so just turn up if you can — or there's always snail mail and the communal landline here — number below. I'm adding a link to the Tir Melys website, to whet your appetite.

Hope to catch up soon, Afan.

He'd replied, saying it was great to be back in touch and that the lack of contact was just as much his responsibility. He'd explained that he needed to get a court hearing out of the way, but then he'd be delighted to visit in August. He tried the landline number now, but it rang out with no voicemail, so he sent an email. Today was Thursday, so he assumed that Afan would pick it up in the next couple of days, in Holybridge.

Hi, Afan. The court case is over now, and decks are cleared. I'll head your way on Monday. It'll be good to catch up after so many years and swap experiences. Tir Melys looks fascinating. Should be with you mid-afternoon.

The door banged and Mark Gill crossed to the table. 'Hi, so sorry I'm late — combination of a lengthy phone call and traffic.' He pulled out a chair and wiped his forehead with the back of a hand. 'This weather's too much and I'm sure the heater was on in my cab.'

'No worries. The rest of my day is blissfully free.'

'Wish I could say the same.' Mark gestured at the wine. 'I hope that's in celebration.'

'It certainly is. Oliver lost and it's over. Jubilation!'

'What a relief! I shouldn't, but I'll have a glass to keep you company. Shall we order?'

They examined the menu and gave their order. Mark rearranged the paper napkins and shoved the stand of olive oil and balsamic vinegar to one side. He was a jumpy, intense man, who spoke, moved and acted rapidly. Even when sitting, he shifted restlessly. He talked constantly in a stream of ideas that were often hard to follow. Swift, who could be still and silent, often watched him with fascination. He'd worked with Mark at the Met, sitting at a desk near him. He'd got used to him suddenly spinning on his chair, clockwise and then anticlockwise when he was on the phone. His nickname at work had been Twitcher.

They clinked glasses. Swift reached into his backpack and handed over a magazine. 'Here, a gift for you.'

Mark laughed. 'Snap! I've got one for you.' He took a magazine from his pocket and placed it in front of Swift.

Swift examined the copy of *Detective Fiction Weekly* from July 1928. It featured *The Cult Murders* by Alan Forsyth. The cover illustration showed a sinister man with brilliantined hair and a waxed moustache. 'Thanks. I don't have this Forsyth. How's my choice for you?'

'Terrific. I have some *Front Page Detective*s, but not a 1943.' The major story in Mark's magazine was *Chinese Beauty and the Bloody Dagger*, with a mysterious woman on the cover.

They sat in silence for a couple of minutes, sipping wine and leafing through their magazines. They both enjoyed crime pulp fiction, although Mark was a more avid collector, and whenever they met, they always discussed their joint interest. They sourced vintage magazines from many sellers, including a shop in Soho that stocked an extensive selection. Swift had spent many enjoyable rainy afternoons in its musty basement. As well as the stories, he enjoyed the adverts: '*Zippo, the gift that never fails.*' '*Enjoy sundown with relaxing cocktails at Laguna Beach.*' '*Inspire his passion when you wear Paris Nights.*'

Mark put his magazine down. 'Did you say you'd heard from Afan Griffith?'

'That's right. He's living in Wales now. I'm going to see him next week.'

'Give him my best, he's a sound man. Thoughtful, too — he sent me a copy of a 1937 *Black Mask* that one time I liaised with him. He did most of the work, really, so it was generous of him.'

'I'll pass that on. I'm not sure why he left Interpol and headed to rural Wales. Do you have any idea?'

Mark was tucking into his mushroom risotto. 'I heard it was something to do with bullying. Not Afan as the bully, obviously. I believe that he had problems with his section boss.'

They talked on about work, while Mark fiddled with the table settings.

'I heard you and Nora aren't together now,' he said.

'That's right. She's seeing someone else.'

'You okay about it?'

Swift said, 'I'm not heartbroken and clearly, neither is she. I'll miss going to the Parterre. I like it there, but it's Nora's favourite bar so . . . best to give it a miss for a while.' He didn't fancy wandering in and spotting Nora and Fitz together.

Mark chased the last grains of rice around his plate and flicked a quick glance at him. 'I never thought you went that well together, to be honest. Hope you don't mind me saying.'

'That seems to have been the general opinion. When it was good it was great, but the cracks showed too often.' He gestured at the magazine. 'Nora objected to my pulp fiction, said all the stories were sexist and misogynistic. I argued that they're of their time and you had to read them in context, but she suspected me of chauvinist tendencies.' And yet she'd moved on to Fitz, who made no secret of being a serial womaniser. Maybe she hoped to change him. Swift wished her luck with that. He added, 'Nora doesn't have much time for kids either and makes no secret of it. She didn't hit it off with Branna and was short-tempered with her at times, so that was another difficulty, and it gave Ruth ammunition to aim at me.'

'Sounds messy and complicated.'

'It was. Branna got anxious about Nora not liking her. I can understand that Ruth would react to that and be protective, but she got so high-handed about it, egged on by Marcel, her partner, who is always quoted as a fount of wisdom.'

Mark pulled a face. 'Ouch! Sounds like you were the filling in the sandwich. Rather you than me, mate.'

'Yeah. It wasn't working with Nora, but I let it drift on, so only myself to blame in the end.' The truth was that since he'd been on his own again, his thoughts had turned frequently to Ruth, wandering down the dangerous path of what might have been. Maybe he'd been using the relationship with Nora as a distraction all along. He forked up his last portion of moussaka. 'How's your love life these days?'

'Non-existent at the moment. All the women I come across are married or just about to be divorced and burdened by anger and regret. Then there are all the bewildered kids in tow and as you've discovered, that can be a minefield.'

'I've gathered that it's the same for women in our age group who are in search of a likely partner.'

'No doubt. I read that the average age for a first divorce is thirty. A woman I met and liked a lot told me that she was grieving for the future she'd lost, and the children she might have had. Took me a while to work that out. Maybe I don't really want to make room for anyone in my life. It's a big adjustment when you've been on your own for a while.'

Swift often had similar thoughts himself and said so. 'Maybe we'll be meeting like this in ten years' time, two middle-aged singletons, exchanging pulp fiction magazines.'

Mark grinned. 'That's supposed to sound sad, but actually, I find it quite appealing. Although I saw an article recently that said that people who live alone stand twice the risk of getting dementia as those with partners, who also have better physical health. Apparently, single households are also a wasteful use of resources.'

'We're pretty damned then on all fronts, from the sound of it. Might as well enjoy the wine while we can.'

Mark raised his glass. 'I'll drink to that.'

Mark had to dash once he'd eaten, but Swift stayed on to have coffee and read his magazine, settling into pleasurable escapism. The villain lurked in the shadows, furious at being jilted by his fiancée and plotting his revenge. He was called Galway Barth, a striking if improbable name.

When he'd finished his coffee, Swift paid his bill and stood outside the café. The wine, food and the close, humid air combined to make him woolly and inert. The suit he'd worn for court clung to him like a suffocating blanket. He shook himself. He'd take his boat out on the river, catch whatever breeze there was, and loosen his leaden muscles.

He caught a bus to Hammersmith, sitting on the top deck by an open window. The plane trees were dull and parched, their leaves dusty. There'd been no rain for weeks, just a smoky-coloured, sullen sky. Surely it would rain in Wales, with its oceanic climate, where they got precipitation even in the driest months. Once, when they were enduring a downpour in Lyon, Afan had told him that the Welsh had numerous descriptions for rain, much as it was said the Inuit had dozens to describe snow. He'd gone through them: *Spotting. Big spaced drops. Short sharp showers. Pouring very quickly. Throwing it down. Fierce rain. Sheets of rain. Fountain rain. Beating rain. Bucketing rain. Maximum intensity rain.* He'd added that the Welsh equivalent of 'It's raining cats and dogs' was, mystifyingly, 'It's raining old women and sticks.'

They'd met soon after Swift joined Interpol. Afan had been a slow-speaking, private man and a highly effective criminal intelligence analyst. He and Swift had liaised on a couple of cases and had worked well together. Afan had been precise and thorough, but with a light touch. They'd become friends, enjoying an occasional meal and walking by the Rhône. Swift had learned that Afan was a fanatical walker and rambled for miles around the region. He had a great love of his country and a passion for male voice choirs, although he'd maintained that he couldn't sing a note, which was shameful for a Welshman. He'd also been a huge fan of Motown. Sounds of the Temptations, Diana Ross and the Four Tops had drifted from his office.

He'd owned an apartment in a nineteenth-century, stone-built mansion in a prestigious neighbourhood. It had a wide balcony overlooking the river Rhône, where he'd grown fruit and vegetables in tubs. In summer, it had been a riot of bright, hot colours and greenery, with peppers and broad beans trained up the railings. He'd spoken now and again of having had enough of the pace and demands of Interpol and his yearning for a simpler, less stressful life. Swift had formed the opinion that although Afan was skilled at his job, he was too sensitive to last in a pressured work environment. He'd referred to losing his parents when he was young and being at a boarding school that he'd hated, and Swift had suspected that he carried deep scars from that time.

Afan had been transferred to Brussels to head up a new unit and although they'd been in touch now and again, the friendship had waned. Swift had left Interpol after being stabbed in the thigh during a raid on sex traffickers and had returned to London. He'd lost contact with Afan, although he'd heard from a mutual colleague that his friend had also given up the job after time off with stress.

He pictured Afan now — tall and gangly, cropped dark hair, small sharp nose with a reddish tip, as if he had a permanent cold, and jug ears — *my only resemblance to Prince Charles.* Since Afan had been in touch, odd memories had come back to him, in the way that they do when the pool of the past has been stirred. He recalled sitting on Afan's balcony in the hot dusk of a summer's evening, drinking aromatic Munica Brune beer while his friend sipped absinthe: the sharp scent of ripe beef tomatoes, the sweetness of honeysuckle, the rippling silver river below and on Afan's sound system, the Neath choir singing 'Myfanwy'. He'd been happy that night, looking forward to seeing Ruth when he returned to London for a visit. That was just before she'd told him that she'd fallen in love with a man called Emlyn and their engagement was over.

Appropriately enough, 'Myfanwy' was a melancholy tale of unrequited love. '*What was it that I did, oh Myfanwy / To deserve the frown of your beautiful cheeks?*' Yet for Swift, it summoned pleasant memories of tranquil, trouble-free times.

CHAPTER 2

The air freshened as Swift drove west, past Swansea and into deep green countryside. The fields were dotted with sheep, some with dark coats. He lowered his window and breathed in the aromatic scent of the hedges. When he stopped the car to stretch his legs, he leaned against a gate and contemplated a flock of Badger Face sheep, so called because of their distinctive black markings. They were comical. He took a photo to send to Branna. He missed her. His clothes were far too tidy and lacking food smears. A few of the sheep halted long enough to return his gaze, and then skittered away among mossy clumps of white saxifrage. The air was cool, the watery blue sky busy with pale grey clouds, and now and again, there were spits of rain. He recalled Afan once saying, '*good summer weather in Wales is as rare as a hen's teeth.*'

He drove on, reflecting on the Tir Melys website. It was in Welsh and English, well designed and informative, albeit a tad smug and with a flavour of virtue-signalling:

Tir Melys translates into English as Sweet Land.

We are a thriving community of smallholdings on a fifty-acre site, with a central communal hub, the Bivium. Our aim is to be part of the ecosystem and work the land with respect. We see ourselves as stewards of the earth, not owners of it. We manage our sweet land innovatively and collectively, always with the aim of being self-sufficient.

Our popularity is such that we have no more space at present for new stewards, but we welcome volunteers and visitors. Be warned — if you're a digital addict this probably isn't the place for you! We have no broadband and no phone signal. (In fact, none of us has a TV). There is one landline in the community house. We find that we're far too busy and content here to notice the lack of these things.

When he was six miles from Holybridge, travelling a narrow back road, he saw the sign to Tir Melys. It was a carved, oval piece of oak fixed to two robust posts in the ground. The name was in green, nestling among painted rosy apples, pointing to a gated lane with a cattle grid inside a black five-bar gate. Swift opened the gate and drove through, closed it after him and carried on slowly along the rutted surface. On his left, he saw a small, single-storey stone building, with worn steps up to a wooden door. It was neglected, with cracked glass in the tiny, high windows, and surrounded by brambles and tall nettles.

He'd had an email reply from Afan on Saturday.

See you on Monday. I live in Croeso Adref (Welcome Home) so once you've parked, take the main path. You'll see the Bivium straight ahead. Go left and you'll find me just off the path, on the right. Door's always open. I'll probably be out working, but I'll be back by sixish, so make yourself comfy.

After driving along the track for a couple of minutes, Swift saw a sign to the car park: *Please Park Here. We prefer to keep cars away from our peaceful homes.* He parked in the small, gravelled space, near the only other vehicle, a red Land Rover, took the rucksack he'd packed from the car boot and followed the path marked by another wooden signpost saying *Bivium.*

The rough path was lined with a rosemary hedge and behind it, apple and pear trees laden with ripening fruit. In the silence, he heard the insistent drone of bees. He recognised the Bivium from the photo on the website. It was a semi-circular timber building with a curving turfed roof, set on a grassy mound of land which was dotted with dandelions, daisies and herbs. Steps led to the outer glassed veranda. He'd expected the place to be busy, but it seemed quiet. He could smell the sea now and hear it too, a distant whisper, just a couple of miles away, over the headland.

He walked on, his rucksack bumping against his back, past a round timber dwelling with a garden framed by tall sunflowers, then by a large, cultivated area full of ripe vegetables and a row of potatoes that had been dug up and left to dry.

To his right, down a slight incline, he saw a single-storey, traditional cottage, with a rough exterior like wattle and daub, a central door and two windows either side, the left one slightly open. The cottage was painted sky blue, with a turfed, bright green roof, in the centre of which nestled a squat chimney. Scarlet geraniums tumbled from window boxes. The vivid colours called to mind a child's crayoned drawing, perhaps the cottage in the woods where the woodcutter gave you refuge when you were lost. A plaque by the front door bore the greeting, *Croeso Adref.* To the left of the door were four large rainwater barrels and raised vegetable beds, planted with broad and runner beans, loganberry and raspberry bushes, tomatoes, potatoes and courgettes.

Swift knocked on the wooden door. When he got no reply, he tried the iron handle and the door opened. He called hello and stepped inside, into a whitewashed room with a grey slate floor. He put his rucksack down and gazed around. A small round oak dining table with two chairs, a twin door, multi-fuel stove with an old-fashioned drying rack holding jeans and shirts suspended overhead, one armchair and a deep, wide Welsh dresser. A door to the left of the room stood open. Swift crossed to it and saw a bedroom with a double bed, bookshelves, a wardrobe and a small en-suite toilet and shower. He touched the stove. It was just faintly warm and the clothes hanging above it were bone dry.

Swift went back outside. At the rear of the house was a large shed with an alloy frame touring bike propped against one side. The door wasn't locked and when he went in, he saw that it was shelved, with a long central table made out of an old pine door. Gardening tools, a spade, hoe and a rake hung from hooks above a tall open cupboard containing packets of seeds, a tub of plant food, canes and twine. The shelves were stacked with plastic buckets, empty bottles and glass demijohns. Jars of pale gold honey were lined up on the table. He picked one up and read the orange and white label:

Tir Melys Honey

Our honey is foraged by our bees from wild blossoms and flowers, including Bramble, Hawthorn, Clover and Bluebells.

We don't heat-treat our honey, thus preserving its natural flavours.

Also on the table were a dozen demijohns fitted with air-locks, with thick sediment in their bases and full of an acorn-coloured liquid. Beside them stood a row of filled bottles, as yet unlabelled, holding a deep amber drink. The labels were in a pile at the end of the table and Swift read the top one.

Tir Melys Orange Blossom Mead

Made by Afan Griffith

Medium-dry mead with a smooth finish

Made to an ancient Welsh recipe

Best served slightly chilled

A pale green jacket was on a hanger to one side of the door. It was elasticated at the waist and cuffs, and a hood with a veil was attached by loops. Grey sheepskin gauntlets dangled on a hook next to the jacket. Swift recognised protective wear for working with bees.

He headed back to the cottage. The temperature had dropped suddenly, and thick cloud was moving in from the sea. It was just gone four, he'd had nothing to eat or drink since a coffee and ham croissant mid-morning, and he was running on empty. He stood in the centre of the room, puzzled. There was no proper kitchen in this cottage and no cooker. Just a small sink with a lidded enamel bucket full of water standing beside it with a note — presumably for his benefit — saying *drinking water*. A microwave, a mini fridge, a kettle and a breadbin stood on top of the deep middle ledge of the dresser. The kettle was half-full of water. He switched it on and found a carton of oat milk in the fridge, which also held cheese and a small tub of butter. There were teabags, mugs, and a tub of home-baked flapjacks in the bottom cupboard of the dresser, which he noticed was riddled with old woodworm scars.

While he waited for the kettle to boil, he scanned the room again. All the furniture appeared home-made or upcycled and there was no sense of personality, no splashes of colour. On the table, he saw a radio and beside it, a photo with a note attached. He picked it up and read Afan's comment. *Remember this walk, Ty? We did about twelve miles along the river and back and stopped to have a drink at the Mistral.* Afan had taken the selfie on a hot July evening in Lyon, by the Lafayette Bridge. He was elegant, wearing a navy linen shirt, Panama hat and designer sunglasses. As usual, Swift's dark curls verged on the wild and his cotton T-shirt had faded in the wash. Ah yes, the days before he had a streak of silver at his temple. He replaced the photo and inspected the two stacks of books on the table. They were nearly all about beekeeping, with a few of mead recipes and a couple about the Pembrokeshire coast. One was a textbook with the title *Brwsiwch eich Cymraeg* — 'Brush up your Welsh'.

He made a mug of tea, added oat milk and took it outside with a flapjack. He decided that oat milk would be an acquired taste, but the flapjack was delicious. He wandered around the vegetable patch, fingering runner beans and picking and eating a couple of juicy tomatoes. The air was breezy and moist. A blackbird sang sweetly nearby. His muscles relaxed. He liked being a long way from everything, and especially Oliver Sheridan.

He glanced back at the cottage. Where was he supposed to sleep, let alone eat, he wondered. He'd worked out that Afan had chosen a simpler life, but this place was basic in the extreme, and the bedroom resembled a monk's cell. He couldn't help wondering about the friend he was going to meet again. Would they have anything in common now?

Perhaps the friendship had belonged to a certain time and place, and this would prove to be an awkward couple of days with both of them searching for things to say.

The Afan he'd known in Lyon had been a cultivated, wealthy man with a taste for the finer things in life. He'd driven a BMW sports car, and had worn beautifully tailored Canali suits, teamed with Louis Vuitton shirts, to work. Swift rarely bought new clothes but he'd admired a jade, square-collared cotton shirt with mother-of-pearl buttons. He'd searched for it online, had seen that it cost nearly £300 and had decided to stick to the more downmarket shops. Even Afan's casual clothes had come from Balmain, and his grey leather walking boots had been pristine and unscuffed. His spacious apartment had been richly decorated with modern art, his treasured collection of antique inkwells, and the many curios he'd picked up in flea markets. A beautiful green Russian antique clock made with Siberian malachite and topped with a gilt Siberian eagle owl had dominated the living room mantelpiece. Afan had also been excited by technology and had loved gadgets and innovation. He was one of the first people Swift had seen with a smartwatch, a Fitbit and a Kindle and he'd loved playing games on apps, particularly Spider Solitaire and Golfshot.

At Tir Melys, Afan seemed to have shed everything from his previous life, with just a radio for entertainment. Maybe he had his possessions in storage. Or perhaps, like a man entering a religious order, he'd shed his worldly goods. Swift remembered Afan's email, telling him to make himself comfy, and wondered if it was ironic.

The sky darkened to a muddy grey. A thin drizzle started. Swift glanced around. In the bleak light, the cottage and garden had a forsaken air. He shivered. He wasn't disposed to premonitions, but he was uneasy. He went back inside and was just removing a sweater from his rucksack, the first time he'd have worn one in months, when a slight man in brown dungarees and a fleece with the hood up appeared through the door.

‘Who are you?’ A Canadian accent, gruff and flat.

‘Hi, I’m Tyrone Swift, a friend of Afan’s. I arranged to visit, but he’s not here. I’ve been wondering where he’s got to.’

The man stared at him with narrow, dark eyes. ‘So have I. I’ve been out looking for him.’

‘Is he not around, then?’

The man shook his head. ‘Come on, we’d better see Jasmine.’

* * *

The man didn’t speak as he led the way back to the Bivium, breaking into a run as the wind whipped up and rain started to hammer down. Swift ran too — with his longer legs, he could have outpaced him, but he stayed just behind. They were both dripping by the time they entered the shelter of the veranda. Swift was aware of light and a smell like fresh sawdust. From somewhere came the plangent sound of harp music.

‘Wait here,’ the man said, and darted away through central folding doors.

Swift used his sleeve to wipe drips from his forehead and neck. A long, deep shelf ran the length of the veranda. The woodcarvings displayed there were unskilled and some of them were downright clumsy. They were mainly of birds, shaped from oak and aspen: owls on branches, hummingbirds, eagles, gannets, puffins and cormorants. There was also a scowling Green Man with a long beard, and an elephant carved from driftwood. At the far end of the shelf was a collection of attractive baskets, planters, bird feeders and trays made of willow.

Through the inner door, Swift saw a large, square room with an open-plan kitchen and a huge oblong dining table constructed from railway sleepers, with driftwood benches. A burly man with his back turned was working at the massive black Aga cooker, and there was a pungent aroma of garlic. Perhaps the smallholders ate communally, which would explain the lack of a proper kitchen in Afan’s cottage.

Swift realised that the harp had stopped. The man who had found him appeared through a door at the far end of the kitchen, followed by a woman. She wore Birkenstocks that clicked on the floor, and an orange felt hat. Her hand rested on the man's shoulder. She had a long face, high forehead and hazel eyes with dark brown rings around the pupils.

'I'm Jasmine Merchant, and this is Bruno Andersen,' she said to Swift. 'Bruno tells me you're Afan's friend.' She gave him a languid handshake.

'That's right. I'm Tyrone Swift. Afan was expecting me this afternoon.'

'Yes, he did mention that you'd be visiting. He booked you a guest room. Let's discuss.'

She made a sweeping gesture with her hand that put Swift in mind of royalty. She led the way back through the kitchen, along a corridor and into a room that had a sign over the door saying '*The Parley*'. It had huge windows patterned with fat raindrops and a floor made of blocks of granite. A tall, elegant beechwood harp stood in the far corner, with a curved, cushioned seat beside it. The dozen or so low stools dotted around were fashioned from sections of tree trunk. Swift felt slightly ridiculous, perched on his stumpy seat, but Jasmine and Bruno were at ease.

'Now, let's see what we have here,' Jasmine said. She was in her early fifties, had a plummy, authoritative voice and was dressed in animal-print yoga wear — high-waisted, grey leggings and a long, shapeless grey sweatshirt with a lime green vest beneath. 'Bruno, what time were you expecting Afan to join you?'

He spoke impatiently, as if she and Swift should already know. 'Around half two. We'd planned to reinforce the hives and inspect for disease. When he didn't turn up, I waited for a while, and then I went to his place, but he wasn't in. So I searched all over, but no one had seen him.' He glared at Swift as if he'd caught him up to no good. 'Then I spotted this guy in Afan's garden, so I went back to see what was going on.'

Jasmine fiddled with the toggle on her sweatshirt. 'Well . . . It seems a bit odd, but maybe Afan decided there was something he needed to do in Holybridge.'

Bruno shook his head. 'The Land Rover's here and his bike's at the side of his shed. He can't have gone anywhere.'

Jasmine's expression was kindly but supercilious. 'He could have gone for a walk?'

Bruno had a broad forehead, a bushy beard and straight black hair that fell in untidy strands. He bit at the side of his thumb. 'Why would Afan have done that? We were working this afternoon, there was a lot to do. He's always reliable.'

'And he was expecting me,' Swift added.

'Yes . . . of course . . . Had you told him you'd be here this afternoon?'

'I emailed him and he replied. He said he'd probably be out working but he'd be back about six.'

Jasmine said, 'Well, there we are. Let's wait and see. It's getting on for five now, so he'll probably turn up by six. I'm sure there's a very simple explanation. I expect something cropped up for him. Or . . . Afan does go off-piste sometimes, we all understand that.'

'Meaning?' Swift asked.

'Oh, he likes to take himself off, have a bit of solitary time. He tramps the countryside and the coast paths for miles, makes the rest of us seem idle by comparison. We don't live in each other's pockets here, but it is hard not to bump into people.'

Swift saw that Bruno was unconvinced. He asked him, 'Have you been all over the site?'

'Everywhere. No one's seen him since mid-morning.'

Jasmine stood in a fluid movement. 'I'm sure Afan will appear soon. Bruno, can you show Mr Smith to his room? He's in Willow.' It sounded like an order rather than a request.

'It's Swift, not Smith,' Swift said. He had to place his hands on the floor to lever himself up.

'Swift, yes. Actually, we use first names here. May I call you Tyrone?'

‘Ty is fine.’

‘Lovely. Well, Ty, perhaps you can wait at Croeso Adref once you’ve seen where you’re sleeping, and then with Afan, join us for supper in the refec. We eat at seven thirty. I must get back to my harp practice, I’ve a concert coming up and I’m doing two new pieces.’

Bruno left the room without a backward glance. Swift followed him along a corridor and up a wide wooden staircase. The first-floor walls were painted a pale tangerine and all the rooms had plant names: Sage, Thyme, Magnolia, Bay and at the end, Willow. Bruno threw open the pine door to a small box of a room, just big enough for bunk beds, a built-in wardrobe and adjacent shower and toilet. The light and warmth compensated for its proportions, although Swift didn’t care much for the egg-yolk-yellow walls and he was dubious about fitting his six-foot-three frame on one of the beds.

‘Not much to see,’ Bruno said.

‘Why is this building called the Bivium?’

‘Jasmine named it. She did all the naming. It’s Latin for an intersection. It’s where our lives join and cross.’

‘Is there anyone else staying here?’

‘Nope. The five rooms are for guests or volunteers who want to stay over, but we don’t get that many of either. The accommodation isn’t the source of income it was intended to attract.’

Swift was surprised. ‘Why is that? It’s an interesting place in terms of conservation and community projects.’

‘Sure, but maybe the far west of rainy Wales isn’t everyone’s idea of a good time. A lot of young people head off to more exotic, sunny countries to practise being green. Although, I guess that with the right kind of energy, a lot more could be done here. There have been various ideas and plans but they haven’t come to anything.’ He fingered his beard. ‘Best if you head back to Afan’s now.’

‘I get the impression you’re worried about him.’

Bruno hooked his thumbs through his dungaree straps and mulled that over. ‘I could set my watch by Afan. He doesn't disappear when work's scheduled without saying anything.' He turned on his heel and made off.

Swift stood for a moment at the window. He could hear the harp again, a light, rippling tune. Now and again Jasmine stopped and replayed a phrase. In the distance were the blueish hills of north Pembrokeshire. He could just see Afan's cottage and Bruno on the path beside it with his pigeon-toed walk, head down against the rain. Beyond Bruno's huddled figure, Swift could make out an apiary with clusters of beehives. The sky was steel-grey now, the rain thinner but drifting and persistent. Swift guessed that it had set in for the night. He gazed at drenched rows of late raspberries and a rowan sapling sagging in the blustery breeze. A small figure in a hooded raincoat splashed through puddles and pushed a wheelbarrow along the path. Hot, arid London seemed a continent away.

It wasn't going to be a night to be out and about.

CHAPTER 3

When they were all seated at the dining table, Jasmine Merchant made introductions, gesturing with her imperious hand movements.

'This is Peter, my husband, Kat Glover, Suki Mehta and Bryn Price. You've met Bruno. Guy and Elinor Brinkworth also live here but they often eat at home. Now, everyone, Ty has come to visit Afan, who is unaccountably not to be found at present. I have explained to Ty that Afan does head off to seek solitude at times and of course, we respect that. Respect is our watchword at Tir Melys. However, Afan was expecting his guest this afternoon, and he's always unfailingly polite and hospitable. I expect he'll rush through the door any minute, full of apologies. We'll have our main course and then if he hasn't turned up, we'll discuss.' She held her hands together in a Namaste greeting and closed her eyes as she intoned, 'We gently caress you, the earth, our planet and home. May harmony and peace bless our land.'

Swift saw that the others listened to Jasmine in the same pose. Except for Bruno, sitting opposite him, who held his hands joined, but glanced at him and rolled his eyes. Swift was surprised. He hadn't noted that Bruno had a sense of humour. Jasmine sat at the head of the table, in a larger chair with a curved back and arms. She might as well wear a badge saying *Head Girl*. She still had her hat on, and Swift wondered if it was an affectation, or if she suffered from a scalp condition. Peter Merchant sat at Jasmine's right, opening and refolding his paper napkin. He was bony faced, with thinning greyish hair and a faded complexion. Bryn, tonight's cook, sat at Swift's left and Kat and Suki sat either side of Bruno.

The evening was gloomy and tall white pillar candles in ornate pewter holders, four of which were spaced along the table, provided the only light. They gave the meal a vaguely ecclesiastical ambience and Swift found this irritating. It was another affectation, with Jasmine playing the role of high priestess.

Bryn wore a long blue-and-white-striped butcher's apron, splashed with food smears and tied below his impressive beer gut. He brought the meal to the table with a great deal of fuss and noise, pretending to play a trumpet fanfare. 'I present my heavenly slow-cooked lamb with herbs. Sweet and tender, like me! I want to see clean plates or there'll be questions! Oh — and a nut cutlet for our plant muncher, Suki. You've no idea what you're missing.'

Suki sighed. 'You say the same thing to me every time, Bryn, but I suppose it amuses you, so I indulge you.'

He laughed and set a huge orange casserole down with a thump, so that the table vibrated.

'We don't need quite so much theatre,' Bruno said.

'Food should be theatre, man! Tuck in, everyone.'

The lamb casserole was served with roast vegetables and home-baked bread. They ate from shallow turquoise earthenware bowls. Suki, a tiny woman with short black hair, had informed Swift that she made them in her pottery. The food was tasty, but Swift was anxious about Afan and had little appetite. There was no sign of him, and Swift couldn't understand his absence. Bruno had returned to his cottage to find Swift and had confirmed that Afan's phone wasn't by the bread bin, where it usually sat. The black cagoule he habitually wore was missing from its peg by the door.

Swift ate silently, listening to the scrape of cutlery. This was an odd, uncomfortable situation, to be a guest where he knew nobody and had no points of reference. He couldn't relax. There were two carafes of elderberry wine, dry and slightly sharp, on the table. Bryn Price helped himself regularly to the one nearest him.

He asked in a forceful voice, 'How d'you know Afan, Ty?'

'We worked together a while back in Lyon, at Interpol.'

Price's eyebrows went up. 'Gosh! Hey, Jasmine, Afan worked for Interpol!'

She paused as she mopped her bowl with bread. 'Indeed. Is that where you work, Ty?'

'I used to.'

'What do you do now?'

His instinct was to keep that quiet. 'I'm self-employed.'

'Well, I hope it's not too quiet here for you after your European connections. No international intrigues at Tir Melys.'

'We had some sheep rustling the year before last,' her husband said with a little smirk. He spoke lightly, with a Home Counties drawl. 'This is great lamb, Bryn. Tasty.'

Bryn grinned and tilted his head towards Suki. 'I could probably name the lamb it came from, but that might upset some people, and I don't want to be accused of insensitivity. The recipe's from my great-nan, with my own little additions.'

Jasmine swept a hand in Swift's direction. 'We aim to be as self-sufficient as possible here, Ty. All our own vegetables and fruit, chicken, eggs and lamb. Wine, too. We take turns cooking and we make all our own bread. We respect the land that nurtures us. We live by Thoreau's philosophy: "Live in each season as it passes, breathe the air, drink the drink, taste the fruit, and resign yourself to the influence of the earth." It's a simple life and a good one.' She had a didactic manner and when she made a pronouncement, she gave a private smile.

Her husband murmured in agreement and Kat Glover patted the table in approval. It was a reasonable and benign philosophy, although self-evident — it would be difficult not to breathe the air. Listening to Jasmine, Swift placed a bet with himself that she'd written the self-satisfied description on the Tir Melys website.

He asked, 'Have you all been here a long time?'

'It feels like only yesterday, but we moved here from London sixteen years ago, and people gradually joined us,' Jasmine said. 'We all grow fruit and veg and then of course, we have our own specialties. Bryn has chickens and sheep, Bruno and Afan keep bees — Afan also makes mead with the honey, Suki's a potter, Kat specialises in woodcraft and is an expert forager. Guy and Elinor are jewellers, Peter makes willow furniture and wine, and I generally manage the site, run healing and therapy workshops and of course, I play the harp.'

Bryn belched and grinned. 'An alternative script that Jasmine could give you is that she and Peter are Mam and Dad, I'm the naughty one, Suki's the normal, balanced one, Bruno's the troubled one, Kat's the problematic one, Elinor's the damaged one, Guy's the scathing one and Afan's the high-minded one.'

'Three cheers for the cod psychology, you should take it up as a career,' Kat told him, sounding annoyed.

Peter Merchant cleared the plates while Bryn brought a huge oval platter heaped with fruit salad and pitchers of cream to the table. He set the platter and a ladle in front of Jasmine with a stack of bowls.

'The Queen was in her counting house, counting out her money,' he teased.

Jasmine glanced at him. 'What's that supposed to mean?'

'Nothing. Just an old rhyme that popped into my head.'

She dished out portions and passed them around. Swift imagined he was back at school. As soon as everyone had a serving, he asked, 'Has anyone seen Afan today?'

Jasmine frowned at his taking the lead on the subject but said nothing.

'I came by the refec for breakfast,' Suki said. She had neat, symmetrical features and her hands were chapped from shaping clay. 'Afan was here, eating muesli and reading. He always brings a book with him.'

Swift asked, 'What time was that?'

'Just gone eight. I made him a cuppa as I was having one myself. I'm not much of a morning person, so we didn't talk as such. I grabbed a roll and honey. I'd finished by a quarter past eight. Bryn came in just as I was leaving.'

Bryn said, 'That's right. I'd had breakfast at mine, but I wanted to check out the ingredients for dinner. We said good morning. Afan headed off while I had my head in the fridge.'

'Has anyone seen him since then?' Jasmine had drawn herself up, taking over.

Kat waved her spoon. Swift had noticed her gazing at him intensely throughout the meal. 'I saw him hoeing the communal allotment around ten thirty this morning. We didn't speak. He just waved and carried on. I popped in to Elinor and Guy's on my way here. They both said they hadn't seen Afan today.'

No one else spoke. The fruit salad was laced heavily with honey and Swift found it too sweet. He took a sip of the sharp wine to clean his palate and asked, 'Did Afan tell anyone his plans for today?'

'Plans?' Kat seemed mystified.

'I told you, he was supposed to work with me this afternoon,' Bruno muttered.

'You see, Ty,' Jasmine explained, 'unlike most other people, we don't usually have "what I'm doing today" conversations. We tend to have the same plans day in, day out here. We work the land and carry out our daily tasks. Each day, each week, each month, we move with nature's cycle. Steady, routine and no doubt mundane, but that's what the land demands of us as its stewards. Occasionally, we go to Holybridge to pick up supplies we can't provide for ourselves, or to sell our products. Sometimes to use the internet in a café there, although few of us have regular need of it.'

Swift asked, 'Were you all aware that I was coming?'

'Afan mentioned it on Saturday evening at our colloquy, but he didn't say what time,' Peter said.

'What's your colloquy?'

'It's our weekly information sharing session, just before Saturday supper. We discuss the past week and the one to come, talk about any challenges or developments we need to make.'

'Although developments are few and far between,' Bruno commented, glancing at Bryn.

Swift wondered about this need for strange names. Why did a place to hang out in have to be called a Bivium, a meeting room the Parley, a chat a colloquy and the kitchen/dining room the refec? Jasmine's choices bore the hallmark of a snob. He wondered what her background was and placed another bet with himself that she'd gone to public school. 'Did Afan say anything else about my visit?'

Peter rubbed his chin. He had deep lines around his mouth. He must have a good ten years on his wife and looked even older, dressed in a fusty cable-knit cardigan. 'He said you were an old friend. He hadn't seen you for a while and he'd booked you a room.'

One of the candles sputtered. Bryn leaned forward, licked a finger and thumb and straightened the wick. He rose and brought a tray with a bottle of mead and tumblers to the table. 'Here. In Afan's absence, the next best thing is his lovingly made mead.' He poured a couple of inches of the drink into a tumbler and handed it to Swift.

'Thanks.' Swift sipped some. He could taste honey, but it was surprisingly tangy and dry.

Bruno and Suki helped themselves while Jasmine asked, 'Given that his bike is here and he hasn't borrowed the Land Rover, does anyone have any idea where Afan might be?'

A general shaking of heads.

'He does go for long walks.' Suki had poured cream into her spoon and was sipping it through neat, rosy lips. 'But not when he's working — in the evenings, or at weekends.'

'What if he's had an accident?' Bryn turned towards Jasmine. He was stocky and tall, and he radiated warmth, as if he'd been absorbing the cooker's heat. Swift could smell garlic on his breath, mixed with the wine.

She glanced at her watch. 'It's getting on for nine. That has to be a possibility. What to do? We'd better all check the site carefully. There's no point in going further afield on foot. It'll be dark soon and visibility will be hopeless in this weather. I'll call on the Brinkworths and ask them to help. Ty, you can come with me.'

Stumbling around in the dark would be pointless, and he had no wish to follow Jasmine's orders in the rain. He asked, 'How far from here to get a phone signal?'

'Couple of miles, as the road climbs to Holybridge,' Kat told him.

'I'm going to drive that way, then. I'd like to check my phone, in case Afan has sent me a text or email. His phone is missing, so presumably it's with him. If he's in trouble, he might have used it.'

'If that was the case, he'd have tried the landline here,' Peter Merchant said.

'Maybe. When I rang it to tell Afan I was coming, no one replied, and it didn't take a message.'

'The answerphone's unreliable and sometimes we forget to switch it on,' Jasmine told him.

'I checked it just before supper, because I was worried about Afan. The answerphone was on and there were no messages,' Kat replied. She nodded at Swift. 'That's a good idea of yours. I'll drive you, if you like. Then you can scan the roads for any sign of Afan as well as checking your phone. I'll just get the keys to the Land Rover.'

Bryn chuckled, and Jasmine eyed Kat shrewdly but said nothing. The others donned their coats while Jasmine allotted them each an area to search. They all had torches in their pockets, used as they were to walking through the country darkness. Swift put his waxed jacket on and watched them file out. Jasmine's ringing voice was still issuing orders as she opened the outer door.

Suki was bringing up the rear and turned. 'I'm sure Afan's okay, Ty.' She smiled up at Swift, touching his arm lightly, but he glimpsed concern in her dark eyes.

* * *

Kat Glover was a terrible driver, the kind who clutched the wheel too hard and used the brake erratically. The rain was driving hard against the windscreen, and she had the wipers on at full speed. This weather fitted Afan's description of *throwing it down*. He glanced across at Kat as the Land Rover lurched. She was mannish, with a dumpy, muscular shape and although she must have been in her late thirties, she wore her hair in two juvenile pigtails tied with dark red ribbon. He'd observed that she had a slight limp and a built-up left shoe as he'd followed her to the car park. She'd had to pull her seat as far forward as it would go so that her feet could reach the pedals.

'What's that place?' Swift pointed to the low stone building near the entrance gate.

'That's St Finnian's chapel, believed to date from the fifteenth century. It's not used for formal worship these days. It has another name locally — the Serpent's Chapel. Local lore has it that it was once used for satanic worship or rituals of some kind. I've no idea if that's true. We patch the place up as best we can, as it's ancient and part of this estate. People from around here call in occasionally and tourists visit. The windows need repairing. We discussed it at a colloquy, but the summer months have been a bit busy. Can you hop out and do the gate?'

Swift pulled his hood up and ran to the gate when Kat stopped. The wind stung his face as he gripped the cold metal bars. The headlights illuminated the silver needles of rain and he glanced up at Kat, hunched at the wheel, a cushion wedged behind her back. She was like a child who's taken her parents' car for a joy ride.

She drove slowly to the road, concentrating on the track. Now and again, she took the end of a pigtail and sucked it. Swift stared out at the wild, hostile night. A line of hawthorn trees were swaying, their branches dancing and dipping, illuminated and then cast back to dark shadow as the Land Rover's lights caught them and moved on. Afan could be lying in any of these hedgerows and you'd never see him. He kept recalling Afan's first email: *there is a sour note that troubles me and plays on my mind.* Nobody would be out in this weather without good reason. It was a night to head for home. He held his phone in his hand and as the road started to climb towards Holybridge, he saw that he had one bar of a signal, creeping up to two. He had no text messages, but he was relieved to see an email from Afan.

Hi Ty, I'm really sorry to do this, but something urgent has come up and I've got to head off and deal with it. Please accept my apologies and can you tell them at Tir Melys. Hopefully, you can enjoy a couple of days there anyway. I'll be in touch as soon as I can. Again, so sorry, Afan.

He checked the time it had been sent: 2.15 p.m. He rang the phone number, but it went to voicemail. He left a message, saying that he'd received the email but was concerned, and hoped that everything was okay. He asked Afan to get in touch, via the landline at Tir Melys if possible. Kat slowed, bumped the Land Rover onto the verge and yanked the handbrake. She turned to him, anxious.

'You've heard from Afan?'

'Yes.' He read her the email.

'Hmm. Very strange, but I suppose at least he's left a message. I wonder what could be so urgent. I don't understand why he didn't say anything to me, reach out about this problem, whatever it is.' She lifted a pigtail and licked the end of it. 'He's okay, that's the main thing.'

'Are you and Afan close?' Swift wanted to pull the hair out of her mouth. It was a revolting habit.

'Well, we get each other. We're on the same *wavelength*, we share things,' she said.

He wondered if she was indicating that they slept together. He couldn't imagine it. In Lyon, Afan had had a partner called Amira Brodeur, a dark, slim woman, pretty and very feminine. Kat seemed to be expecting him to enquire further and when he didn't, she wiped the inside of the windscreen with the back of her hand.

'I'll head back, shall I?'

'Fine, yes. Has Afan seemed worried about anything recently?'

She tapped her stubby fingers on the wheel. 'I don't think so. We talk pretty much every day and he hasn't mentioned anything. He had some leaf spot on his early tomatoes and that bugged him, but I don't suppose that's what you mean.'

'No, it isn't. Would Afan go somewhere and leave his door and a window open?'

'Oh, we don't lock anything at Tir Melys, there's no need. I wish he'd said something to me, I'm sure I could have helped. We're all there for each other in the community. But you shouldn't worry too much. He's clearly okay, he's just got this thing to deal with, whatever it is. I expect he'll tell us all about it when he gets back.'

Swift didn't reply. He and Afan should have been sitting by the glowing stove, drinking wine and catching up while the weather did its worst outside. This wasn't right. He couldn't fathom why his friend would have left on foot to an emergency. He held the door handle as Kat executed an awkward three-point turn and drove into the dismal night. His gut twisted with anxiety.

CHAPTER 4

After fifteen minutes of lying in his bunk bed, Swift decided that he wouldn't get a wink of sleep. Not only was it not long enough, but the mattress was so thin, he could feel the slats beneath. There was a proper bed at Afan's and he might as well use it, given that its owner didn't need it for now.

He rose, put his clothes back on, fetched his toiletries and his rucksack and headed downstairs. It was just after midnight and the Bivium was silent. He passed through the refec, which was now spotless, with just a tureen of fruit in the middle of the dining table. The digital display on the oven gleamed bright blue in the dark and the fridge hummed quietly. He could still smell lamb juices and garlic. When he'd returned with Kat, Jasmine had declared in a mock military fashion that everyone could stand down.

'It's rather inconsiderate of Afan,' she'd said, 'but I suppose if it's an emergency, he has his reasons. Does this email say how long he expects to be gone?'

'No. It's vague,' Swift had told her. *And Afan was never vague. He was always clinically precise.* 'Did he ever walk to Holybridge? He must have walked somewhere, as he had no transport — unless someone picked him up.'

Bryn had answered him. 'The coastal path cuts by the west of Holybridge. Afan used to do that walk into the town sometimes. I've gone with him a couple of times, although he usually preferred solitary rambles. It'd take about an hour. There'd be taxis there and the train station.'

Swift had said, 'Why would Afan have walked for an hour to deal with an urgent matter when he could have asked for a lift or called a taxi?'

'Good question,' Peter Merchant had commented, 'no idea of the answer. It doesn't make a lot of sense.'

Swift had asked Jasmine if she had any next of kin details for Afan. He'd never heard his friend mention extended family. She'd shaken her head and seemed to have decided to take the question as a criticism, pointing out sniffily that this was a community of independent adult members, not a record-keeping fiefdom. Bruno had grinned at that.

When Swift stepped out of the Bivium, the rain had stopped and the air was chilly. A sickle moon glittered occasionally through scudding clouds. There was a plaintive *maah* from a sheep, otherwise the darkness was like a silent cloak. He'd borrowed a torch and swept it along the path and clumps of purple foxgloves, making his way over the sodden ground. He came to where the path branched to Afan's cottage and as he turned with the torch and the beam danced, he thought he saw a shadow, a shape slipping away down the side of the shed. It was gone in an instant. He ran along the path, sliding on wet grass, and walked around the shed, past Afan's bike. There was no one and when he stood listening, no sound. He looked in the shed, but it was exactly as it had been earlier.

He opened the cottage door, switched on the light and stood on the threshold. The room was the same and when he gazed around, he couldn't see that anything had been moved. But he recognised a difference, a trace of recent warmth, of human sweat and breath on the air. The photo that Afan had left on the table was undisturbed, and he tucked it into the inner pocket of his jacket.

There was a key hanging above the door, and he locked it before he went to bed. Afan's bedtime reading was *Wolf Hall*. A sticker on the front told Swift that it had cost him £2.50 in Holybooks Preloved. The bookmark, a creased post-card of Caerphilly castle, was a quarter of the way in. He read the back. The handwriting was spidery.

I found this recipe for Elderberry and Meadowsweet mead. Sounds yummy. Shall we try a batch? We could go foraging early one morning (just as the sun is rising!) K xx

1 gallon spring water

2 ounces dried meadowsweet leaf and flower

8 ounces dried elderberries

1/2 teaspoon pectin

1 teaspoon yeast nutrient

1/2 packet of yeast

1 1/2 36-ounce jars of honey

Afan had always been an avid reader, sometimes confess-ing at work that he was tired because he'd been unable to put a book down until the early hours. Swift lay in the man-sized bed, gratefully stretching his legs and wondering why Afan hadn't taken his book with him. He was weary but sleep eluded him. He cast his mind back to when he'd been with Afan in Lyon, trying to remember if he'd ever mentioned relatives. He drew a blank.

His eyes grew heavy, but he kept thinking about that email. It bothered him. It didn't make sense. Why that, and not a phone call or a note? Afan would have realised that he might not see the email for some time. He would surely have left a note on the kitchen table, wanting Swift to find it as soon as he arrived. He wasn't a man to cause unnecessary alarm and especially to an expected visitor.

He drifted in and out of sleep through the night. He had vivid dreams. In one, Ruth sat by the Rhône in Lyon with him. She wore a wedding dress and a circlet of flowers in her hair. He went to take her hand, telling her how happy he was to be her husband, but she frowned and told him he'd got it wrong. She'd married Emlyn, they were on their honeymoon and he would be here any minute.

* * *

Swift woke just after half six and peered out of the bedroom window. The rain had cleared, and the sky was an intense, cloudless blue. Somewhere, a cockerel crowed loud and long. He went to the bathroom and listened to the toilet make its loud, sinister groan. Bruno had explained that it was a macerating system, as the waste had some way to go to the main drain. He showered under a slow trickle of lukewarm water and dressed, then he made a cup of tea and wandered barefoot into the garden. He picked and ate tomatoes and loganberries. Jasmine had told him that he should help himself to breakfast in the refec. He decided to walk around the site first and get his bearings properly. He donned his jacket, closed the windows, locked the door and set off.

The dwellings all had turfed roofs and chimneys but had been constructed in different styles. There was another cottage like Afan's, two hexagonal structures, painted bright pink with porthole windows, a cabin with a triangular front and a house that resembled a Viking longhouse, made of varnished timbers and with oregano, sedum and sea thrift growing on the roof. He passed several long polytunnels and a large, fenced area with henhouses inside.

The climbing sun was drying the drenched earth and the air smelled rich and loamy. Past the Bivium and through a wooded area of hornbeam and larch, he saw an elevated, handsome period farmhouse, fronted by a paved courtyard. It was stone-built, weathered grey and brown, with pargeting on the plaster around the sturdy oak front door. The courtyard was dotted with lemon trees in blue earthenware pots. Dark green willow planters containing purple fuchsias stood under the windows. Peter Merchant was standing in the centre of the paving with his back turned, his bare right foot against his left calf, arms reaching up with steepled hands. He wore a T-shirt and baggy tracksuit bottoms — a scrawny scarecrow. It seemed that the Merchants lived in the big house. Swift was puzzled about how this place fitted together.

He decided to walk as far as the chapel and hoped it would be open. The rutted path towards the entrance gate was deep in puddles. Swift was regretting his lack of wellingtons. He should have borrowed Afan's, which he'd seen near the front door. He brushed the back of his hand along the tops of drenched ferns as he walked. His back was to the sun and he was glad of its warmth on his neck.

The chapel door had a simple latch, and it was open. On the right of the doorframe, Swift saw that a fish symbol had been carved into the stone. Inside was a shadowy space of about fifteen feet square with a vaulted roof. The walls were limestone, the earth floor dry and caked. A wooden collection box was fixed to the back wall with a laminated card above.

Welcome to St Finnian's chapel

The Tir Melys community cares for this holy place

Please leave a donation towards its upkeep

He put a pound coin in the box. There was just a small stone altar with two wooden benches before it. Swift walked around the bare altar and then sat on one of the benches. The air was chilly but not damp. The chapel had a benign atmosphere, not particularly holy, but calm. He heard the door open behind him and turned to see Bruno entering, his dungarees tucked into wellingtons. He was carrying a bunch of wildflowers. He halted abruptly when he saw Swift, and then came and sat beside him.

'You're an early bird,' he said softly.

'So are you.'

'I call in here now and again. It's peaceful. A bit gloomy, and freezing in the winter, but peaceful.'

'If you want to be on your own, I can go.'

'No, no, stay as you are.' Bruno seemed friendlier this morning. 'No sign of Afan?

‘No, but if he’s had to deal with an emergency, I wouldn’t expect him to be back yet. I’ve been wondering why this is called St Finnian’s chapel. Wasn’t he Irish?’

‘He was trained in a Welsh monastery, in Glamorgan, in the fifth century. There’s no evidence that he ever actually hung out here. A handful of hermits used it over the centuries, I believe. There’s a cleft in the stone to one side of the altar, leads to a small chamber. It’s supposed to be a hidey-hole where hermits used to conceal themselves if they heard someone coming. The chapel isn’t in use anymore. Just a bit of interesting heritage.’

‘Kat told me it’s also called the Serpent’s Chapel.’

Bruno laughed. ‘Kat likes a bit of drama and embellishment. There’s some local stories that satanic rites were enacted here, possibly in the seventeenth century, but it’s all a bit vague. Might have been the teenage Goth equivalents of the time, having a bit of fun.’ He stretched his legs out, crossed them at the ankles. ‘Afan comes here sometimes to meditate.’

‘He was a private kind of man when I knew him in Lyon. Is he religious?’

Bruno said, ‘Not religious in any formal sense. I used to work with horses back in Alberta. Sometimes, Afan reminds me of a nervous horse, skittish if you get too close.’ He pulled a face and tugged at his beard. ‘He probably comes here to hide away from Kat.’

‘Because?’

‘Kat’s a bit keen on Afan. She’s laid siege to him ever since she arrived. He’s too kind to tell her straight that he’s not interested, and she’s not the type to take a subtle hint. He’s sensitive about her damaged foot, doesn’t want her to think that puts him off. She’s convinced that they have an attraction. She makes him little carvings and bakes him cakes, buys him books on bees, pops up when he’s off for a walk, to keep him company. It’s a source of some amusement to us all.’

It sounded oppressive. ‘It can’t be too amusing if you’re Afan.’

'No, but . . . I told him, buddy, she's not the kind of woman to get nuance. He's too much of a gent.'

'You work together a lot?'

'Sure, yeah, as a team. We invested jointly in the beehives and equipment. We're pretty much self-taught about bee-keeping so we share information. Afan did a course recently in Holybridge, and that was very helpful. I'm pretty pissed at him just taking off, because there's a lot to do. Nectar flow slows down in August, so we have to check for mites and take precautions against robbers.'

Swift was surprised. 'People come to steal the honey?'

Bruno smiled. 'No, not people, mainly other bees and wasps.' He yawned. 'I couldn't sleep last night, thinking about Afan. It seems strange, the way he vanished without saying anything. Not like him at all. What could be such an emergency that he couldn't have dropped by and told me?'

'I've had similar thoughts.'

Bruno glanced at him. 'I don't suppose there's any connection, but someone went missing from around here about four months ago.'

'Who was that?'

'His name was Morgan Callender, a young guy. He was one of our volunteers.'

'Were the police involved?'

'Yeah, they came here. Jasmine wasn't best pleased. Morgan was living with his family and there'd been problems. Apparently, he'd told friends that he'd had enough and was planning to leave home. I heard he left a note. That's what the police believed had happened — young guy decided to take off. I suppose they checked it out.'

It could mean something or nothing. Swift asked, 'Did anyone ever hear from him?'

'No idea.' Bruno ran his fingers through his hair. 'Afan mentions you now and again, he holds you in high regard. One time when we were working, he said that you're one of the few people he's ever trusted.'

Swift was embarrassed. He'd had no idea that Afan had valued him in that way. It made him regret the loss of contact. He said, 'I've always found Afan a good man, kind and reliable.'

They sat in silence for a few moments. Bruno had placed the wildflowers on his lap. Swift could smell the rainwater on them.

He asked, 'How did you get from Alberta to Pembrokeshire?'

Bruno hesitated before replying. He sounded cagey. 'A circuitous route. I kind of tripped over this place and it suited. My mom was from Wales, she emigrated to Canada as a war bride, so I guess I was maybe following an umbilical cord. There's a Welsh word, *hiraeth*. It means homesickness or nostalgia.' He got up and placed the flowers on the altar, making a little bow. 'These are just a general offering to the gods, whoever they may be, asking that they keep our bees happy and our honey rich and bountiful.'

Swift followed him, walking around the altar to the stone wall. He saw that there was a concealed opening, about five feet high and just wide enough to enter. He ducked and went in. Immediately, the air grew colder. A couple of paces brought him to a cavity, about four feet square, reaching up to the roof. He imagined a hermit scuttling in here when he heard footsteps or the sound of voices. You wouldn't want to loiter for long, it would chill and cramp your bones, but then he supposed that hermits would have been used to discomfort.

Bruno peered in at him. 'Boo! Good place for hide-and-seek.'

They walked back together. Bruno became quieter, more his taciturn self from yesterday. Swift wanted to ask him more about the set-up at Tir Melys but gauged that the time wasn't right. When he commented that he was surprised that Afan's house had no proper kitchen, Bruno replied that a couple of cottages were built that way to keep costs down and because the Merchants wanted to encourage communal eating. Anyone who wanted could have a takeaway supper and heat it through in their microwave. When they reached the Bivium, he turned abruptly away with no farewell, leaving Swift to enter the refec for breakfast.

* * *

A large, heavy woman with wispy shoulder-length curls and a smiling, eager expression was sitting at the dining table eating scrambled eggs. She wore black leggings and a voluminous cream and brown kaftan, circled by a woven belt which emphasised her girth. On her lap was a tiny dog, with a long silky beige-and-white coat, a round face and a black button nose. She introduced herself as Elinor Brinkworth and picked the dog up, waving one of its paws at Swift. Her fingers were so plump that her gold wedding ring was embedded in the flesh.

'Meet Frankie. He's my lickle cuddle buddy.' She pronounced his name *Fwankie.*

Swift greeted them both and explained that he'd come to visit Afan. His last close encounter with a dog had resulted in a nasty bite. Admittedly, Frankie was like a toy in comparison to the Alsatian that had been instructed to attack him, but he decided to keep his distance.

'Let me make you some breakfast,' Elinor said, beaming. 'There's porridge on the hob, or you can have muesli, bacon and egg, scrambled egg on toast — or maybe you prefer your eggs boiled, with soldiers? Just say, and I'll sort it for you.'

'There's no need. I can help myself.'

'Are you sure? You're a bit on the slim side for such a tall man. You could do with a proper breakfast to set you up. It's no trouble at all and you are our guest. I'm sure Afan would do the same for you if he was here. Isn't it odd, that he's gone off so suddenly without telling anyone? I suppose it must have been something very urgent. I do hope everything will be okay for him.' She started to get up, Frankie fussing in her arms.

He said firmly, 'Please don't bother. I can manage fine.'

He helped himself to porridge from a slow cooker, coffee, toast and marmalade. The kitchen was well stocked, with pots and pans hanging from brass hooks and a walk-in cupboard, its shelves lined with cooking aids: a bread maker, electric mixer, pasta machine, pressure cooker, raclette and fondue sets, a toasted sandwich maker, spaghetti pot and several utensils that Swift didn't recognise. The cupboards were full of jars of herbs and home-made cordials, preserves and pickles.

Elinor called out to him as he found what he needed. 'There's jam, honey and marmalade in the right-hand cupboard and butter and various other spreads in the fridge. Just shout if you need anything.'

He wished she'd stop fussing. He collected his food, put it on a tray and brought it to the table. Elinor was feeding Frankie shreds of scrambled egg.

'You're the self-sufficient type, I see,' she said. 'Do you live on your own?'

'I do, yes.'

'How come you're single, a handsome man like you?'

He smiled at her, his eyes saying *back off*. 'It's a long story and it's also by choice.'

The dog glanced back and forth between them as they talked, his nose twitching. Elinor chucked him under the chin, and he wriggled in ecstasy. She wore a long silver and agate pendant decorated with an ivy garland. It rose and fell on her round, squashy bosom when she moved.

'Ooh, that sounds interesting, doesn't it, Fwankie? You'll have to tell me some time. I couldn't imagine living on my own, with no one to chat to and share things with. If Guy, my hubby, goes out for more than a couple of hours, I get anxious. He cycles, takes off most days for a spin. I tell him not to be gone for more than two hours or I'll be climbing the walls. He says I'm a fusspot, but it's just the way I'm made. It's the only time I wish we had a phone signal here, so that Guy could call me. He's out cycling at the moment, that's why I decided to have breakfast in here. I was hoping I'd have some company and hey presto, in you walked!'

Swift smiled. If he was Guy, he'd probably be gone for most of the day.

'I do hope Afan is okay,' she carried on. 'We're worried about him, aren't we, Fwankie?' She had protuberant blue eyes and a tremulous voice, as if all her speech was a question.

'Yes, I hope so too. Which house do you live in?'

'Cuddfan, just by the polytunnels.'

The house that resembled a Viking dwelling. 'Oh yes, I saw it. You have a handsome roof garden. Does that take a lot of maintenance?'

'It's lovely, isn't it? It's well designed so to be honest, it's not hard work. We were keen to help biodiversity and create a natural habitat for flora and fauna. And of course, it's another way of reducing our carbon footprint.'

'It fits well into this landscape.'

The dog tried to climb onto the table, its tiny paws scrabbling. 'Now, now, Fwankie, don't be naughty. Aunty Jasmine doesn't allow doggies on the table.' Elinor rubbed noses with her pet and fed him a sliver of toast. She winked at Swift. 'Jasmine doesn't like me feeding him at the table, but she's not here and I'm sure you won't tell tales.'

He asked, 'Does Jasmine lay down the rules?'

'Well . . . I wouldn't quite say that. But it's her place — hers and Peter's, so you have to observe tenancy conditions. Not that there are that many.'

'You're tenants? I assumed you owned your homes here.'

'No, we're tenants. We moved here last year. The Merchants own all of this.' She pointed vaguely and Frankie whined. 'It's their baby, their dream, their development, their risk. They bought the farmhouse — it's seventeenth-century and gorgeous — and the land. Then they decided to set the farm up as smallholdings.'

'How long are your tenancies for?'

She scratched the dog's head. 'Ooh, Fwankie, he's a nosy one, isn't he?'

'Sorry. I didn't mean to intrude.' Although it helped explain Jasmine's lady-of-the-manor style.

‘Oh no, that’s okay. Five-year tenancies, renewable. We pay a reasonable rent, you see, enough to cover our utilities and something for the communal pot. Really, it’s all about the cooperative. And there aren’t that many rules and regs. Guy and I adore it here. We’re jewellers, we have our studio near the house. It’s a dream come true for us, being in this paradise, living off the land. And we hope our other dream is going to come true too, don’t we, Fwankie?’

Things were becoming clearer for him. The picture painted by the website was somewhat misleading. He buttered more toast, watched closely by Frankie, whose nose quivered. Having accused him of nosiness, Elinor turned out to be one of those garrulous people who spill out their personal information to strangers. She started to explain that she and her husband were applying to become adoptive parents.

‘I’ve got a useless womb, you see. It was hard to accept at first, because all the women in my family are amazingly fertile and pop out *bambinos* as if they’re shelling peas, but I’ve come to terms with it now. Guy and I believe that we should offer the chance of this amazing life here to an unwanted infink. That’s why we chose Tir Melys, it’s such a lovely place to raise a littl’un. Everything happens for a reason, doesn’t it? I mean, we did discuss a surrogacy arrangement, but Guy was against it and said it just didn’t seem right, with the world in the state it’s in. There are thousands of kiddies waiting to be adopted in the UK, aren’t there, Fwankie? The whole thing takes at least six months and we’re three months in. We’ve done stage one, all the checks and references and self-assessment questionnaires. Guy grumbles about it all. He doesn’t like the way we’re being scrutinised, but then he’s never been keen on bureaucracy and he’s got high standards — he has a doctorate, you see.’ She stated this proudly. ‘Some of the social worker’s reports have had spelling and grammar errors and Guy’s been sarcastic to him about it. He corrected one report in red pen and sent it back! We have to go to preparation classes and have a lengthy assessment done by Terry, the social worker. Guy says it’s a bit like being dissected in a laboratory, put under a microscope, but I've said to him that they have to be very careful. So, it's complicated and we're keeping everything crossed like mad. It's a bit of an emotional tightrope. You'd love an ickle playmate, wouldn't you, Fwankie? If we're successful, our little cherub will be the first in the community for a while. Between you and me, Jasmine's not that keen on having kiddiewinks here, although she's got one son, but he's all growed up now and lives in London. But there's no rule against them and I'm sure she'll love our little bundle of joy as much as we will.'

Swift was battered by this gale of information. The dynamics of the Brinkworths' marriage sounded intricate. He rallied and managed, 'Best of luck with it all, I admire you.'

'Thank you. I appreciate that.'

He finished his coffee. 'Would you say that Afan is happy here?'

She blinked at the change of subject. 'That's an odd question.'

'Is it? As you all see a fair amount of each other, I assumed you'd have a view.'

'Oh, right — well, he seems happy. He's never looked *unhappy*. He's one of those level-seeming people, unflappable, a man who doesn't really show emotion. Not like me, I wear my heart on my sleeve. I cry at the least thing, don't I, Fwankie? Old films, *EastEnders*, any of those programmes about finding lost family. Guy says I'm like a tap. Still, we can't all be the same, can we?'

Swift agreed that this was the case.

'Mind you,' Elinor carried on, 'I'm not as bad as Bruno. You can never tell if he's going to smile or bite your head off. I shouldn't really say that, because he has depression, but it can be difficult, gauging his moods. There's been times when he's really upset me. I've only been checking he's okay and he's snapped, told me to lay off. Guy says it's my own fault, and I worry too much about other people. I suppose it's my maternal instinct expressing itself. Bruno takes medication of course, so most of the time his illness is under control and working with the bees must be very soothing.'

She stopped speaking as Kat Glover clumped in, wearing a khaki body warmer over a short-sleeved checked shirt. She made a beeline for Swift.

'Any news of Afan?'

'No, unless he's phoned the landline here.'

She shook her head. 'I checked it. I made sure the answerphone was switched on last night.' She sighed heavily. 'I checked my place carefully as well, in case he'd left me a note and I'd missed it. Whatever's happened, he must have been in too much of a hurry to tell me.' She twisted a pigtail around her finger.

Swift was impressed by her well-developed biceps, which were on show this morning. Her eyes were red and watery, and he wondered if she'd been crying. He stood and cleared his breakfast things from the table.

'I'll stay around for a couple of days. I'll make sure it's okay with Jasmine.'

Elinor fluttered her fingers at him. 'Of course it will be, won't it, Fwankie? Jasmine loves visitors. We all do.'

CHAPTER 5

The Merchants' house was also called Tir Melys, giving its name to the land. Swift went to lift the heavy brass knocker on the door, but paused as he heard their raised, angry voices through an open window. Mainly Jasmine shouting the odds, with Peter sounding cross but resigned.

'What else can we do, Peter? You haven't come up with any better ideas and we've been talking about it long enough. The bank won't lend to us and even if we found one that would, the kind of interest they'd charge would be crippling. Giles is going to need the help and soon, if he's going to sort this bloody mess out.'

'But I love this house. I've devoted my heart and soul to it. We've put down roots here. I don't see why Giles can't sort himself out. It's not as if he ever comes here or takes any interest in us. This will cause so much upset and bad feeling . . .'

'This is a business as well as our home, when all's said and done, not a charity. We have to put our family first and make a decision. You'd procrastinate till the cows come home.'

'This is awful. What will people say? Such an upheaval!'

'Yes, it is awful, but don't make me into the bad cop here. We just have to face facts. Giles needs the help, and we don't have a lot of choice.'

As soon as he knocked, silence fell. After a good half minute, Peter Merchant opened the door, said hello and asked him in. As they entered the kitchen, Jasmine was stuffing paperwork into a drawer. The atmosphere was stiff with tension, but she managed a tight smile as they sat at the table. She wore a different yoga outfit today, in deep greens, and another felt hat in the same style, in a paisley pattern. When Swift asked if it was okay to stay on for a while, she said of course, although her tone was cool. She and Peter had bowls of porridge topped with bananas in front of them. The porridge was congealing and the same colour as Peter's cardigan. A cafetière stood in the centre of the table, but Swift wasn't offered any coffee.

'We ask for a contribution of ten pounds per day, if that seems fair,' Jasmine said.

'More than fair. I'll stay at Afan's for now, if that's okay, rather than in the Bivium, as there's a bigger bed.'

Peter Merchant ate fussily, stabbing the lumpy porridge with his spoon. He had an anaemic pallor but perhaps it was his colourless eyes that made him seem insipid. 'I suppose you're hoping that Afan will be back soon.'

Swift saw a flash of gold filling in his mouth. 'That's the idea. If I hang on, I'll get to catch up with him as intended.'

Jasmine gave him a narrow stare. 'How long are you planning to be with us?'

'A couple of days at least. Then I'll take stock, based on what's happening with Afan. I hope he'll be in touch soon.'

'Well,' she said, 'you needn't be at a loss for things to occupy you. We can always make use of an extra pair of hands in the community. Every season is busy here. I can draw up a little plan for you.'

I bet you can. He didn't mind helping out, but he wasn't proposing to spend his time being bossed around by Jasmine. 'That's okay. I'm sure I'll pitch in when I'm ready but first, I want to visit Holybridge and get my bearings.'

'As you wish,' she said, stirring her porridge.

The kitchen was cluttered and homely, decorated in a rustic style with low ceiling beams, open shelving, a cream Aga, piles of magazines and newspapers and a worn farmhouse table. There were vases of dried blossoms and wildflowers dotted around. Swift admired a sturdy willow armchair sitting at an angle to the fire, and an elegant white willow chaise longue with scalloped edges resting below a window.

He said, 'This is a lovely house.'

'Thank you,' Jasmine said more graciously. 'We're privileged to call it home.'

Swift saw her husband's mouth twist as if he was in pain. He asked, 'Did you make the willow furniture?'

'All my own work,' Peter replied.

'It's handsome.'

'Thanks. I take great pleasure in it.'

It was a magnificent house, sturdy and imposing, with sloping, timbered ceilings and deep windows. There was an open fire burning in the kitchen hearth, with pots and pans hanging from a rack overhead. The deep, wide fireplace reminded Swift of those he'd seen in the kitchens at Hampton Court. He pictured a pig roasting on a spit while a sweating kitchen boy turned it. The Merchants might cosily refer to themselves and all the smallholders as 'stewards', but they had ultimate control over this community, and the house stamped them as the landowners.

Swift addressed Peter. 'What made you decide to move here from London?'

The man's face brightened a little. 'I'd done my time in banking. We wanted a simpler life. I've spent many happy years with my wine and willow. Yes, good years, well spent. I read my poetry. Every morning I wake up and I'm grateful to be here in this little corner of heaven.'

There was a strange silence. Peter slumped a little in his chair while Jasmine chewed.

'I understand that a young man, Morgan Callender, went missing a couple of months ago,' Swift said.

Jasmine snapped, 'Who told you that?'

'Bruno.'

'I see. You never need to tune into the news here, there's always someone broadcasting. Yes, Morgan vanished from his home in Holybridge. He didn't live here. He was an occasional volunteer and not a particularly reliable one.'

'You must have been worried, all the same.'

'We were concerned, of course,' Peter replied, 'and sorry for his family, but we heard that he left a message saying that he'd decided to leave home.'

Jasmine pulled a face. 'He was a dissatisfied young man and when he did bother to turn up, he never finished a job properly. The police reckoned he'd taken off to London, or some other city. They see a lot of that. There's not much around here for youngsters. We have one other volunteer — one who hasn't taken off to the bright lights — who comes a couple of days each week. Her name's Caris Murray and unlike Morgan she's reliable, although she was friendly with him. I'll ask her to cast an eye over Afan's garden while she's here. Just to tidy it and pick any ripe produce for the kitchen. So if you see her, you'll not be concerned.'

'By the way, there's a natural spring at the back of the house,' Peter told him. 'We've seen maps that show it's been in use for more than two centuries. The water has a high calcium content, so it's good for teeth and bones. You can bring a bucket if you want any water from there for cold drinks. We generally use harvested rainwater for cooking, etcetera — it's fine as long as you boil it. Every home has rain barrels and of course we have a central reservoir.'

'Presumably, you'll be eating in the refec while you're here,' Jasmine said. 'You need to put your name down for supper by ten in the morning. The book's by the fridge in there. Now, if you don't mind, we've a lot to be getting on with.'

He went back to the refec and put his name in the book for supper. Bryn, Kat and Suki had already written in it. He didn't particularly want to eat with them all, but he didn't have much choice for now and he'd better show willing. He saw that Bruno would be cooking. A note in tight, backward sloping writing said, *Tonight's menu is homity pies with salads and plum crumble*. He'd never heard of homity pie. It sounded American.

He walked back to Afan's, going over the snippet of quarrel he'd overheard, wondering who Giles was and what it was about. It sounded as if the Merchants were in financial trouble. Did Afan know about it and was it the sourness he'd referred to?

He was on edge and decided to take a walk along the coastal path and find a phone signal. He hoped to have some further message from his friend. He'd noticed a local guide lying on top of the other books on the kitchen table, and he guessed that Afan had left it there for him. He sat in the surprisingly comfortable wooden armchair. It was on rockers and the back was shaped like a hand, with the fingertips forming a headrest. He turned to the maps in the guide and scanned the section of path that ran from Tir Melys to Holybridge. He read that it was a challenging trail, with regular ascent and descent, requiring good fitness: '*The landscape is wild and remote, with eight stiles to cross and steep gradients. The terrain is tough. About two miles along this section, you will note a Neolithic burial chamber, Carreg Trefin.*'

He put on his walking boots, tucked a bottle of water and a flapjack into the deep pockets of his waxed jacket, took a pair of binoculars from the back of the door and set off. He passed Bryn Price and Bruno. They were deep in conversation, mending a fence on Bryn's smallholding. Bryn waved, calling that the rain would hopefully hold off for a couple of hours.

In this southerly direction, the Tir Melys land ended in a narrow meadow dotted with purple bell heather, witch hazel, corn marigolds and comfrey. Scores of bees clustered around the blossoms and sheep were grazing by the far hedge. A stile at the end led onto the coastal path. Once Swift was on it, the ground started to wind and rise steeply, and a sharp breeze buffeted him. Goats wandered on the vertiginous cliffs above him, among tiny red sorrel flowers that turned the grass scarlet. At the top of a steep climb, he stood and trained the binoculars on the glittering sea below, sure that he could see bottlenose dolphins. Choughs, guillemots and kestrels wheeled overhead. The light was intense, vibrant. He could see why Afan had chosen to settle here after he left the anxiety and stresses of his job. It would have offered the prospect of a peaceful haven, of daily self-sufficiency and these natural wonders to roam. But he still thought that a few home comforts wouldn't go amiss in Afan's rural sanctuary.

He panned the horizon with the binoculars, his mind drifting to the man he hadn't seen for years. He remembered Afan's kindness on his return to Lyon from the harrowing trip to London, when he'd been ambushed and bruised by Ruth's news that she was leaving him. Afan had said little, but had bought him a drink and listened, his dark eyes pensive and gentle. His friend had been kind too when he'd been stabbed in the thigh during a raid on sex traffickers. Afan had returned from Brussels to Lyon for a conference, and he'd visited Swift in hospital, bringing good coffee, books and newspapers. To his discomfort, Swift couldn't recall repaying any of these kindnesses. He shouldn't have allowed the friendship to drift.

A ping on his phone told him he had a signal. He turned his back to the sun and saw that Ruth had sent him a photo of Branna frolicking on a beach, her arms thrown wide, captioned *Hi Daddy!* As always, when her photo was being taken, she was gurning for the camera. He laughed, felt a pang of separation and then filmed the cliffs and sea and sent the video for Branna with the caption, *Can you spot the dolphins?* There was no email or text from Afan. Swift rang his number, but it went to voicemail. He left a message, saying that he hoped everything was okay, and then sent a text.

Contact me when you can. In the meantime, I'm keeping your bed warm.

He walked on, stepping over three stiles, now climbing, now descending. Sweat dampened his neck and his lungs were expanding. He was panting as the path twisted left and then levelled out. About fifteen metres ahead, on a grassy slope, he saw the Neolithic burial chamber, a rough oval slab set aslant four supporting stones. The prehistoric dead would have had a fine, far-reaching view of sea, sky and cliffs. Branna would like a photo of this as well. She had a taste for the ghoulish — she'd been interested in death and why people had to die since learning about Anne Boleyn's beheading. Recently, she'd questioned him closely as to why some people were buried and some 'burned up'. He approached the chamber and was raising his phone, ready to take a photo, when he stopped in his tracks.

Someone lay within the shelter of the chamber. He couldn't see the head, which was hidden by a supporting stone. It looked like a man on his back. His first reaction was that this was someone who'd decided to take a rest after a strenuous walk, judging the chamber a useful shelter, out of the wind and inevitable rain. He called out twice, and then feared that this figure wasn't going to respond. His chest tightened. He climbed the slope and knelt down.

The man wore jeans and a black cagoule. His arms were folded across his chest. Swift's heart was heavy with foreboding. He took a breath and leaned into the shadow of the cairn. It was Afan. Afan with a leaner, weather-beaten face and a goatee beard. His eyes were closed, his expression peaceful. He could have been sleeping. There was no obvious injury. When Swift touched his arm, his body was stiff with rigor. A turquoise mug sat at the right side of his head and on the left side was a matching bowl. A paperback book with a deep yellow cover lay propped on his crossed hands. The title was *Hives and Honey*. Had Afan decided on suicide and arranged himself here, waiting for death? He searched carefully around the body, but could see no note, no bottle or empty tablet packet. Swift gazed for a few moments at Afan's older but familiar face and was shaken by grief.

A chill dizziness came over him. He sat on the hard ground of the slope, among fragrant broom with his head lowered between his legs. He took deep breaths until the world stopped spinning, then raised his head slowly and gazed up at black and white razorbills swooping to ledges on the climbing cliffs above. The only sounds were birdcalls, the rustling breeze and the restless sea. Afan was at rest here in this isolated burial place. Now he'd have to be dissected and examined on a pathologist's slab. *I should have come to see him sooner.*

He took his phone out, but the signal had vanished again. He retraced his steps fast along the path until a bar appeared, and phoned emergency services. Then he rang the landline at Tir Melys but no one answered, so he left a message, saying that he had found Afan's body and the police were on their way. He wondered if there was someone there who wouldn't be surprised by this news.

He walked back to Carreg Trefin and sat by his friend. Towering, black-grey clouds were moving in fast from the Irish Sea. The breeze strengthened and whipped the water into tall white crests. It started to rain, a slanting, soaking drizzle but, lost in thought, he barely noticed.

* * *

It was almost an hour before the police arrived. Swift gave his details to a DS Spencer and a brief description of how he'd found Afan's body. It took a lot of fumbling and repeated questions for the sergeant to record the information with his thick fingers. It was pouring now. (He heard Afan say, *sheets of rain.*) A dripping, grumpy-sounding DI Weber, who was the lead investigator, told him that he could head back to Tir Melys but he wasn't to give any details about Afan's body or its exact location.

Before he left, he turned back to the group of colleagues huddled around the cairn, the photographer bending close to the body. He was reluctant to go, but he'd only be in the way and he didn't want to get off on the wrong foot with DI Weber. She was a shrewd, rugged woman with her right arm in a cumbersome plaster and sling and she leaned on a curved walking stick. An elastic band, stretched across her chest between the buttons, secured her stockman's full-length coat. Even with the injured arm and the stick, she was formidable.

Swift's hooded waxed jacket had kept his head and torso dry, but his legs were drenched, his jeans clinging and heavy. He was fit from regular rowing but by the time he reached the meadow, he was tired to the bone. When he opened Afan's door, he was shivering, numb and drained. He stripped off his clothes, towelled himself dry, changed and hung the wet jeans and jacket over the stove. The cottage was chilly, so he lit a fire in the stove, using the last of the logs in a wicker basket beside it. He stood at the table, running a comb through his tangled curls, and observed the books. He couldn't recall exactly how many there had been when he'd first arrived, but he was sure that he'd seen one with a deep yellow cover and it was missing. He needed a mug of tea but didn't fancy oat milk, and he wanted to make the community aware of the awful news, so he found his leather jacket and set off for the refec.

Kat was standing in the doorway, leaning against the frame with arms crossed, hugging her body. She was ashen. She stammered, 'I just picked up your message. What's happened?'

'I found Afan's body. Let's go inside.'

He followed her into the kitchen. A man with mottled, dry skin, a hipster beard and long blond hair tied in a topknot was sitting at the table, checking wooden bowls of golden and purple plums.

Kat blurted out, 'Guy, Afan's dead! Ty found him!' She started to cry, deep loud sobs.

Guy Brinkworth stared, his fingers hovering over a bowl. He had an androgynous appearance and such sparse, pale eyelashes that his eyes seemed naked. 'When was this?'

'In the last hour or so,' Swift told him.

Kat was leaning against the table, howling now. 'Afan, oh, Afan,' she repeated.

Swift pulled a chair out for her. She smelled hot and sweaty. 'Sit down, Kat.'

Guy grimaced with a weary expression at Kat slumping onto the chair. 'What happened to Afan, was it an accident?'

'The police might be able to tell you more. They'll be arriving soon. I'm Ty Swift. I came to visit Afan but he wasn't here. Could you go around the site and ask everyone to come here? I should stay with Kat.' He was probably already stepping on DI Weber's toes, but at least he could tell everyone about Afan's death at the same time.

Guy looked disgruntled but stood, saying dispassionately, 'For goodness' sake, Kat, stop screeching and get a grip. You sound demented. We all know you like to emote but creating a scene doesn't help Afan or any of us.'

Her head jerked up and she glared at him, her face the colour of one of the dark plums. 'You heartless bastard! How on earth does Elinor put up with you? You're a cold, cold fish.'

Guy shot back, 'Better than being a shark, always lurking in the shallows to trap people. I wouldn't be surprised if Afan killed himself to get away from you.' He grabbed his coat and left the room.

Kat put her face in her hands and continued crying, more quietly now. Swift was used to strange reactions to bad news, but he was shocked by the acid exchange. He crossed to the kitchen and put the kettle on. He found teabags and a plastic box full of home-made spicy biscuits. While he waited for the kettle to boil, he opened the cupboards and checked out the crockery. He made the tea in a red earthenware pot and took it to the table, where he poured two mugs.

'Here, drink this. There's sugar if you want.'

Kat was chewing on the end of a plait. She reached out a hand for the mug of tea and said pleadingly to him, 'What happened to Afan? Please tell me.' She had a hair stuck to her bottom lip.

'All I can say for now is that I found his body. I'm sorry, you'll have to wait.'

'But . . . how did he die?'

'Kat, I don't know.'

'What Guy said — he didn't kill himself, did he? Afan wouldn't do that.'

He repeated, 'I can't tell you.' If you were minded to end your life, then Carreg Trefin might seem an ideal location.

'Oh my God, what will I do without him? How will I fill the terrible gap this leaves?'

This struck him as stagey, but it could be the shock making her sound like a ham actor. She looked terrible, her eyes raw and popping. Whatever Bruno and Guy said, Kat had been under the impression that Afan was an important person in her life. Swift drank his tea and ate a couple of biscuits. It was just the warming tonic he needed — and the sugar was warding off the shock, giving him energy.

Kat blew her nose and dabbed her eyes with the tissue. 'Afan was going to let me help him make a new mead. Just a small, trial batch. I'd found him an old Tudor recipe using elderberries and meadowsweet. I was really excited about the two of us working together.' Her eyes welled up again.

He said nothing. He recalled the postcard he'd found and that note of entreaty, *we could go foraging early one morning.* He suspected that Afan hadn't wanted to take Kat up on her offer. The hair-sucking alone would be unappealing. She'd constructed a fantasy about herself and Afan that bore little relation to reality. He sat in silence, feeling hollow and lost, while Kat sniffled and sighed.

The others started to troop in, bringing the dampness of rain with them. Suki first, followed by Bryn and the Brinkworths, with Elinor clutching Frankie in one arm and holding on to her husband's waist with the other. Bruno, Jasmine and Peter arrived together. They were all sombre and they glanced silently at Kat, who by now had a pile of damp tissues in front of her. Jasmine sat in her chair at the head of the table.

'What on earth has happened?' She glared at Swift as if he was the cause of the problem.

'I went for a walk along the cliff path, towards Holybridge. I found Afan's body. I called the police. They'll be here soon.'

'But what *happened* to him?' Jasmine said crossly.

'The police will tell you.'

'But . . . did he have an accident or something?' Suki was stroking her left hand with her right. She had little pale marks on her earlobes, where she'd worn studs.

'I honestly have no idea how he died. Even if I knew, or could guess, I couldn't tell you. The police would be very annoyed with me, and with justification.'

'He hadn't been ill recently,' Suki said, 'and he's always been in pretty good health, except for winter coughs. Maybe he had a heart attack, or a stroke.'

'I suppose you're familiar with police methods from your time with Interpol,' Peter said to Swift.

'Of course, and I used to work in the Met.' He'd revealed the information deliberately and noted the sharp glance that Bryn gave him.

'Interpol, the Met — you do have an interesting background.' Jasmine tucked some strands of hair under her hat. 'This is terrible news, hard to believe. Poor, poor Afan. He loved that walk on the coast path.'

'How long has he been dead?' Bryn asked Swift.

'The pathologist will determine that.'

Kat gulped back a sob. 'We should have searched the path last night. I'll never, ever forgive myself for not looking there. He was out there all night, all alone in the dark and cold and rain.'

Swift wondered how she could know that, but supposed that it was a natural assumption, given that Afan had gone missing the day before.

Peter said, 'We couldn't have gone up there in the dark, Kat. It would have been far too dangerous, and we had no reason to believe that we needed to search for Afan earlier in the evening. You can't blame yourself. This is all very puzzling, given the email you received, Ty.'

'It is, yes,' Swift agreed. He didn't want to be drawn into too much discussion for now.

Kat pointed at Guy. 'He said the most awful thing, that Afan might have killed himself!'

Guy stared at her. 'It's a possibility. No point in ignoring it.'

Jasmine said, 'I really don't believe that Afan would do that. Please, let's not speculate about what's happened until the police can tell us something definite. It's not helpful and it's distressing.'

Elinor had tears in her eyes. 'Afan was such a good man. He was always kind to Fwankie and said hello to him.'

The dog heard its name and started yapping loudly and turning around in her lap. Guy Brinkworth tutted with irritation, picked him up and dropped him on the floor with a firm 'Stay!' His wife bit her lip but didn't say anything.

Jasmine stood. 'Well, we need tea and coffee while we wait for the police. This has been a terrible shock for us all. Peter, can you help me? And can someone give Kat some clean tissues. Kat, dear, try to calm yourself.'

There was a bustle of activity. Suki found a box of tissues and put them in front of Kat. She sat beside her and patted her arm, but Kat flinched away. Suki made a little helpless gesture to Swift.

They sat in silence for a while with their hot drinks. The only sounds were the chink of crockery and Kat's shuddering breaths. Bryn was drinking gooseberry wine and had shoved a glass in front of Kat, muttering that she should drown her sorrows.

'I wonder when the news will get out locally,' Jasmine said.

'Worried it will be bad for business?' Bryn stared down into his glass.

'Of course that's not what I mean. It's just that there might be reporters or other nosy people to deal with. It's going to cause a stir, that's for certain. Ty, what's your view, from your police experience?'

'Hard to say. The local police will decide when to make it public. It won't be a priority, but they won't sit on it either.'

Elinor held her mug to her chest, cradling it. 'Afan was so happy here. He once said he'd found his own Garden of Eden.'

'The snake's arrived here now all right, and we'll all be suspects as far as PC Plod's concerned,' Guy said. 'We can say goodbye to the quiet life for a while. They'll be traipsing all over the place and sticking their noses into our business.'

'I'm sure that Afan would have been more considerate and gone further afield if he'd realised he was going to cause you inconvenience,' Suki snapped.

Kat gasped and covered her face with her hands. Silence fell again and Bryn, who was on his second glass of wine, started to sing softly in a pleasing tenor:

'*I don't ask for a luxurious life,*
The world's gold or its fine pearls,
I ask for a happy heart,
An honest heart, a pure heart.
A pure heart full of goodness
Is fairer than the pretty lily . . .'

The door banged open and DI Weber strode through, with DS Spencer and two constables in tow.

'Great song, Calon Lân, and that's a good voice you have there,' she told Bryn.

She introduced her team and checked that everyone who lived at Tir Melys was present. DS Spencer wrote down all their names. He stood very close to his boss, glancing at her nervously with thick-lidded, sleepy eyes. He had full red lips, floppy fair hair and a face that still held traces of puppy fat. His suit was too tight, straining across his shoulders. DI Weber informed the group that Mr Griffith had died from a stab wound and his body had been left near the coast path. His wallet was in his pocket but there was no sign of his mobile phone.

'I understand that you must all be very shocked, but we have to ask questions and make a nuisance of ourselves, and we have to work as quickly as we can. We'll try not to be too intrusive, but a man's life has been taken, so I'm sure you'll all bear with us.'

Kat started to cry again. Ignoring her, the inspector said that the police needed to search Mr Griffith's home and speak to everyone. She asked them all to stay where they were for now and told Swift that she wanted to talk to him first.

'You can use the Parley room if you wish,' Jasmine informed her, on her dignity. 'Ty can show you where it is.'

DI Weber spent a few minutes with her team. Then Swift led her through from the kitchen. She stared at the name on the room door.

'Parley as in Native American parleys with fork-tongued white man?'

'That's right.'

'Hmm.'

Inside, she poked at a low stool with her stick. She was nearly six feet tall, rangy and slim with a spatter of freckles on her cheeks and a mane of caramel brown hair caught up in a clip. With her trousers tucked into DMs, the little satchel slung across her chest and her walking stick, she might be taken for a shepherd rather than a detective. She propped her stick against the wall and sat down gingerly, muttering *verdammt*! She stretched out her feet. Her boots were patterned with red and green flowers.

'These stools are ridiculous. What's the point of furniture you can't get comfortable on?'

'Perhaps they're intended to stimulate discussion,' he said. 'Do you want me to get you a chair?'

'No, it's okay for now.'

'How did you get injured?'

She frowned at him. She had mobile, expressive eyebrows. 'None of your biz, but I fell a couple of weeks ago, broke my arm badly and sprained my ankle. The ankle's still dodgy. The stick helps me to balance.' She undid the elastic band and shrugged off her coat. She wore a baggy navy T-shirt over black jeans. 'I'm sorry about your friend. Very hard on you to find him like that. Talk me through how you come to be here.'

Swift explained his background with Afan, how they'd met in Lyon and the invitation he'd followed up. He detailed events since he'd arrived.

She eyed him appraisingly. 'So, you hadn't been in touch for ten years?'

'Yes, just over ten.'

'You don't have information about any family we can contact?'

'No. Afan once mentioned that he'd been orphaned but he never talked about any other family members. He seemed . . . alone in the world.'

She raised an eyebrow. 'Was it one of those typical male friendships, then? The kind where you do manly activities and never talk about anything personal?'

Her words rankled, partly because they'd touched a nerve, but he snapped back, 'It was a friendship. Friendships are varied and different, they're not all cut from the same cloth.'

She seemed to approve of his reply. 'So, back to when you arrived here. What time was that?'

'Just after three o'clock. Afan wasn't around, but I assumed that he was working.'

'So you went for a walk along the coastal path this morning because you thought that Mr Griffith might have contacted you?'

'That's right, and I needed a phone signal. I wanted the exercise as well. I hoped that Afan would have left me another message. It seemed out of character, the way he just took off when he was expecting me, and without trying to phone me or leaving a note.'

'Can you send me the emails you had from him?'

'I will, but there's no Wi-Fi or phone signal here so it'll have to wait.'

DI Weber shook her head, sounding testy. 'This place would drive me bonkers, being so cut off.'

'It's part of the attraction for the people who live here.'

'If you say so.'

'It's what they say. Any idea what was used to stab Afan?'

She shifted her injured arm and winced. 'Not yet. But there was little bleeding and whoever did it zipped his cagoule up for him after stabbing him.'

'The murder was planned. The blue bowl and mug by Afan's head — that crockery is made by Suki Mehta, who lives here. It's used in the kitchen and I believe she sells it.'

'She does. I've got some at home. Gave me a bit of a shock to see the same bowl I have my soup from.'

'I checked the communal kitchen cupboards when I got back here. Crockery sets usually come in even numbers and there are twenty-three mugs and bowls.'

'Okay, thanks. Of course, I presume it's also used in some of the homes here.'

'Probably. Afan has a set in the dresser. There are four mugs, bowls and plates.'

'Okay, thanks. DS Spencer tells me you're ex-Met. Did he get that right?'

'Yes. I'm a private investigator now.'

'Hmm. In London?'

'Mainly, but wherever the work takes me.'

'And you've no idea what Mr Griffith wanted to discuss with you?'

'No. I never got the chance to talk to him. There's something else you need to be aware of. I'm sure that the paperback resting on Afan's hands was on his kitchen table yesterday afternoon when I arrived. It's a distinctive colour.' He told her about returning to the cottage late the previous night and glimpsing a fleeting figure. 'That could have been the killer, fetching the book.'

DI Weber said, 'Risky.'

'Risky and strange.'

'So if this literary killer did take the book, they didn't have to break in?'

'No. They leave their doors open here.'

'Of course they do. You've only been here about twenty-four hours, but have you picked up on any animosity towards Mr Griffith?'

'Quite the opposite. He seems to have been well liked. He was a quiet man when I knew him in France. Kind, too. He hadn't changed, from what I've gathered. He kept bees, made mead, loved walking and often used the coastal path.'

'Sounds idyllic, but someone didn't like him. What can you tell me about the set-up here? I live fifteen miles the other side of Holybridge. I've heard of it, but I've not been here before.'

'The website is instructive, but it doesn't tell the full story. There's the farmhouse, where the Merchants live, and the smallholdings. When I read about it online, I assumed that the smallholders owned their houses and land. But the Merchants own the place and the stewards, as they're called, are tenants on five-year leases. Jasmine seems to be top dog. Kat Glover had unrequited feelings for Afan.'

'She's the mannish woman with the Pippi Longstocking pigtails and the weepy eyes?'

'That's right.' He'd decided not to mention the argument he'd overheard between the Merchants for now. DI Weber could do her own legwork. He added, 'They sometimes have volunteers who work here. One of them, a Morgan Callender, went missing a while ago.'

'Thanks, I'll check that out. Right, I'll leave it there for now.' She lifted her right foot and rotated the ankle carefully, wincing slightly.

Swift shifted on the back-breaking stool. 'I've been staying in Afan's cottage. The bed is much more suitable than the guest accommodation here. Is it okay if I continue to stay there?'

'I don't see why not. You can't go back there until later, when Spencer and forensics have finished the search. And to reiterate, you don't tell anyone about the location of the body in the cairn, or the presence of the crockery and book.'

He didn't like being patronised. 'I do understand how a police investigation works.'

She reached for her stick and said, 'Yes, but it's a while since you were a proper cop.'

If she was setting out to annoy him, she was succeeding. 'Being a private investigator doesn't mean I've forgotten my previous training. I rely on it. If you bother to check me out, you'll see that I've racked up some successful investigations. Sometimes, I've solved crimes when the police have failed.'

She narrowed her eyes at him. 'Don't get uppity with me. You could be Holmes, Morse and Maigret combined for all I care. I'm running this investigation, so my rules apply. I could kill for a coffee. What's it like here? Is it a proper job or something they make from acorns?'

He couldn't help smiling. 'It's ethically sourced from Colombia and a medium blend. I've had worse.'

'Sounds okay. Just to make it clear — you might be ex-Met and, according to your own publicity, a gold-standard PI, but you're a suspect until I rule you out. No special favours.'

'Of course. I wouldn't expect any favours,' he said.

She levered herself up, using the stick. 'I'll speak to Jasmine Merchant next. Can you ask her to organise coffee and then to come through — oh, and ask her to get two chairs brought in, otherwise I'll be carried out of here on a bloody stretcher.'

CHAPTER 6

It was late afternoon. The weather had settled into watery sunshine followed by sharp bursts of rain. Swift couldn't go back to Afan's yet, but he was restless and frayed. He walked up and down the veranda, gazing out at the saturated land. Suki was in her garden, ignoring the showers, picking runner beans and throwing them into a wicker basket on her arm. She moved slowly, halting now and again, staring into the mid-distance. As soon as the rain stopped, birds started calling and singing in a loud chorus. Wrens and robins darted to the ground for worms and insects. A vibrant rainbow shimmered to the west, lighting the sky. It was a peaceful, pastoral scene and at any other time, he'd delight in its loveliness. But today, he couldn't take any pleasure in it. Sadness weighed on him and he was conscious of the years that had gone, years when he could have seen Afan. He'd let them pass, caught up in the workaday world.

Someone had planned and made a ritual of Afan's murder, placing him in an ancient burial site with grave goods he'd need for his journey to another world. Was it done in mockery, or as a gesture of solace and respect, or maybe as a form of sacrifice? The fact that his cagoule had been zipped up over his wound indicated a kind of care, affection even.

He grew tired of pointlessly tramping the veranda, so he went inside and offered to help Bruno with preparing supper. The man must have known Afan as well as, if not better than, anyone here. Bruno had caught his hair into an elastic band. He'd just taken a bowl of pastry covered in clingfilm from the fridge and didn't seem keen on help but accepted grumpily. Then he made a rueful face and pointed an imaginary gun at his temple.

'Sorry. I'm being crabby. Talking to the police was exhausting and it put me on edge. So many questions, and this horrible sensation that they're trying to trap you. You've had a crap time today, finding Afan, and none of us have exactly sympathised. It's terrible for you.'

Innocent people could feel cornered when faced with a police enquiry, but Bruno's reaction seemed excessive. 'Thanks. It's not the meeting I was expecting with Afan. I'd anticipated laughter and the pleasures of catching up. It's not the first time I've found a body, although it's a different kind of shock when it's a friend.'

Bruno was startled. 'Wow, really? How many dead people have you dealt with?'

Too many. 'I don't keep count. If you're a detective, you have to expect that it might happen.' He remembered his girlfriend Kris Jelen. He'd found her body in her flat, where she'd been killed by a man who'd been paid to harass him. Then there was Ben Ramsay, the young man who'd been suffocated and left in Swift's house. Ruth had had Branna in her arms when she found his body. She still used it as a stick to beat him with. He couldn't blame her. He could hear her now. '*It's a dirty job that you do. Doesn't the taint of it bother you? I worry about it impacting on Branna as she grows up and finds out about some of the things you've been involved with.*'

Bruno said, 'Yeah, I guess. Afan didn't do that kind of work in Interpol, did he? No way can I imagine him dealing with violence and the dead.'

'No, Afan was a senior officer in criminal intelligence. He dealt with information about the people who traded in crime. He examined and liaised on international data about criminal activity: times, locations, backgrounds, activity in sex and drug trafficking and illicit markets, stuff like that.'

Bruno unwrapped the pastry. 'Amazing, the things you find out about folk. It's all a long way from beekeeping in rural Wales. I had no idea. He didn't talk about what he'd done before he came here. Mind you, neither did I.' He sprinkled flour on the worktop. 'Jasmine asked for us all to eat together tonight, but I've no idea if anyone will have an appetite. The pies will keep for a few days if they're not eaten. Well, if you want to lend a hand, you can prepare a couscous salad. The ingredients are on the counter there.'

Kat was still sitting at the table, staring down, alternating the pigtails to her mouth. Now and again, she groaned softly.

'I wish she'd go home,' Bruno muttered, glancing at her. 'I asked her if she wanted to help with the food, but she didn't reply.'

'She's in shock.'

'Yeah. We all are, but chewing her hair isn't going to help any. I'm amazed she hasn't got stomach trouble. I googled it. It's a kind of OCD thing, called trichotillomania. I'm not one to talk, I have my own problems, but I wish she'd get therapy.' Bruno was rolling out the shortcrust pastry with deft movements. 'I just don't get it. Afan was the sweetest, gentlest guy. Why would anyone want to kill him? I mean, if his wallet wasn't taken, it wasn't a robbery.'

'No, that wasn't the motive. Had Afan had any disagreements with anyone, here or locally?'

'None that I heard about. He just kept bees, made mead and grew vegetables. A steady, trouble-free, day-to-day routine. It's not the kind of life that leads you into disputes with people.'

Not entirely true, given Afan's email. Bruno was painting a rosy picture that didn't quite add up. Swift observed him as he dusted the rolling pin with flour. Did he have a reason for painting that picture? Was it a smokescreen?

Something had troubled Afan and he'd fallen foul of someone. And from what Swift had seen of this community, they were like a squabbling extended family with some prickly members. They were isolated, too, spending a lot of time in close proximity. That could provide fertile soil for resentment, and resentment could ripen into murder.

Bruno rubbed flour from his fingers and turned to him. 'Was it really Afan who sent you that email, saying that something urgent had come up?'

Swift quartered tomatoes. 'No, I think his killer sent it, to delay any concerns about him.' *So the killer knew I was visiting, which indicates that it was probably someone who lives here or has contact with Tir Melys.* 'How many volunteers come here?'

'At the moment, just Caris Murray. She's here at various times.'

'What about Jasmine's counselling and therapy — that must bring people here?'

'That's more her wish list than a reality. Nobody signed up for her recent course. Maybe there's not much need around here, or maybe she's not much good at it. I'm not sure her heart's been in it the past couple of months, and empathy isn't her forte. She has a thyroid problem, which saps her energy a fair bit, so I guess that's a factor. She sleeps most afternoons, can't make it through the day without a nap.'

'You don't like her much, do you?'

Bruno grunted. 'Not particularly. She's patronising and her grand style can be jarring. Afan and I used to laugh about it. He'd refer to her as "the chatelaine". She's particularly grandiose when she gives her harp concerts, dressed up in Celtic-themed gear. She sells tickets for them locally, so people come here for those. She's a good player, but anyone would think she was a virtuoso.'

Swift reached for a bowl of cooked peas and added them to the tomatoes. He popped one in his mouth. It was fresh and sweet. 'Did Afan know many people in Holybridge?'

'I'm not sure. He went there fairly regularly, to the bookshop and the café, for Wi-Fi.'

'He did a beekeeping course, didn't he?'

'That's right, this April. He was going to Welsh lessons too, once a week on Fridays. He'd forgotten most of what he'd learned at school. You can chop some spring onions for that, then the couscous can go in. It's ready in the fridge.' Bruno cut two circles of pastry and laid them in greased pie dishes, raising and patting the sides. 'Afan was so clued-up about the bees. I'll be scratching my head without him.' His voice caught and he passed a forearm across his face. 'The police were searching the kitchen cupboards. What was that about?'

'They make all kinds of searches. Part of their process.'

Bruno stiffened. 'I suppose that means they'll do background checks on everyone here as well.'

Talking about the police again had rattled him. 'That's right. Does that bother you?'

Bruno didn't answer, cracked an egg into a mug and whisked it with a fork. Swift read his silence as a yes.

Homity pies turned out to originate from Devon, not America. Bruno put a mixture of cooked potatoes, onion, spinach, cream and grated cheese in each dish and then grated nutmeg on top. He covered the pies with pastry lids, crimped them down and brushed a glistening egg wash over each.

'I reckon we might be eating late so I won't put these in yet. That salad could use a bit of mint, if you like, and then you could make one with leaves. If you don't mind, I'll just work now and not talk. I'm okay with company up to a point, then I get irritable.'

'I've noticed.' Swift found him a likeable man, despite his changeable moods.

'Yeah, I'm so subtle. I have depression. That's not an excuse. Just the way I am. I have good, intermediate and bad days. Today's so-so.'

Bruno switched on the radio to a Welsh station, Dragon Radio, and they worked on in silence, listening to Fleetwood Mac, Bob Marley and Katherine Jenkins. Swift found the monotony of chopping and mixing therapeutic. His mind cleared and quietened in the way it did when he was rowing.

It was just after eight o'clock when the police left. Bruno lit the candles and they all sat down to eat. There was an air of relief and exhaustion around the table.

Jasmine closed her eyes and made the Namaste greeting. 'We gather as a sorrowful community this evening. This is a dreadful time for us all, and we have to remain strong and help each other through it. We miss Afan, our dear friend and fellow steward. We will continue to honour the land in his memory.'

Swift scanned the table. They all had their eyes closed, including Bruno, but Bryn Price spoke to Jasmine as soon as she'd finished.

There was a challenge in his voice. 'We *are* continuing with our stewardship of Tir Melys then, Jasmine?'

Jasmine stiffened. 'Of course we are. I don't understand what you mean, Bryn.'

They were all gaping at him. He poured himself a large glass of wine, holding their attention. 'Just checking. I heard a rumour that you might be planning to move on from here.'

There was a shocked murmur as his blustering voice carried around the table. Kat gasped and placed a palm to her heart.

Jasmine took a sip of water. 'Where did you hear that?'

'Oh, just around and about.'

'You shouldn't listen to gossip,' Peter Merchant said. He put a hand over his wife's. 'We've all had enough of a shock today, Bryn, without you worrying people unnecessarily.'

'It's not true, then?' Bryn asked. He sounded as if he was enjoying himself.

Jasmine had rallied. 'It certainly isn't, and I've no idea where such a lie has come from. This community is dear to our hearts. Really, Bryn, you must trust us more than that.'

'I'd say I've worked out how much I can trust you.'

Guy tilted his glass at Jasmine, a little smile on his lips. His hair was loose and flowing down his back, enhancing his androgynous air. He was wearing a chunky silver and gold ring with a zigzag topaz stone and a matching plaited necklace. 'As you always say, Jasmine, respect is our watchword at Tir Melys.'

Jasmine tugged her hat down. 'Exactly. Now let's eat, although I have to confess, I haven't much appetite.'

'Homity pie was one of Afan's favourites,' Kat whispered.

They were all silent while they helped themselves to the food. Swift tried some of the gooseberry wine. It was almond-coloured, light and refreshing.

'The police were asking me about my pottery, where I sold it.' Suki said. 'They counted my crockery and asked how many of each item I usually had. Weird.' She was wearing a sari this evening, white polka dots on black cotton, with a white T-shirt under the folds.

'Were they all accounted for?' Swift asked.

'Yes. What was that about? Why did you ask?'

'I just wondered,' he said easily.

'I told them I broke a couple of pieces in the kitchen a few months back,' Kat said.

'Most of us have some of your pottery,' Elinor told Suki. 'Terry, our social worker, admired it when he came last week. I told him it's for sale in Davis's in Holybridge. He really liked it, didn't he, Guy? He said he was going to buy a set.' She smiled brightly at her husband. Frankie was in place on her lap, subdued.

Guy finished chewing and said in a bored voice, 'I couldn't say, I didn't take much notice. I try to ignore Terry's irritating voice as much as possible, especially when he mispronounces words. If he says "perogative" instead of "prerogative" and "mischeeveeus" instead of "mischievous" again, I'll start howling. And don't get me started on his atrocious grammar, getting "their/they're" and "your/you're" mixed up in his reports.' He spelled the words aloud. 'Apostrophes are too high a mountain for Terry to climb. It's hard to believe that a dullard like him is responsible for deciding if highly educated people should adopt a child. I wouldn't let him make a decision about Frankie's welfare.'

'His heart's in the right place and he's very kind and understanding,' Elinor said.

Guy snorted. 'What an accolade about a supposed professional. But then, your standards are lower than mine, Elinor, and you think that emotions rank higher than intellectual rigour.'

'Oh, I'm so sorry . . . I didn't mean . . . so stupid of me . . .' Flustered, Elinor dropped her fork on the floor. Frankie barked and she shushed him.

'Best to engage brain before you speak,' her husband advised. 'Returning to the subject of Suki's pottery, I don't suppose her sales are at the top of her agenda on a sad day like this.'

'At least Elinor's got a brain, Guy, instead of a head full of spite,' Bryn said.

Swift would never have put Guy and Elinor together as a couple, but perhaps it was a case of polar opposites attracting. He was skinny, with girlish, prissy features, and a long nose that he used for looking down. She'd piled her plate with food, whereas he had small portions. Swift couldn't help remembering the rhyme, *Jack Sprat could eat no fat, his wife could eat no lean.*

Elinor rubbed her fork on her paper napkin. 'It was horrible, being questioned by that detective, having to give an account of where you've been and what you've been doing. Why is it that the police make you believe you're a suspect even when you're completely blameless?'

Bryn folded his arms. 'Is anyone completely blameless? I doubt it. Most of us have things we'd rather keep quiet about. I bet even you have, Ty.'

Swift said, 'Of course. Most of us have committed some kind of petty misdemeanour: sticking a postage stamp upside down, beeping a car horn without good reason, parking on the pavement. Luckily, not many of us commit murder.'

Jasmine cleared her throat. 'We all need to gather here at the Bivium at ten tomorrow morning. The police are coming back to fingerprint us. DI Weber seemed to find it odd that we didn't have next of kin details for Afan.'

‘He was born in Cardiff,’ Kat said hoarsely. ‘I remember him saying that and I told the sergeant. I asked Afan once if he wanted a Mother’s Day card because I had a couple of spares, but he said he was without a mother to send one to. That was ever so sad. I really felt for him.’ She was picking at her food and pushing it around the plate.

Bruno threw her a withering glance. ‘Is it sad, necessarily? Afan was in his forties. Lots of people have lost a parent by the time they reach that age, and from what I knew of him, he wouldn’t have been maudlin about it.’

‘You didn’t know him like I did, none of you did,’ Kat said meaningfully.

Guy sniggered. ‘In your dreams.’

Kat pointed her knife at him. ‘*You* couldn’t stand him. You weren’t fit to clean his shoes.’

Bryn tapped his glass. ‘Now now, children, play nicely at a time of mourning. What will our guest make of us?’

Jasmine spoke quietly. ‘Yes, this isn’t a time for bickering. Please show respect for Afan and our visitor. We should all bear in mind that Ty has had the biggest shock today and he’s dealt with it very well indeed.’

Swift concentrated on his pie. Even when she was trying to be kindly, Jasmine couldn’t help but sound condescending.

Bryn sat back with his forearms stretched on the table. ‘I wonder where Afan’s phone is.’

‘In the sea, I expect. It would be the obvious place to chuck it. And the weapon, whatever it was. I doubt the police will ever find either.’ Guy turned to Swift. ‘You haven’t told us much about how you found Afan. Was he right on the path? Could you see the stab wound?’

‘The police have asked me not to discuss it.’

‘It’s just as well I didn’t find him,’ Elinor said. ‘I’d have been a nervous wreck, wouldn’t I, Fwankie? I’d probably have collapsed on the path and then I’m such a blabbermouth, I’d have told everyone the details. I can’t keep anything to myself.’

'Yes, you do prattle on,' her husband said. 'Emotionally incontinent Elinor.'

'How quickly things change,' Bruno said softly. 'If Afan was here, you wouldn't be speaking like that to Elinor. Better be careful, Guy. The police might think you had a strong motive for not wanting him around.'

A silence fell. Elinor folded in on herself, stroked Frankie's ears and kissed his forehead. He looked up at her adoringly and then settled his head on his paws. Swift wondered if he was keeping a low profile this evening because Jasmine was present.

Peter filled his glass with water and said, 'I was wondering if maybe someone, a tourist or a walker, no one local at any rate, met Afan on the path and they had an argument for some reason. It might have been someone on drugs, or perhaps a schizophrenic person who should be in hospital and whose medication wasn't controlled. You do hear of such random things happening.'

'And this random person just happened to be carrying a weapon?' Bryn laughed.

'Interesting that you should choose someone with a mental illness as the murderer, Peter.' Bruno stared at him. 'Not that you're into stereotyping. Mad, bad and dangerous.'

'I didn't mean it in that way,' Peter said hastily.

'Really? Putting it more politely than Guy, which is no great effort, maybe you should think more carefully before you theorise.'

Kat banged a hand on the table. 'Can't you all just shut up! Stop going on about things that don't matter and being nasty to each other. Afan's dead, he's never coming back and all you can do is squabble!' She shoved her chair away from the table and stomped out of the room.

Guy broke the silence. 'Kat won't be wanting pudding, then.'

Suki glared at him. 'You're embarrassing yourself and the rest of us. What must Ty make of us?'

'I should imagine he's used to witnessing the tension created by a murder,' Guy told her. 'It's not a time for worrying about social graces.'

Suki fired back, 'Not that you're blessed with those.'

'Hush, everyone, please! You are too much sometimes, Guy,' Jasmine said to him. 'We need to be kind to each other at a time like this. I suggest we finish eating and all get an early night. It's been an arduous day. I'll call on Kat and make sure she's okay. Remember, DI Weber said that we should all start locking our doors, especially at night, until this investigation is over. It goes against the grain, but best to do as she asked.'

'I wonder why she spells her name Weber and not Webber?' Elinor said. 'What do you think, Fwankie?'

'She's from a German family, hails from Haverfordwest,' Bryn told her. 'Her Dad came here from Hanover in the Eighties, something called an Erasmus scholarship, and he decided to stay. You'll like her, Guy, what with her coming from an educated family and being a graduate herself. She's trilingual and speaks proper and all, not like some of us dunces. She'll make sure your statement is typed up with no spelling or grammar errors. I heard her swear in German. Impressive, eh?'

Guy folded his arms and sighed.

'I hope she's more professional than her dress suggests,' Jasmine said. 'I'd say she gets her clothes from a charity bin and those Doc Martens are the kind of boots teenagers wear. At least the sergeant had a suit on.'

Apart from Elinor, they'd eaten little of the main course. Bruno carried it away to the fridge and brought back the plum crumble. Most people took just a spoonful and they ate in silence. Frankie fell asleep and snored softly. Swift enjoyed the sharpness of the fruit and realised that the shock of finding Afan was starting to wear off. The residents were all preoccupied and weary. This community had suddenly found itself in peculiar circumstances, and that stress could bring out the worst in people. Yet the more he saw of them and listened to their backbiting, the less he understood why Afan had wanted to make his home among them.

He glanced at the Merchants. Jasmine was staring into space, chewing at her bottom lip and Peter seemed to have aged ten years in a day. He wondered what they were up to and why they were concealing it from their tenants.

* * *

At Afan's cottage, the stove was still glowing. Swift fetched logs from the stack by the shed and fed them in. Flames were soon dancing. The police had searched neatly, and the books were in two straight piles on the table.

Swift went through the cottage carefully, searching in the dresser and the wardrobe and the bookshelves in the bedroom, unsure what he was hoping to find. Anything that might indicate what Afan had been concerned about, although the police would probably have got to it first. It didn't take him long, with such sparse possessions.

The wardrobe contained a couple of pairs of jeans and jumpers, half a dozen T-shirts, two waterproof, fleece-lined trousers, a long coat similar to DI Weber's and half a dozen cotton shirts from Marks and Spencer. No Louis Vuitton. On the floor, ranged against the back, he saw a couple of Kat's clunky bird woodcarvings. They were as far as it was possible to imagine from the beautifully crafted antiques that Afan had owned in Lyon. Poor Afan, unwilling to exhibit them but too kind or embarrassed to get rid of them. In front of them were one pair of elegant brown leather shoes and a pair of hiking boots. Swift picked up a shoe and saw the label, *Chaussures comme des Gants*. Shoes like gloves. He recalled when Afan had had them handmade in Lyon, from calf leather. One evening, when they'd met for a walk by the river, he'd just come from a measuring session in the shop along the quays. Afan's feet had been narrow and he'd had difficulty finding shoes that fitted. As they'd crossed the Pont Bonaparte, he'd said that he liked to spend his money on comfort. Swift was glad now that he had, but wondered at the life change that had led him to give up his luxury for the austerity of Tir Melys. Perhaps, in the words of the song Bryn had sung, he'd been seeking a happy heart.

The wardrobe had a set of three drawers down the left-hand side. The top held underwear and socks, the middle one contained folded wool scarves and in the bottom one were odds and ends: a tape measure, a small torch, a hammer, assorted hooks and nails, superglue, a couple of padded envelopes, folded carrier bags, a large pair of scissors and underneath all of these a plastic box containing seven sets of keys. Each set had a large mortice and a smaller Yale. They had tags, numbered one to six, and one labelled '*FD*'. Swift was surprised that the police hadn't taken them. DS Spencer had been in charge of searching the cottage — he must have a sluggish brain as well as sleepy eyes.

Swift had hoped that he might find a password for Afan's email account but from what he knew of his friend, he'd have recorded it securely online. There were no personal or financial papers and no copy of a will. Swift was sure that careful, methodical Afan would have made one, and it would reveal if there was a next of kin. He presumed that any such personal documents were in DI Weber's possession now.

He sat on the bed and rummaged through the bookcase. He found mainly novels, local history and biographies of famous Welsh figures: Owen Glendower, Dylan Thomas, Aneurin Bevan, Henry VII and Katheryn of Berain, who he'd never heard of. He read on the blurb that she was called the mother of Wales, because of her many notable descendants. The cover photo showed a serious, pale woman wearing a Tudor ruff. The first three biographies were dog-eared, second-hand paperbacks from Holybooks Preloved. The Berain was a newly minted hardback and when he read the flyleaf, he saw Kat's handwriting. *From one Kat about another Kat! Hope you enjoy xx*. She was persistent in her wooing, and the book looked unread. On the bottom shelf, there were a couple more books on learning Welsh and a pamphlet printed by

Holybridge Beekeepers Club. Swift flicked through it and read the introductory paragraph.

The hum of bees is music in our gardens.

Honeybees have existed on our planet for far longer than human beings. From the very earliest human records, there is evidence that people have sought their honey. There are several primitive Stone Age cave paintings apparently showing people robbing bees' nests. Some people say they can even see in some of the pictures that a man is carrying a smoking torch — evidence that even at this early date smoke was being used to pacify the bees.

We call ourselves beekeepers but in reality, we work with the bees and we depend on their industry and skill.

He saw a couple of notes in the margins in what he assumed was Afan's writing. *Only work with locally sourced bees. Best to have a hive tool that's a bright colour.*

It was gone eleven and he should really have been getting to bed, but he fancied a nightcap first. He'd seen an opened bottle of blackberry mead in the dresser. He poured some to taste. It was rich and fruity. He was about to sit by the stove with it when there was a knock on the door. Suki stood outside with the rain whipping at her back and her sari flapping.

'It's late, but do you mind if I come in for a minute?'

'Of course.'

She hung her coat on a hook. 'I won't stay long. Afan was on my mind. I was twitchy and I saw that your light was on.'

'That's okay. Murder makes people anxious. I was just having a glass of mead. Would you like one?'

'Please.'

He gave her a glass and pulled two chairs to the stove. They sat quietly for a few minutes, drinking. He felt the warmth of the drink and the companionship ease the tensions of the day.

'I never liked mead before I tasted Afan's,' Suki said. 'He was modest about his talents but whatever he set his mind to, he did it well.'

It was an epitaph that his friend would have appreciated, and he told her so.

Suki sat with her toes tucked behind the bar below the chair. She was wearing a tasselled cream poncho over her sari and drew it around her like a blanket. 'I was worrying about what Bryn said.'

'About the Merchants selling up?'

'Mmh. Thing is, Bryn can be a bit of a troublemaker. He likes to stir things up. But he's also quite good at sniffing out gossip. He comes from Holybridge and he knows everyone and all the family histories, going back generations. He drinks at one of the pubs and chats to all and sundry.'

'Why don't you ask him directly what he's heard?'

'I might. He's weaselly, though. You don't always get a straight answer from Bryn.'

'Jasmine assured everyone that it was untrue.'

'Hmm. But . . . well, there's nothing to stop them selling if they want to, and all of our tenancies come up for renewal in November. There has to be three months' notice on either side.'

Swift stretched his legs and yawned. 'Why would they want to sell?'

'I've no idea. They've always seemed very settled and committed to the Tir Melys project. Although . . . I have wondered recently if their enthusiasm has flagged. Partly to do with Jasmine's health. She seems to have lost some of her energy. It's a shame that we haven't developed more activities for the public to access. I can see Jasmine's point of view, though. She maintains that we don't want to spoil the natural beauty and peace that we have here with lots of coming and going.'

They didn't sound very settled when I heard them this morning. 'Maybe you should talk to Jasmine and Peter on your own or raise it again at the colloquy.'

'Yes, I might do both.' She glanced around. 'I haven't been in here for a while. Nothing's changed. Afan liked to keep it simple — far too minimalist for me. My cottage has the same layout, but I like my decorations. Afan lived a bit like one of the hermits who used to inhabit the chapel. We had a good chat about tomato varieties the last time I came over. I'd have visited more often, but Kat wouldn't have liked it.'

'What's it to do with Kat?'

Suki shook her head and sipped her drink. 'She'd been courting Afan since she arrived here. He wasn't interested, but the problem is that unless you're really direct with Kat, she doesn't get the message. We all tiptoe around her because of her lameness and then there's her woodcarving . . .'

'It's not very good.'

'It's awful and embarrassing, but she's convinced it's accomplished. She's never been able to sell any, except for the odd piece here and there. Guy being Guy, and proud of never mincing his words, told her that she should find a market with blind people — which was very cruel, but only what we were all thinking. Those two can't stand each other.'

'I've noticed Guy's sharp tongue.'

'He's like that with everyone, although Elinor comes in for the unkindest comments. I don't understand how she puts up with him and I'm puzzled as to why he married her, given that she seems to irritate him so much and he clearly doesn't regard her as his equal.'

'Maybe that's the reason. He needed someone to patronise and torment.'

'And she is a bit of a victim, our Elinor. Guy likes controlling her. He monitors her and snoops on her when she's talking to people, despite apparently regarding her conversations as trivial.'

'Tell me more about Kat and Afan.'

'Kat saw me leaving here the evening I came over, and she pretty much warned me off seeing Afan. I tried to tell her that I had no designs on him, and anyway I have a partner. He's in Italy at the moment, but we've been together for a while. I could see that Kat was jealous and annoyed, so I stayed away. It's a small community and I didn't want to cause any tensions. I wouldn't want Kat as an enemy.'

Swift could see the problem — Suki was pretty and dainty, especially in her draped sari, and her pottery was skilfully made. 'Does your partner usually live here with you?'

'No, he's based in Cardiff. He's a scuba diver, so he travels a lot. He got a major contract to work in Genoa. He'll be back at Christmas.'

'You must miss him.'

'Yes, I do. But overall, it works for us. Are you married?'

'No. Almost, once.' He often wondered how life might have been if Ruth hadn't left him and they'd married. They'd probably have made a success of it, but in that alternative universe, Branna might not have existed and he couldn't imagine life without her now. No point in tormenting himself with *what ifs*. He wrenched himself back to the here and now. 'How did Kat acquire her limp?'

'Oh goodness, she was keen to tell us all soon after she arrived here. She used to be a weightlifter and a gym trainer. She was using a squat machine, and the weight fell on her leg and broke it in three places. She had to have several operations, and in the end, they removed some bone, hence the built-up shoe. When she recovered, she came here. Her injury was awful, but she trades on it at times. I've noticed that her limp is more pronounced when she's not getting enough attention. I suspect that she was a better weightlifter than woodcarver.' She smiled wryly. 'I'm sounding catty now, and I've probably shocked you, but she can be hard work.'

'She seems very cut up about Afan.'

'Hmm . . . well . . . she saw a rosy future. Sad, really. It was never going to happen.'

'The French have an expression, "*la douleur exquise*". It translates as "the exquisite pain".' Afan had told him that when he was grieving for Ruth. It had summed up his emotions exactly.

'The French always do have the right expression for these things, somehow.'

'Did Afan have a partner during the time he lived here?'

'He never mentioned anyone, never brought anyone here.' She laughed. 'Bryn has a friend, Dilys, who visits him now and again. She's from Swansea and she has a husband there. It's obvious when she's staying because there's loud music from Bryn's — blasts of Iron Maiden and Motorhead. Jasmine complained to him once and he told her not to be po-faced.' She put her empty glass down. 'What I said about Guy earlier wasn't entirely true. He was never sarcastic towards Afan, hence Bruno's comment at supper.'

'Why was that?'

'I'm not sure. Afan had this way of showing that although he was quiet and kindly, he didn't tolerate bullshit. If Guy started being unpleasant while Afan was around, Afan would just fix his gaze on him and Guy would grind to a halt. I'm blabbing on now, like Elinor. I'd better go and let you turn in. I'm a bit of a night owl and I have to remember that most people aren't.'

Swift said, 'Thanks for calling in. If Kat spots you, at least you won't get into trouble for visiting me. You don't usually lock your doors here, but are there any places on Tir Melys that are kept locked — that you'd all have keys for?'

Suki shook her head. 'Nowhere, no. Why do you ask?'

'Oh — probably something and nothing. By the way, who is Giles? I heard Jasmine refer to him.'

'Giles is the Merchants' son. He's in London. He lived here for about two years when they bought Tir Melys and he made it clear that he couldn't wait to get away. He resented the move from London. It was probably unfair to uproot a teenager in that way. He and Peter don't get on too well. Giles is a bit of a mummy's boy. Anyway, he headed back to London as soon as he was eighteen. He rarely comes here — in fact, it must be three years since I've seen him, and all he did then was moan about the weather and the lack of broadband. He's nothing like his parents.'

'Not a country lover?'

Suki smiled. 'Not at all. Giles is a city dweller, through and through. Sharp dresser, likes the good life. He owns a business, some baking enterprise.' She got up and reached for her coat. He saw sadness in her eyes. 'Thanks for the chat. It's good to be able to talk about Afan with a friend of his who doesn't live here. Different perspective.'

'Any time. Night now, don't get too wet.'

He stood at the door and watched her hurry home. Had she called in for more than a chat and a glass of mead? He'd sensed some subtext beneath her friendly approach. He suspected that she was someone who controlled herself well. He locked up and rinsed the glasses, recalling Afan's clear gaze in meetings. He'd turned it on a couple of unfortunate colleagues who'd tried to bluff their way through badly prepared briefings. His friend had been a good example of the power of silence. Perhaps Guy Brinkworth had had reasons for resenting that power.

He considered the keys in Afan's wardrobe. They might be important. He decided to tuck them away in a more secure place until he found what they unlocked.

He opened a window. The moon was high and full, and the rain was clearing. The sky was bright with stars and he could see Venus, casting its dazzling silver light in the heavens.

CHAPTER 7

Swift enjoyed a solitary breakfast the next morning, and his heart sank when Elinor appeared with Frankie just as he was finishing his coffee. She seemed startled and a little feverish. Her hair was a snarled, uncombed mess.

'We overslept, didn't we, Fwankie? And naughty Daddy Guy went out on his bike without waking us. The social worker's visiting later this morning for the next phase of our adoption,' she told Swift. 'I do hope Guy will be back in time. He was late once before for one of these appointments when he'd gone cycling, and it doesn't give the right impression. He sat through the interview all sweaty and a bit pongy, to be honest. I could see Terry wrinkling his nose although he didn't say anything. He's very open and friendly, but you can never guess what a social worker's thinking and making notes of. Are you okay after your awful shock? Have you had enough to eat? Can I get you anything? The eggs will be fresh from the hens this morning.'

'I've eaten, thanks. You get your own.'

With Frankie under one arm, she helped herself to a brimming bowl of porridge and four slices of toast piled with strips of bacon and brought it to the table. She saw Swift looking. 'I'm an anxiety eater. I wish worry made me go off food.'

He made no comment. She'd become enormous if her stress levels didn't diminish soon. She and Guy would be like an old-fashioned sideshow act — the Fat Lady and the Thin Man. He watched as she ate greedily. Her acerbic husband didn't appear as eager to be a parent as she did, cycling off as a passive-aggressive ploy and a means of sabotage.

Elinor started to talk about the adoption again and seeing how nervous and anxious she was, he listened for a short while. She explained that this stage of the process was where they had to talk through why they wanted to adopt, the kinds of children — '*infinks*' — that they would best be able to care for, and their overall strengths and suitability. She was drawing up a list of these aspects and she kept leaving it on the table, hoping that Guy would contribute. He just said it was mumbo-jumbo and why wouldn't a married couple, well-educated with a good income and living in idyllic surroundings, be suitable? Swift wanted to ask her if she'd considered the possibility that her husband didn't in fact want children, but that would be a painful conversation and it was the social worker's job. He assumed that Terry must have spotted the problem.

When she drew breath, he excused himself, saying he had things to do. Elinor continued a monologue to Frankie while Swift fetched milk and bread from the kitchen to take back to the cottage. When he left the room, Elinor was staring into space while Frankie licked at her cereal bowl.

Swift drove into Holybridge late in the morning, and parked near the bookshop, Holybridge Preloved. He checked his phone and saw that the news of Afan's death had been released to the press, with a head-and-shoulders photo of him that must have been copied from his passport. It was the clean-shaven, urbane Afan he used to work with. That meant that the police had either found next of kin or established that there was none. He skimmed a report.

Murder has taken place in a peaceful coastal setting in the beautiful Pembrokeshire countryside. The body of Afan Griffith was discovered yesterday on the coast path, three miles from Holybridge. Mr

Griffith, 45, had been stabbed. He lived and worked at Tir Melys and was familiar to the community in Holybridge. Mr Griffith went missing some time after mid-morning on Monday.

DI Sofia Weber has appealed for information from anyone who spoke to Mr Griffith recently, saw him on the coastal path or saw anyone acting suspiciously in the area.

Swift strolled around, getting a sense of the market town. It was thriving and prosperous, a popular holiday destination with the middle classes. That explained the organic grocery, wholefood and herbal remedy shop, upmarket outdoor clothing outlet and artisan bakery. There was also a market running the length of the main street, and Swift could see at a glance that there was no tat for sale.

The bookshop was double-fronted, painted a faded green and cream, with a striped canvas awning that had seen better days and a bright, busy window display. One window was full of community notices and posters for parent and baby groups, allotment holders, church meetings, craft workshops, book clubs, Holybridge historical society, an over-sixties club, a walking group, and one which caught Swift's eye.

Welsh classes, all levels

Don't be shy, get started or brush up on what you've forgotten

Ask in the bookshop for details

He also spotted a poster with the Tir Melys logo.

Harp Concert by Jasmine Merchant

24 August, 7.30 p.m., the Bivium, Tir Melys

Refreshments available

Tickets £5 from Holybridge Preloved or on the door

All proceeds go towards the stewardship of the Tir Melys community

Inside, the shop was crammed with floor to ceiling shelves of second-hand books. Near the door stood a scuffed pine table holding a thermos jug of coffee, a tray with milk and sugar and a wooden tree of mugs beside it. A narrow bench like a church pew sat next to it, below the window. A young woman wearing square black glasses, and with her hair tucked into a bandana, was unpacking a box of books and examining the spines. She greeted him when he entered. She had an engaging smile.

'Hi there! I have to go through this box carefully. I got it as a job lot at a car boot sale and some of the books are too knackered to price up. Just browsing, or can I help?'

'You might be able to help. My name's Ty Swift. I'm a friend of Afan Griffith. Have you heard the sad news about him?'

She froze, a book in her hand. 'Oh yes, just this morning! I'm so sorry. I was really shocked. He was such a lovely man.'

'I'd arranged to stay with Afan at Tir Melys, but he was missing when I arrived.'

'Oh, gosh! When did you get there?'

'Monday afternoon.'

She put down the book she was holding. 'How awful for you. What will you do now?'

'I'm staying around for a bit. I want to see his murderer caught.'

'Of course. Let me just get this out of the way.' She bent and moved a box to one side. A lock of black hair fell onto her forehead and she swept it back under her bandana as she straightened up.

Swift found her fluid movements attractive and wondered if she'd had the same effect on Afan. 'Were you close to Afan?'

She came towards him. 'As friends, you understand. One of the lovely things about running this shop is that some customers become friends too. He bought quite a few books here and sometimes we'd chat about local history, and particularly medieval Pembrokeshire. He was very erudite, really knew his subject. Did he have any family around here? They must be in bits.'

That answered one of the questions he had for her. 'Not that he ever mentioned.'

'Oh, I see. That's sad. I suppose the people at Tir Melys were his family in a way.'

'I expect so. Have you had much to do with the community?'

'I've been there a couple of times.'

'Afan seems to have been very involved there.'

'He waxed lyrical about the bees and mead making. He brought some of his apple mead to our Welsh class for a tasting session once. It went down a treat. Just as well we saved it until the end, or we'd have learned nothing!'

'Were you in his class?'

She pushed her glasses up her nose. 'I'm the teacher. We meet in my flat upstairs. Afan came to my class on Fridays, although he didn't attend regularly anymore.'

'Why was that?' Bruno had said that Afan came to lessons every week.

The woman went to the door, checked that there were no other customers on the way in, and came over to the service desk. She moved confidently, dusting her hands on her jeans. Her light verbena scent was pleasant. 'Would you like a coffee? It's free.'

He didn't want the conversation to stall. 'Maybe in a minute, thanks.'

She perched on the desk edge, swinging a leg. Her pretty, sapphire earrings danced as she talked. She had extraordinary eyes, deep-set and a pale blue grey. He found them mesmeric. 'Just help yourself,' she said. 'It's freshly made. My name's Gwyn, by the way, Gwyn Bowen. Afan was vague about the lessons. He just said that he was a bit busy at Tir Melys and it was difficult to fit everything in.'

'When did he start missing lessons?'

'Around early May. There was something not quite right.'

'Why was that?'

She ran a finger along the desk edge. 'I dunno. He sort of looked sideways when he was speaking to me. Seemed on edge, not being quite straight. I was a bit annoyed, frankly, because it disrupts the class dynamic if people don't come regularly. I wasn't thrilled when he only turned up now and again. I said as much to my friend Caris, but she told me I was being a control freak.'

'Would that be Caris Murray, who volunteers at Tir Melys?'

'That's right.'

'I haven't met her, but I expect I will. I'm staying at Tir Melys at the moment.'

'This must be such a blow for you. And poor Caris — I haven't had a chance to speak to her yet. She'll be so shocked. She liked Afan a lot and often spent time with him at Tir Melys. She's had a tough year. Morgan, her friend — or maybe boyfriend, it was always hard to work those two out — went missing not long back. The word is he's in London, but it was all very sudden.'

'Is that Morgan Callender who used to work at Tir Melys as well?'

'Yes. Caris has gone very quiet since it happened. Maybe she cared more about Morgan than she let on. I don't see as much of her these days, her mam's got a bad heart so she has to keep an eye on her. It beats me how she copes, to be honest. I understand, because my dad's poorly with dementia, but he's in a care home so at least I don't have day-to-day responsibilities.' She gave a rueful smile. 'Sometimes we've joked that we could move my dad in with her mum and they could sort of prop each other up. Then Caris could share my flat with me. Wishful thinking.'

Swift thought about the wider context to Tir Melys. Afan must have come across other people when he visited the town. 'Is there anyone else around here who knew Afan, or did he ever mention anyone from his younger days in Wales?'

She took off her glasses and cleaned them with the hem of her shirt. Her eyes shone large and clear, her lips curved generously. 'I'm not sure,' she said. 'He knew people through our classes, but I wasn't aware that he saw them outside of lessons. Tir Melys was very much his focus.' She paused and rubbed her neck. 'Now you mention it, there was a guy who'd met him back in the day in Cardiff. He stopped by here last year asking for a book. There were a couple of bottles of Afan's mead on the desk and this guy saw Afan's name and said he wondered if it could be the same person. I had photos of one of our classes on my phone and I showed him one with Afan in. He said they'd done sports together in Cardiff, way back. I told him about Tir Melys and he seemed surprised that Afan had decided to come back to Wales. I mentioned it to Afan, but he didn't seem interested.'

'Do you remember this man's name? Was he from around here?'

'Oh, now you're asking. He was on a minibreak with his family, I remember that, because he had a young girl with him, and she was bored. She knocked over some books, fidgeting around. He wasn't living near here. He was from the Glamorgan area.'

Swift wanted to ask more, but a man in walking gear came in and headed straight for the desk, enquiring about ordnance survey maps for the Brecon Beacons. Swift moved away, helped himself to a coffee, and then browsed the shelves. The shop was well set out, with clear sections and little cards below some books, with reviews and recommendations for other similar titles. He picked out a Gillian Flynn that he'd not read and from the history section, a slim volume called *Holybridge Old and New*, printed by a local press.

He waited to pay and asked Gwyn where there was a café with Wi-Fi.

'Blasus is good. It's where Afan used to go. Just on Castell Street, turn right out of here and round the corner. Oh, listen, I've remembered that the guy I told you about ordered a book, so he'd have given me his details. When I've got a spare minute, I'll go through my orders from last year and check with him if I can pass on his name.' She squared off a pile of leaflets on the desk. 'Who'll tell us about Afan's funeral — I mean, if there's no family involved?'

'I'm not sure. If he left a will, it's up to the police to find out if he had a solicitor and what his wishes were, if any. I'll pass on any information that comes my way.'

'Thanks. Give my best to the people at Tir Melys. This must be a terrible time for them.'

It was one of those unpredictable days of warm sun and quick, hard showers when you're hot one minute, chilly and soaked the next. Swift took his jacket off as he walked to Blasus, which was busy with the buzz of conversation. It might have been preserved in aspic since 1968. The walls were covered in multicoloured, psychedelic swirls and posters of Che Guevara, Jimi Hendrix, Janis Joplin, Diana Ross and Bob Dylan. Behind the counter was a huge pink and yellow tapestry covered in flowers and proclaiming *Peace & Love*. The chairs and tables were orange plastic, and his eye was drawn to a splendid, gleaming red jukebox with *Stereo* engraved on the glass door. Joan Baez was singing 'Sad-Eyed Lady of the Lowlands'. He expected to find that superannuated hippies ran the café, but there was a man in his twenties serving at the counter. He had a horseshoe moustache, long hair and wore a striped headband. His flowered shirt was tucked into blue jeans and his name badge, in the shape of a peace symbol, said *Sam*.

Swift ordered coffee and a club sandwich and paid for half an hour of internet use. 'This is a fascinating place. There aren't many internet cafés left these days. Do you get a lot of custom?'

'Plenty. It's a little goldmine. Tourists come in, of course, but lots of locals use us. Once you leave town, Wi-Fi is either slow or non-existent in lots of places. There's always talk that it'll be massively improved, but it never comes to anything — which is good for Blasus. Phones don't always cut it if you want to do some online business, research or play games. Loads of students come here. And then there's the social angle. We run "Learn to surf the web" classes for older people on Wednesday afternoons, and we have live music at weekends.' Sam grinned enthusiastically. 'I love working here. You get all sorts, all generations. How did you find your way to us?'

'Gwyn at the bookshop directed me here.'

'I'll give her a free herbal tea next time she's in. She envies our busy trade sometimes. I'm sorry for her. Most of her days seem slow, no matter what she does to attract customers. She's worked so hard, trying to make the shop a success, put her heart and soul into it but . . . People buy books online, don't they, even second-hand ones?' He pointed to the computers. 'Our speedy Wi-Fi probably does her out of a lot of trade but that's the cut and thrust of business for you.'

There was nothing laid-back and woolly about Sam. Swift reckoned that the 'tache and long hair were part of his brand. 'Did you know Afan Griffith?'

'Of course. Afan was a regular in here. He always had tea and a cheese toastie. We heard what's happened this morning. Truly terrible. Are you a family member?'

'No, a friend of his.'

'I'm ever so sorry. Afan was a quiet sort of man. He'd always lend our older customers a hand if the computer baffled them. Why would anyone want to kill him?'

'Hopefully, the police will find out.'

Sam said, 'If you want another coffee, it's on the house.'

Swift was touched. 'Thank you, that's kind.'

'Least I can do.'

The computers were grouped at the far end of the room and he stopped to examine the jukebox on his way. *Rock-Ola* was inscribed in red lettering across the top. There were about a hundred records inside and he put two pounds in the slot and selected 'Ain't No Mountain High Enough' and 'Sunny Afternoon'.

He checked his email and saw that Ruth had sent two. The first had more photos of Branna, this time at a fairground, sporting a yellow sun hat and perched in a cup and saucer. He replied, explaining what had happened at Tir Melys — he could imagine Ruth's raised brows — and saying that he'd be in Wales longer than he'd expected. He added that there was no phone signal or Wi-Fi where he was staying — he pictured Ruth's exasperated expression again — and said that he'd call around seven tomorrow evening.

He informed Branna that the joke Welsh name for a microwave was 'popty ping'. When he opened the second email, his mouth went dry.

Hi, Ty. I just wanted to say that Marcel and I are getting married next year, probably in the spring. We've been discussing where to live, and I've decided to move to Guernsey with Branna. We want to have children, and this is a lovely place to raise a family. I've checked the job market here, and I should be able to get a part-time lecturing post. I understand that you'll find this difficult, but you can see Branna regularly and FaceTime etc. every week. It will be so good for her to have siblings and play on the beach after school. There are excellent facilities here for children with hearing problems. I wanted to give you the heads-up because Branna is very excited about the wedding and is already being bossy about what I should wear and the large role she wants to play. You can imagine. I hope that you can be happy for me.

He'd considered this possibility, like a train hurtling down the track towards him. It had caused him sleepless nights. How could he challenge Ruth's decision? She had the right to lead her own life and she was Branna's main parent. Her lecturing job was routine, with timetabled hours, whereas his days were unpredictable, with work often occupying his evenings. Ruth had grown away from him since meeting Marcel Vaudin and become more judgemental of him and his work. Marcel had a house on a beautiful island, above idyllic Fermain Bay. There was no contest between living there and North London, especially if you had one child and wanted more. He didn't bother replying. There was nothing to say for now. FaceTime was fine, but on a screen, he couldn't make Branna laugh by rubbing his chin on her neck or feel the warm weight of her when she climbed on his back. He saw a bleak future. He and Branna would have intermittent meetings, like ships that pass in the night.

His lunch arrived. The sandwich smelled delicious, but he couldn't face it now. He shoved it to one side. He'd ask Sam to box it up and he could eat it this evening. The coffee was strong and bracing and he drank it gratefully, his hand unsteady.

He forced himself back to the other tasks he needed to complete. He forwarded Afan's emails and his replies to DI Weber and checked that, other than email, Afan had no social media presence. He read through the Tir Melys website again but didn't glean any new information. He was curious about the Merchants' finances, so searched for Giles Merchant. This threw up a number of candidates, but based on Suki's information, the most likely was a website for a business called Scrumptious, operating from Putney. It was a cake-making outfit and featured a photo of a beaming Giles Merchant in a chef's hat, balancing two iced sponge cakes in either hand. He resembled his father but had his mother's imperious gaze.

Hi, I'm Giles and I set up Scrumptious Cakes in 2012. We deliver delicious cakes, cupcakes and other sweet treats throughout London. Our clients are individuals, businesses and events organisers. We'll tailor our cakes to your needs and make suggestions if you're not sure what you want. All our goodies are made to order by our highly skilled bakers, using only the finest ingredients.

Go on, get in touch. We bet you want to!

There were photos of beautiful cakes in all shapes, sizes and colours, themed for engagements, weddings, birthdays and anniversaries. Beneath them were links to YouTube videos of cakes being made and decorated, with some recipes thrown in. Swift watched one. The theme was a rainforest, and it was visually striking in emerald-green, blue and red icing, topped with multicoloured trees and butterflies. He recalled Jasmine's worried comment, *Giles needs the help, and we don't have a lot of choice.* Perhaps Scrumptious wasn't as successful as the publicity suggested. He sent himself a link to the website and sat pondering. He decided that he wanted to talk to Caris Murray. It seemed odd that both she and her boyfriend had volunteered at Tir Melys and had met Afan, and the two men were now gone, one of them dead. In Swift's experience, odd was always worth pursuing.

At the counter, Sam told him that wrapping the sandwich up was no problem. 'It's not that you didn't like it, then? Our food's highly rated.'

'I'm saving it for later, thanks. Did Afan seem bothered about anything recently?'

Sam was assembling a brown cardboard box. 'I don't think so. He'd come in, ask for his usual, put a record on the jukebox and use a computer.' He handed the food across.

'Thanks.' Swift was about to go, and then turned back. 'What music did Afan play?'

'His favourite was Motown. He always chose Martha and the Vandellas, "Dancing in the Street".'

Swift was gladdened to hear that something about Afan hadn't changed. He went back to the jukebox and selected the record. Sam smiled at him and raised the glass of water he was drinking in a toast. '*Lechyd da*! To Afan.'

Swift opened the café door and almost fell over DI Weber, who clutched at her arm protectively, losing her grip on her stick. Swift caught it for her and handed it back.

'Thanks. I expected to see you,' she said. 'You'd been to the bookshop before me too.'

'A DI doing all the legwork?'

She frowned at him. 'I hope you're not meddling.'

'It's natural to care about a friend who's been murdered.'

'Hmm. Well, while we're passing the time, I can inform you that you're not a suspect. Are you going to be back at Tir Melys later this afternoon?'

'I can be.'

'There's things I want to discuss. I'll see you at Mr Griffith's place around half four. Have the kettle on. Now, I don't usually ask men to open doors for me, but I'll make an exception today.'

On his way back to his car, Swift stopped at the organic grocery where he bought orange juice, two cartons of vegetable soup, some tins of baked beans and apples. The mini fridge at Afan's had just two compartments, so he had to limit his supplies. He could get bread and milk when he needed it from the kitchen at Tir Melys. He didn't want to have to eat in the refec all the time and be beholden to the community, and he particularly didn't want to fulfil Jasmine's expectation that he'd dine with them daily. It was useful to get a handle on the general dynamic and relationships of the community and observe them close up. If Afan's killer was at the table, he didn't mind breaking bread with them now and again, especially if it helped to catch them, but he was no martyr and he couldn't face nightly suppers.

The road back curved around the coastline. Swift stopped the car in a lay-by and gazed out at the hazy horizon and a wide stretch of sandy beach. The unpredictable weather and brisk breeze meant that it was almost empty. As often happened with sudden death, Afan's was causing him to reflect on the years that had slipped by so quickly, years without contact, and his life during that time. Losing Ruth, then meeting her again and helping her during her difficult marriage. Setting up his own investigation agency, discovering that Ruth was pregnant with their child and then finding out that Branna had hearing loss. The death of his close friend Cedric, the deaths of others, both friends and victims and his failed relationship with Nora. He was tired and unsure, wondering if he had taken wrong turnings.

He pictured his daughter playing on a sunnier beach, running towards the waves and shrieking when they rolled over her legs. She'd be chanting, 'Silly old sea, you can't catch me!'

Tears ambushed him. He blinked and drove on.

CHAPTER 8

There was a round plastic food box by the cottage door, with a note on top. Swift expected to find that mother hen Elinor had left it and would have signed Frankie's name alongside her own, but when he unfolded the paper, he saw that he had a different benefactor.

Thought you might like this chicken hotpot. It's my trusty standby recipe and Afan really loved it. Just needs five mins in microwave. Enjoy! Kat xx

He put his supplies away. The chicken hotpot wouldn't fit in the fridge, so he'd have to eat it tonight. He opened the lid and sniffed. It smelled good, but he wondered if Afan had really liked it. He doubted that he'd have thrown it away but pictured him eating it reluctantly, possibly under Kat's watchful, intense gaze.

He was hungry now, so he ate the club sandwich from its box and checked the time. It was three o'clock and he'd noticed a young woman working on the communal allotment alongside Elinor. He decided to check if she was Caris Murray. When he opened the door, he saw her coming towards him. She wore jeans, green wellingtons and an old sweater that hung loosely, exposing one rounded shoulder.

Her thick, bobbed hair was streaked with blue and swayed as she walked.

'Hi, are you Mr Swift?'

'That's right. My name's Ty.'

'I'm Caris Murray. Elinor told me you were here. She said you found Afan. What's happened is so awful, I still can't believe it. You must be in bits.'

She took off a gardening glove and they shook hands. She wore a pretty silver thumb ring, shaped like a feather. Her manner was rough and ready, but she seemed shy, catching his eye fleetingly.

'That's right, I found Afan on the coast path.'

She had wide, chiselled cheeks and was remarkably pale and strained for someone working in the open air. Perhaps it was the shock of hearing about Afan.

'He told me you were coming. He said it had been a long time — too long.'

'It had,' Ty said. 'I was looking forward to our catch-up.'

She rubbed the heel of a wellington along the ground, dislodging a chunk of mud. 'Afan showed me a photo he'd found of you both. He said it was taken in France.'

'He'd left the photo on the table. That's where we met, in Lyon.'

'Yeah. He said you were both at Interpol, when he was working in criminal intelligence.'

'That's right.' It was interesting that Afan had told this young woman information that he hadn't shared with the members of the community. He must have trusted her. 'Did he tell you that in confidence?'

Her eyes were dark, thick-lashed and hard to read. 'Yes. I loved listening to him talking about it. I never expected to meet someone who'd worked at a job like that.'

'Do you want to come in for a cup of tea?'

'No, I don't have time, thanks. I'm . . . I'm really sorry about Afan. I liked him a lot. What will . . . What will happen to his things?'

'You mean the things in his cottage?'

She shifted from foot to foot. He had the impression that she was taut with tension and might bolt at any minute. 'Yeah, his possessions.'

'I can't say. Why, is there something of yours in there?'

'No, no. I just wondered, like. I suppose the police will deal with all his personal stuff.'

'It depends. They were asking if Afan had any family or next of kin.'

'He didn't, he had no one,' she said quickly and then grimaced, as if she'd revealed too much.

'Afan told you that?'

'Yeah.'

'Have the police spoken to you yet?'

She stiffened. 'The police? Why would they want to speak to me?'

'They'll be speaking to anyone who knew Afan, especially people with an involvement here. Afan might have appointed a solicitor as his executor.'

'What's that?'

'Someone who carries out your wishes when you die, sorts out your estate. Were you close to Afan? You seem to have been, from the things he told you.'

'Oh . . . well, we'd chat when we were working the crops. Sometimes I helped him with bottling the mead. He was an easy person to get on with and so interesting. Well, I've got stuff to finish before the rain starts again.'

'I met a friend of yours this morning.'

She'd turned to go but halted, and the little remaining colour drained from her face. 'Yeah?'

'In the bookshop. Gwyn Bowen.'

'Oh, Gwyn. Right.' She relaxed and gave a nervous laugh.

What had she been expecting him to say? 'She mentioned that Morgan, your boyfriend, was missing and you've had a difficult time.'

She stared at her feet. She seemed to find her wellingtons fascinating. 'Yeah, I've been better. Morgan and me were kind of on/off though, not exactly devoted. More like mates most of the time, really. But I'm sure Morgan's gone to London. He talked a lot about living there. He left a note in his bedroom saying that's what he was planning.'

She was lying and she wasn't much good at hiding it. 'He went away without telling you and he hasn't been in touch since? Doesn't sound much of a relationship, even just for mates.'

He'd intended to goad her, and it worked. She looked up at him quickly, but he could see fear rather than anger in her eyes.

'It was what it was. You can't hold someone back from what they want.'

'Did you meet through volunteering here?'

'No, we knew each other before that, we were at school together. I've got to go. If you want to harvest what you want for now from Afan's garden, I'll collect any other ripe stuff another day and process it for the kitchen.'

She walked away quickly, and he watched her rigid shoulders. What had that been about? Caris had come for information, but he'd no idea why. She was well informed about Afan yet didn't want to admit it, and she was deeply worried. When people were moved to share personal information, those confidences were usually a two-way street, and he was curious about what Afan might have learned from her.

He found a wooden bowl in the dresser and picked tomatoes, raspberries and some late strawberries. The wigwams of runner beans were heavy with ripe pods. Caris had several hours' work ahead of her when she came to harvest.

* * *

DI Weber was sitting in the chair with a back like a hand, rocking back and forth. She wore thick purple wool walking socks rolled down over her DMs, a red elastic band secured her coat buttons and there was a hole in the side seam of her trousers, just below the knee. He appreciated a fellow scruff, but Jasmine would be appalled.

She said, 'Your friend wasn't into home comforts, was he?'

Swift brought her a mug of tea. 'I was taken aback when I arrived. It's such a contrast to how he used to live when I knew him.' He described Afan's beautiful flat in Lyon.

She sipped the tea. 'That's not a bad brew. So, why the huge life change?'

'No idea. I wasn't in contact with him during the process that brought him here.' He recalled what Mark Gill had told him. 'A friend of mine from the Met knew Afan slightly. He said he'd heard that Afan left Interpol after an issue about bullying. I gathered that he was off work suffering from stress.'

'I see. We appreciate, don't we, Mr Swift, that someone's life often explains their death.'

'We do and you can call me Ty. At least you haven't called me Mr Smith, like Jasmine did.'

The DI snorted. 'She's a madam, that one. Very haughty. You can call me Sofia as you're not a suspect and we're kind of in the same line of work. We spotted your car on the motorway by Swansea at 1.15 p.m. on Monday and the post-mortem says that Mr Griffith died between midday and 2.30 p.m. The email to you was sent from his phone at 2.15 p.m., so I'd guess the killer wrote it just after the stabbing and before they got rid of the phone and the weapon.'

'That does point to the killer being from here, because it was someone who knew that Afan was expecting me and who wanted to delay us worrying about his absence. He'd told them all that I was visiting.'

She grimaced. 'Ah yes, they mentioned it at the "colloquy". But Mr Griffith did go into Holybridge regularly. He could have told someone there about your visit. Although if you're right about a shadowy figure fetching the book to place on his body late Monday night, that suggests someone resident here. I agree with you about the reason for the email, although whoever stabbed him must have grasped that it wouldn't be too long before his body was found. It's late summer and that stretch of path is fairly well used.'

Swift had placed a plate of fruit on the table. Sofia took a glowing strawberry and murmured with pleasure as she ate it. 'Nothing like fruit that's just been picked. I can taste the sun and rain on it. I couldn't live in a place like this, but there are odd moments when a flight of fancy makes me half believe I could. All the Tir Melys residents say that Mr Griffith was content here. This cottage does have a peaceful, if spartan atmosphere.'

Swift said, 'I'm not sure that I buy into the happy community angle that they try to promote. I've observed a number of personality clashes already. Something was troubling Afan's contentment. I've been giving some thought to the huge change in his lifestyle. He went through a difficult time when he left Interpol. That kind of trauma can make you re-evaluate your life and take a different direction. I was stabbed when I worked for Interpol and that made me rethink my career. That's why I started my own private investigation agency.'

Sofia cradled her broken arm, rubbing the plaster as if she could ease it through the hard casing. 'I googled you and fair dos, I could see you've had some results.'

'Thanks. I've had a few casualties as well, things that keep me awake at night.'

She shrugged. 'You stir shit, you get some on you. I've had my moments.' She took a sharp breath, clearly in pain, and reached into a pocket of her voluminous coat. She took out painkillers and tried to pop two from the pack with her left hand. It slid to the floor and Swift picked it up. 'Thanks. Can you get them out for me? I'm right-handed and I'm finding that my left one is a hopeless supporting act.'

Swift put the capsules in her hand, and she swallowed them with a draught of tea.

'This bloody arm gives me bloody gyp.'

'It's hard, conducting an investigation when you're below par. I caught a parasitic infection when someone tried to drown me in the Regent's Canal, and the job was quite a struggle for a while. Is it a good idea to be at work with a broken arm?'

She rolled her eyes. 'We're down to a skeleton staff as it is, so I persuaded the doctor to say I could work. I wanted to as well, I'd rather be busy than loitering at home. But I'll be honest with you, I'm a bad-tempered DI at the moment. I hate not being able to drive myself. I either have to listen to DS Spencer's passion for ten-pin bowling or get cabs. I prefer the cabs.'

Swift understood her need to be active, but a murder investigation was a tall order when you were hampered with a badly broken limb. He wondered how many murders she'd investigated — there wouldn't be that many in this area. 'Just don't take your bad mood out on me.'

She sighed. 'I'll try to reserve my irritation for that numpty Spence, who has been placed on this earth with the sole purpose of trying my patience. He moved out from his mam's recently and he's like a chick that's fallen out of the nest.'

'High time he moved out, surely? He must be in his late twenties.' Swift had left home at eighteen and never gone back there to live.

'Agreed, but he didn't want to. His mam told him it was time to stand on his own two feet. He has abandonment issues.' She rolled her eyes. 'He's curiously old-fashioned, which is occasionally endearing, but the rest of the time I want to wring the chick's neck. Now, back to business. Your friend was stabbed in the chest with a screwdriver, which we haven't found, probably because it went into the waves with his phone. It caused a severe internal haemorrhage with little external bleeding. He was killed just a few feet from the cairn, and then his body was dragged in there. His solicitor is in Cardiff and I'm going to speak to him in the morning. He confirmed that Mr Griffith had no next of kin but left a will and that he's his executor.'

DI Weber seemed very open with her information this afternoon and he decided to reciprocate. He told her what he'd learned in Holybridge and his conversation with Caris Murray.

'She came to see me, and she was fishing for information about Afan.'

'Maybe she's hoping he's left her something.'

'Maybe. But there was something else — she seemed to know things about Afan that he hadn't shared with any of the others here.'

A glint came into Sofia's eye and she wiggled her eyebrows. 'They might have had a relationship. He could have been consoling her after the boyfriend vanished. Older man . . . shoulder to lean on.'

'They might have, although no one here has indicated that, and Suki told me he didn't have a partner. It wouldn't be easy to keep it under wraps in this community. Also, Caris is just eighteen, according to Bruno. I can't imagine Afan going for a woman that much younger.'

She glanced out of the window. 'Oh, I'm not so sure. There'd be ways to keep it under the radar. You could be tending the garden and then you'd pop into the house or the shed for a while. And clearly, your friend had changed a fair bit since you knew him. Maybe Caris's youth made him feel rejuvenated.'

Swift could see her point, although he was dubious. 'I suppose. Afan could have met her in Holybridge. Maybe that's what he was doing when he was supposed to be at his Welsh class.' He was still reflecting on Caris's comments about her on/off boyfriend. 'Did you find out anything about Morgan Callender?'

She rubbed her eyes and yawned. 'I've asked Spence to check it, so I might hear something this side of Christmas if I'm lucky.' The light was grey outside, and her freckles seemed darker in the dimness. She crossed her legs, hugging her arm. 'As you've gathered, DS Spencer is my cross to bear and not a lot of use to me. Willing and likeable, but not too sharp. *Pendafad*, my mam would say. A sheep-head. He was transferred to me a couple of months back from another team. The idea was that my experience would rub off on him. It might, given at least ten years and a miracle. Now, you strike me as an astute kind of man with brains to spare, and I gather that you're keen on staying around here and asking your own questions. Am I right?'

'You're right.' He could guess where this was leading. He hoped that he was reading Sofia correctly.

'Good. You'll have plenty of opportunity for hanging out, chatting with the community and picking up bits of gossip. So, Ty Swift, my proposal is that we work in harmony. I can't say together because I have to be careful what info I pass to you, and I don't dare use any official communication channels. Let's say as much of a reciprocal relationship as possible. How does that sound?'

'Attractive. Will DS Spencer be party to this arrangement?'

'He won't. He's one of those limited people who have to do everything by the book. The few brains he has would be in a spin if I told him. What do you think?'

He'd now received confirmation that Afan had had no next of kin. There was no family to represent him and make sure that his killer was caught. Afan had been in his corner more than once when he'd needed help. After a long silence, his friend had contacted him when he'd needed assistance, presumably because he'd valued Swift's investigative skills. Swift had been too late to give that help. Or maybe not. Maybe he could give it now. 'Okay, that sounds good to me.'

'I thought it might. What's your instinct about anyone here as the killer? Could it be Kat, with her unfulfilled romantic yearnings?'

He reflected on those scratchy suppers around the table. 'It could be any of them. A community like this must have hidden tensions as well as some obvious ones. Kat isn't liked much, Bryn Price loves to stir things and Bruno seemed tense at the prospect of the police being around. The Merchants have financial problems and the Brinkworths' marriage isn't the happiest I've seen. Suki seems straightforward, but maybe she's too good to be true.'

'Let's assume that the killer came back in here late on the night of the murder to fetch the book and take it back to his victim's body. That was a real gamble. Why take it?'

'Regret? Trying to offer Afan comfort in death? It suggests that the motive wasn't hatred. More that he couldn't be allowed to live.'

'Hmm. Strange.' Sofia picked up a strawberry by its hull and handed it to Swift, then took another for herself. The way she made herself at home reminded him of Nora but, thankfully, that was the only resemblance so far. 'I saw Elinor Brinkworth earlier, walking that dog that's like a soft toy,' she continued. 'She was down in the mouth. She used the dog as a comfort blanket when I interviewed her. I've noticed more people using animals like that these days. What's it all about?'

'In Elinor's case, I suppose she's signalling her maternal wishes and making up for the affection she doesn't get from her husband,' he said. 'There's increasing use of emotional support animals recently.'

'Lucky old Frankie, getting cosseted like that.' Sofia tapped the table with her good hand. 'This strikes me as a place where you might run from something or somebody and hide yourself. I've got Spence carrying out background checks on all of them. He's not too bad with a limited, specific task and he's handy with a computer.'

'As we're now sort of co-working, did you find any of Afan's financial information here?'

'Absolutely zilch. Must have dealt with it all online, so our techies are investigating the computers at Blasus. I couldn't do that myself. I have online accounts, but I like bits of paper with figures written on. Seems more tangible.' She yawned and shook her head. 'I need to go. I want to catch Caris Murray if I can. Here's my personal mobile number. I can't give you a badge but keep in touch, Lone Ranger.'

She handed him a scrap of paper with her number and strode out, smacking her stick against the ground, her coat flapping in the breeze. The sky had lightened, and the sun was hazy but warm. Swift was weary but his mind was busy.

He massaged his temples. He'd take Afan's bike out and get some exercise. He needed to decide what he was going to say to Ruth, and the terms he wanted to negotiate about Branna and the future.

He was cycling towards the chapel when he saw Elinor coming out with Frankie on a lead. She was wearing a baggy wraparound cardigan over a patchwork smock and blowing her nose. He slowed as he neared her, and he saw that her eyes were watery.

'Oh, hello. I was just in the chapel for a bit. It's a good place to be quiet. You off for a ride?'

'That's the idea. How did you get on with your social worker?'

She picked Frankie up and cuddled him close. 'It was a bit difficult. Guy arrived back very late for the meeting and said he'd lost track of the time. I could see that Terry was fed up. He asked Guy if he was fully committed to the adoption, and then Guy lost his cool and said he resented being interrogated in his own home by a government flunkey with poor literacy skills. Then he asked why Terry never called him by his proper title — he's Dr Brinkworth, of course — and Terry said it would be best to set up another meeting and he'd have to bring his manager.' She gulped and dabbed her eyes. 'I'm worried now, in case this goes against us.'

'I'm sorry it didn't go so well.'

'Guy has a short fuse, hasn't he, Fwankie? He doesn't suffer fools gladly and he never reacts well to stress, that's the problem.'

'And what about you? This is stressful for you as well.'

'Yes, I suppose.' She glanced back at the chapel. 'Afan was very understanding when I talked to him about it all a while ago. I visited the chapel, and he was there. He just listened, really. He did ask me if I thought that Guy had the patience to raise a child. He said that his dad had been very self-centred and short-tempered, a frightening man. I told him that Guy isn't that bad, he just gets wound up. He's terribly intelligent you see, and very talented, so he sets high standards for himself and others.'

Swift sighed inwardly. 'Guy's lucky to have you. You're very understanding.'

'Oh, well — he puts up with me going on about things.'

'Did you tell Guy that you'd talked to Afan about the adoption?'

She blushed and seemed startled. 'Oh no, I didn't mention it. That was just for me, a bit of reassurance. Guy hates to think that anyone's prying into our lives or making judgements. That's why he finds working with the adoption people so difficult.' She was clutching the dog tightly, in a smothering hold, but he didn't seem to mind. 'I must get back. I want to make sure he's okay now. He takes these things to heart. People don't see it, but he feels things very deeply.' She buried her face in Frankie's head and set off.

Swift cycled on, enjoying the breeze and the warm early evening scents. He pictured Elinor in the seclusion of the chapel, confiding in Afan as if he was a minister. It sounded as if Afan's father had been a bully, just like Guy Brinkworth. Would Afan have spoken to Guy about his behaviour? If he had, Guy might have reacted badly, resenting Afan's disapproval. His short fuse might have flared into violence. Swift couldn't believe that an adoption agency would deem that Guy was a suitable parent. It would be a terrible blow for Elinor, but he reckoned that Terry should advise her to forget about the hassle of adopting a child with her testy, egotistical husband, and stick to mothering Frankie.

* * *

He'd just eaten some of the chicken hotpot, which was rich and good but far too salty. He'd decided that he couldn't manage any more and would bin the rest, when there was a knock at the door. Kat was outside, holding a package in baking foil.

'Hello! Did you enjoy your chicken?' She was through the door without being invited, standing by the table and scanning his plate. 'Oh, you haven't finished, have I interrupted?'

'It was lovely, thanks. Very filling. I can't manage any more for now.'

'I used to make one for Afan every couple of weeks. I'd have left it on the table, like I usually did, but the door was locked, so poor little me couldn't get in.'

He stood with his back against the dresser, arms folded, unwelcoming. 'The police have advised you to lock your door, so I hope you are.'

'I certainly am not! Not worrying about security has always been one of the lovely things about living here. I can't imagine why anyone would want to harm me, and I'm not afraid of anyone either.'

You'd have no reason to be afraid if you're Afan's killer. 'Okay, that's up to you.'

'Exactly. If you put the rest of that chicken in the fridge, it'll be fine for tomorrow. Just make sure you heat it through thoroughly.'

'Thanks for the tip.'

She thrust the package towards him. 'Here, some lemon and honey cake, one of my specialities. Afan's honey, natch.'

'That's very kind of you, but you really shouldn't go to so much trouble.'

'I like baking and it's therapy. I'm so sad about Afan and it's hard to settle to anything. It's something to do, otherwise I'd just be sitting at home and crying.'

If he refused the cake, he'd be denying her grief. He took it, sensing that she was relentless and in her own way, formidable. She reminded him of Branna when his daughter was in one of her obdurate moods.

She sat in the armchair and hooked one leg over the side. Her skin-tight jeans strained against her bulging calf muscles. 'I always sat here when I came over to see Afan. He'd make a cup of tea and we'd have a slice of whatever cake I'd brought.'

He didn't want her company, but he thought he'd better take the hint. 'I was about to put the kettle on. Would you like a cup now?'

'Lovely, yes.' She watched with that concentrated, unblinking gaze of hers as he prepared tea. 'It seems so weird, to knock on the door and you open it, instead of Afan. You're a similar height and build, so it's a bit spooky, in a way.'

'Many things seem strange when someone dies. It's odd to be staying here, using his things and sleeping in his bed.'

She stared and then said, 'Afan always used the striped mugs for tea.'

'Okay.' He sighed inwardly and put back Suki's mugs that he'd taken out of the dresser. He replaced them with striped ones.

'I saw that DI Weber came to visit you earlier.'

'That's right.'

'Did she have any news?'

'She just wanted to ask me a few follow-up questions.' He brought the tea over, and plates for the cake. He cut two slices and handed her one.

Her jaw clicked as she ate. 'I suppose you know lots about Afan, given that you worked with him in Interpol. What was he like back then?'

The cake had a strong lemon flavour but it was soggy — more like a pudding, and he could have done with a fork to eat it.

'He was a good person to work alongside and well respected in his job. How would you describe the Afan you knew?'

She swallowed and took a sip of tea. Then she said solemnly, 'Serious, fascinated by nature and particularly bees, and very kind. Too kind, in a way.'

'Oh? What makes you say that?'

She bit into another chunk of cake. 'Some people traded on his kindness and saw him as a soft touch. He was his own worst enemy. He didn't like to turn people down.'

From what he'd heard and witnessed, she might have been describing the way she'd treated Afan herself. 'People here, at Tir Melys?'

She fingered the end of a plait. 'I don't want to say anything that causes trouble.'

He left a pause to see if she'd continue, but she was examining the ends of her hair and he guessed that she wanted to be persuaded. 'Of course you don't, and I understand that. But I can see how fond you were of Afan. None of us like to think that a friend is being made use of.'

She pursed her lips, her eyes fixed on him. It was like being stalked by a watchful predator. She wanted more. He obliged.

'I'm sure you looked out for Afan. I can tell that you're that sort of considerate person. He'd have appreciated it.'

She seemed to deem that sufficient flattery. She swung her leg from the chair arm and leaned forward slightly. 'It's true. I tried to care for him, but his soft heart meant he wouldn't listen. That Caris Murray was always moping and wheedling her way around him. Her boyfriend, Morgan, used to tag along with her sometimes when she came to work here. He was a waste of space, couldn't focus on anything for more than two minutes. Both of them come from rough backgrounds and I suspected they were on the make and take. I'd see the two of them talking to Afan, very hugger-mugger. When Morgan took off, Caris was telling Afan her sob story. If she saw me coming, she'd switch to speaking Welsh, which was very rude. I saw Afan giving her money once. He was in his shed, bottling mead and I needed some honey. I was about to go in when I saw Caris in there with him. He was handing her a bunch of notes and I heard him saying, "*that'll tide you over*." She kissed him on the cheek and told him he was a diamond. I went back to see him after she'd gone. I didn't say that I'd seen her take the money, but I told him he was too generous and trusting.' She fell silent.

'How did Afan react?'

She found that memory less pleasing. Her expression grew pinched. 'He got a bit tetchy and told me that people's lives were often complicated in ways that others failed to understand. That was all he'd say.'

Kat wouldn't have liked Afan taking an interest in any woman but her. Caris's fine cheekbones would have been irritating. 'I don't understand why you thought Morgan and Caris were "on the take." Volunteering doesn't seem a very lucrative occupation if you're out to exploit people, and there's nothing valuable here to steal.'

She sniffed. 'That sort always have an agenda. There was definitely something going on, I could tell.'

Swift got up and fed logs into the stove. Given that Kat was a woman with her own agenda, she'd been right in spotting that something was going on. It sounded odd and difficult to fathom. Afan had been unfailingly kind and generous, but he'd never been a walkover. Swift was miles away and then realised that Kat was issuing an invitation. She'd got up and moved towards him, her hands clasped behind her back.

'I've got a proper kitchen at mine, Ty. You're staying for a bit, aren't you? Why don't you come round for supper Friday evening?'

'I'm not sure of my timetable yet.'

'Oh, okay. Well, I hope you can. I'm making lamb tagine and it's pretty good, if I say so myself.'

No doubt it was another of Afan's favourites. When she'd gone, Swift tidied up and put the rest of the chicken and the lemon cake outside in the compost bin. He locked the door behind him with relief. Kat's visit had been useful, if hard work. He decided he'd like to visit Caris Murray on her own territory.

CHAPTER 9

Swift was back in Holybridge the next day. He cycled in against a strong head wind, wondering how many times Afan had made the same journey. It was strange, following in his footsteps, talking to the people he'd lived among, shadowing his absence. At seven that morning, Swift had been woken by a sound at the front door and, dazed from sleep, he'd imagined for a few moments that Afan would appear, asking why Swift was sleeping in his bed. When he'd drawn back the curtain, he'd seen that it was Bryn Price, leaving a box of freshly laid eggs on the doorstep.

He stopped at the bookshop to see Gwyn Bowen. The place was empty, and she was taking books off shelves and dusting them. He had the impression that she was occupying herself with busywork and supposed that she had to do something to fill the hours. It would be disheartening to spend all day in a shop few people frequented. She gave him the details of the customer who'd met Afan. His name was Dale Toft and he lived in Ogmore-by-Sea, about twenty miles west of Cardiff.

'I hope he can help you,' Gwyn said.

'We'll see. Are you friendly with the people at Tir Melys? You said that you haven't been there often, but maybe they come in here to shop.'

She gazed at him with her limpid eyes like pale crystals. 'I don't know them that well, been there a couple of times. I was at one of Jasmine's concerts several years back. Bryn comes in sometimes, usually to gossip rather than to buy.'

'Have you seen Caris since she heard about Afan?'

She wiped a ledge and squared off a couple of paperbacks. 'We spoke on the phone. She's gutted. It's hard to find the right words when someone's so upset.'

Gwyn seemed muted today and disinclined to talk, so he left her to her cleaning. His next stop was Blasus café, where he ordered home-made lemonade from Sam. He chose a random selection on the jukebox, pressing odd numbers. He was rewarded with Dionne Warwick, the Everly Brothers, the Hollies and Chris Montez.

He sat at a computer and started a search. He'd decided that the only way he could work alongside Sofia Weber was to operate as if he was conducting his own investigation. If there were crossover points and information to trade, that was fine and mutually beneficial. As Sofia had said, a victim's life often explained their death and he wanted to track back in Afan's life, following the thread that had led him to Tir Melys. In Lyon, Afan had been close to Amira Brodeur for quite a while and must have shared details about his life. He'd never told Swift why they'd parted, but he'd indicated that his move to Brussels had caused a fracture. She'd worked as a personnel officer for the national police in the city and when Swift found her, he saw that she was still with them, as a communications manager. He switched to Facebook and sent a friend request. He contemplated the message he should send. It was difficult, informing someone about a death at such distance and Amira might have forgotten him. She and Afan might have stayed in touch but for all he knew, they'd parted on bad terms and Amira wouldn't welcome the contact. He stared at the screen for a moment, then started typing.

Hi Amira, I hope this finds you well. I might need to jog your memory. We met when I was working for Interpol. I was friendly with Afan and the three of us had a drink a couple of times. I've been back in the UK for a while now and I work as a private investigator. I regret that I have some very sad news concerning Afan. He has been murdered. I found his body on Tuesday. I'd like to talk to you. I'm adding my email address if that's more convenient, and my phone number although at the moment, I'm staying in a place with no signal.

I'm sorry to contact you in this way. I hope to hear from you.

Kind regards, Ty Swift.

He drank the sharp, refreshing lemonade and googled the Holybridge Beekeepers Club. The contact was a Sion Hughes. He rang the number and spoke to a wistful-sounding man, whose voice dropped when he explained who he was.

'I'm so sorry,' Hughes said. 'That's an awful shock for you, coming all the way from London and finding that Afan's been murdered. I heard that a friend found him. Was that you?'

The grapevine was humming. 'It was me, yes. I wondered if I could come and see you? It's good to talk to people who knew Afan, helps me form a picture of his life here.'

'Well . . . If it will help you, of course. I'm free around half two this afternoon.'

Swift noted the address and directions and logged out of the computer. He heard a familiar voice and turned around. Bryn Price was at the counter, ordering a snack and talking in Welsh to Sam. Swift walked over, nodding hello. He ordered coffee and a ham sandwich and asked Price if they could have a quick chat.

'I suppose so. I don't charge for my time,' Price said. He smelled beery, and his straining gut and double chin suggested he enjoyed his drink.

They moved to a table by the side window. Afan's padlocked bike was leaning against it.

'Good bike, that,' Price said. 'Afan bought it from a cousin of mine who shelled out a fortune for it and then lost interest in his new hobby. Afan said it rides well. It's got good quality tyres. You won't have had to adjust it much — you're a similar build to him. In fact, you could give people the willies, if they see you on it. They might think Afan's ghost is cycling around.'

'If they do, I can reassure them that I'm flesh and blood. It's very comfortable, rides smoothly. I just needed to alter the saddle tilt a bit.'

'I'd say you're fitter than Afan. He took plenty of exercise, but he didn't have your physique. Do you work out?'

'I have a boat and I row regularly.'

Price said, 'That'll be it. I get plenty of exercise working the land, but I never drop a pound because I like exercising my arm as well.' He grinned and made a drinking motion. 'Afan used to get bronchitis every winter. It would go on for weeks. I reckoned he'd have been better off living in a warm climate than in rain-soaked Wales.'

'Did he ever tell you why he came back?'

'I can't remember that he did.'

It was the first time that Swift had seen Price close up in daylight. He had bloodshot eyes and a square head with close-cropped, sandy hair. The eyes might be bleary, but they missed nothing.

'I saw you on the computer,' Price continued. 'I looked you up earlier. You didn't tell us you're a private detective. "Self-employed" indeed!'

'It didn't seem relevant,' Swift hedged.

'Not at first, I suppose, but you might have said something after you found Afan.' Price smirked. 'Maybe it suited you not to tell us. Private eye staying private and all that jazz.'

Sam arrived with their orders and Swift waited until he'd gone. Price slathered brown sauce over his sausage roll.

Swift said, 'I assumed someone would check on me. It's what people do these days.'

Price chewed a mouthful of food and said scathingly, 'I suppose you're playing detective now, snooping around at Tir Melys. I've seen how you absorb everything that's going on. Maybe DI Weber has you on the payroll. A helping hand for the one she can't use at present.'

Swift was startled and wondered if Price might have an inside contact in the police. It would be easy enough in a town like this. If Price had murdered Afan, he had the shrewdness to be elusive. Swift kept a poker face. 'If only. I never play at being a detective, my work is too serious for that. Does my job bother you?'

'Me? No. If you want to grub around in other people's rubbish, that's your choice. As long as you don't step on my toes, I don't care.'

'I want to find out who killed my friend. I presume you want me to.'

'Course. Afan was a decent man. Just because I don't blub and go on about him like a drama queen doesn't mean I'm not sad.' He grinned again. 'Speaking of drama queens, I saw you had a visit from Kat last night. Careful there, Ty. Once she's got you in her sights, she's hard to shake off and you're easy on the eye. I reckon she's got the hots for you.'

Swift ate some of his sandwich and stirred his coffee. He smiled back at Price. 'I can take care of myself, but thanks for the warning. You all seem to keep a close eye on each other at Tir Melys. Kat saw who'd visited me, you knew she'd been to see me. You might as well have net curtains.'

Price winked. 'You understand how it is. Tir Melys is like a tiny village. Sometimes it pays to notice what your neighbour's up to.'

'Have you anything particular in mind?'

'Maybe, maybe not. I guessed that would interest you, see. I will own up to keeping an eye on Elinor. She can be a pain in the arse, but she has a good heart, and I don't like her husband. Let's just say that her eyes are red-rimmed too often. I might well punch Guy very hard one day. I've been near it a couple of times. It'd give me huge satisfaction.'

With his bulk, Price could do a lot of damage if he decided to get handy. 'Guy's provocative.'

'He is, and a bloody snob. Thinks he's God's gift to us because he has a doctorate. He loves to correct anyone who uses the wrong word or phrase.' He finished his food, burped and leaned back. 'One of the things I valued about Afan was that he could handle Guy. I once saw Guy blush so red I thought he'd expire. He'd said something horrible to Elinor at supper and Afan gave him this killer stare and said, "*None can be called deformed but the unkind*". I asked him about that afterwards. It's from *Twelfth Night*. Anyway, I applauded, and Guy said nothing more that night.'

'He was probably even nastier to Elinor when they got home.'

'Probably. She chooses to be married to him. There's no understanding people.'

'If you like to keep an eye on what your neighbours are doing, did you ever notice anything unusual or troubling about Afan?'

Price's eyes glinted. He was enjoying the game. 'That would be telling.'

Swift sipped his coffee. 'You'll have to answer if the police ask you that question.'

Price winked. 'Well, that's different, isn't it? One has a duty to answer their questions. I wouldn't want to be on the wrong side of the law, but I'm not answerable to you.'

'I'll answer my own question, then,' Swift said. 'There was something going on with Afan, something bothering him.'

Price tilted his head sharply. 'Did he tell you something, then?'

'Maybe.' Swift deliberately changed the subject and tried hooking another line. 'I heard that the Merchants have financial troubles.'

Price made a buzzing sound. 'You're as busy as one of the Tir Melys bees.'

'I get around. If it forces them to sell up, it'll be a major blow to everyone.'

'You're right there, no word of a lie. But that's the landed gentry all over, isn't it? Londoners like the Merchants who fancied a patch of Wales, where land's cheaper and they could squire it over the locals. It's been the way in Pembrokeshire for centuries, with *fforinyrs* coming in. They call this county "little England". The Brinkworths are the same — they've chosen to favour us with their company, but Guy believes we're backward, leek-munching troglodytes. Distinct lack of PhDs around here.'

'You think the Merchants were lying, then, when you challenged them?'

'Let's say I'm surprised that Jasmine's nose didn't grow. I'm working on it — hold the front page.' Price tapped his nose and folded his arms on top of his gut. 'I've got lots of irons in the fire in Holybridge. My family have been here for generations. My name comes from the Welsh, *ap Rhys*. It means son of Rhys.' He laughed. 'I told uppity Guy that his name means "farm". He didn't like that one little bit. Far too common. It's too easy to get a rise out of him, but I do enjoy it.'

'How come you're living as a tenant at Tir Melys if your family are from here?' He saw a frown gathering on Price's face so added, 'If you don't mind me asking.'

'Messy divorce, and I do mind.' He hummed for a few seconds. 'If you're fishing for snippets of gossip, here's a morsel to go with your sandwich. Suki and Afan were in here one day. I saw them through this window as I was passing. They were having lunch and it wasn't a comfortable conversation. She had a face like thunder, and he was staring miserably into his mug.'

'When was that?'

'Dunno exactly. In the spring sometime.' He turned to Sam, who was cleaning a table. 'Hey, Sam, I was telling Ty here that Guy Brinkworth is well up himself. Far too good for the likes of us. What's he a doctor of again? Something phoney-sounding, like one of those qualifications you can buy on the internet.'

'Parapsychology.' Sam laughed. 'It's pretty much regarded as a pseudoscience. Maybe Guy was able to predict his grades.'

'We had a right giggle when we found that out,' Price said. 'I mean, what kind of doctorate is that and what bloody use is it to anyone? I might have a bit of respect if his subject was something handy, like land management or conservation. He probably couldn't get a proper job, which is why he pitched up at Tir Melys, hammering out his jewellery. Anyway, his PhD doesn't seem to help him use his psychic powers to find out who killed Afan.'

He and Sam started to banter back and forth, with Sam calling, 'I knew you were going to say that.' Price waved a mock warning finger at him and went to the jukebox, where he selected Led Zeppelin. Swift paid for his meal, went outside and unlocked the bike. He glanced through the window when he straightened up. Price was gyrating beside the jukebox, making the peace sign, while a couple of customers clapped.

He was a braggart, but he might be a useful one.

* * *

The bike handled well with its broad tyres, but Sion Hughes hadn't mentioned that his house was four miles from Holybridge along a series of winding, narrow roads that climbed uphill all the way. The inevitable rain arrived ten minutes after Swift left the town, but it drifted softly and he pushed on, breathing hard, finding the wind and wet exhilarating.

Hughes lived in an unremarkable modern, pebble-dashed bungalow facing a broad valley. The ordinariness of the house was transformed by the view and the front garden, which contained tall steel and bronze sculptures of spindly trees standing in a circle within a ring of white rocks. Some of their branches intertwined. Swift stood and inspected them for a full minute. They were eerie and beautiful. Kat could learn a few lessons from the sculptor's skill and simplicity.

The knocker on the door was made from rusted iron, in the shape of a bee. Hughes opened the door carrying a phone. He looked like Paul McCartney after a couple of years on the razzle. He had the same pixie features and boyish smile, but his face was deeply lined, and a pronounced dewlap hung beneath his chin. He wore black jeans with a leather fringe vest over a pink T-shirt, and a rainbow-coloured hemp necklace. He was slim and erect, with thin, silvery hair skimming his shoulders. Swift introduced himself and they shook hands.

'Hey, man, you've caught some raindrops,' Hughes said. He even sounded like Macca. 'Come on in.'

The living room was painted pale grey and had a picture window with cream and grey wooden blinds looking over the verdant valley and Hughes's extensive apiary. The floor was white oak. Two Eames lounge chairs in brandy leather with matching footrests faced the window, separated by a low walnut table. One wall was covered with a canvas print of a section of a beehive, crowded with worker bees. Opposite it sat a sleek black home entertainment system. Built-in bookshelves framed the recessed, log-effect electric fire which flickered on a low, comforting flame. Swift caught the sharp whiff of marijuana.

'Sit down and chill,' Hughes said. 'Would you like tea? I don't have coffee — bad for my blood pressure.'

'I'm okay, thanks. I've just come from Blasus, in town.'

Hughes gave an approving nod. 'Good food and service?'

'Yes, and great music.'

'Glad to hear it. I own it.'

'I had no idea.'

'Yeah. I based it on my favourite hangout in San Francisco back in the day. A Haight-Ashbury/Holybridge fusion but with better service and no hash in the brownies — more's the pity. Young people are far more clean-living than in my day. You have to move with the times, even if your bones creak while you're doing it.'

His allusion to the birthplace of 1960s counterculture explained his hint of Californian drawl and the hippie-themed Blasus. The whole time, he was fiddling awkwardly with the back of his phone.

'Hey, could you fix this for me? It's fully charged but it keeps dying. They told me to take the SIM card out and put it back in. I get how to do it, but my arthritic fingers won't cooperate.'

The fingers on his right hand were gnarled and curved inwards. Swift took the iPhone, checked that it was switched off, removed the SIM and then replaced it. Hughes hummed while he did it, in his light, faded voice. Swift turned the phone back on, and the screen lit up.

'There you are, good as new.'

'Brilliant, man! I wish someone could get my circuits moving again so easily. Thanks a bunch.'

'That's okay. I see you get a signal here. There's none at Tir Melys.'

'Yeah, I couldn't stand that. I like to know I'm connected, especially here on my own, with my seized-up hand and creaky hip.'

Swift pointed. 'You have a great view to compensate for the isolation.'

'Yeah, isn't it? I spend a lot of time just sitting here. Afan called in once and we shared a joint and gazed at the wonders. He said it was heavenly. I'm very sad about what's happened. He was one of the good guys.'

'Did you ever visit him at Tir Melys?'

'Not at his cottage. I went to one of the harp concerts last year, at his invitation. Jasmine played well, although I find the harp a bit samey when it's played solo — after a while all the melodies start blurring. I prefer it when it's used with vocals, like Queen did, and the Beach Boys and Eurythmics. I worked as a studio technician in the music industry, so I'm probably a bit of a stern critic. The medieval-themed evening wasn't really my scene, although I enjoyed the mead and nibbles. But I made the effort. They're doing good stuff at that community. There was some butch chick following Afan around all evening, making sure she sat very close to him.'

'How did you meet him?'

'I saw him in Blasus a couple of times. We get regular custom from the people at Tir Melys. They all need their internet fix, even if they pretend not to. Then he enquired about beekeeping courses. He came to one earlier this year, about natural beekeeping. We had a lecture on using horizontal hives, which was fascinating — explaining how we can try to mimic bee behaviour while we manage them. Afan was particularly interested in successful wintering.'

Hughes became energised as he spoke about winter preparations: strengthening colonies, leaving as much honey as possible for the bees, the importance of varroa floors, pollen supplements, pest treatments, insulation, mouse guards, use of Gas-Vaps and feeding fondant and syrup. It went over Swift's head, he got lost in Hughes's ramblings and suspected that he could talk for hours on his favourite topic. He half-listened, reflecting that this was the kind of handsomely designed and furnished living space that he'd have expected to find at Afan's home. Luxuriously simple and relaxing. The chair was the most comfortable he'd sat in since leaving London. Hughes must have seen the bewilderment on his face because he trailed off.

'I'm going on too much about my pet passion, aren't I? Verbal diarrhoea is one of the pitfalls of old age and living alone. Sorry, man.'

'You did lose me there. I can tell you live and breathe it. I imagine that it must be an incredibly demanding occupation.'

'It's wonderful, because you get so much back from the hard work. Afan and Bruno used to bang on about bees almost as much as I do!'

'Bruno said he's going to miss Afan's expertise.'

'He will, but I got the impression he's no mean beekeeper himself. He has his troubles and working with bees, you have to be focused and calm.'

Swift gazed out of the window. A watery sun glinted on the washed vista spread out below. 'Did Afan ever seem worried about anything? Tir Melys is a small community — there might have been tensions or arguments.'

Hughes was sitting with one skinny ankle resting on a stool, the other leg straight out. 'He never mentioned any falling-out and he always seemed in good spirits. I suppose he must have had an enemy — someone took his life.'

'It's unlikely to have been a stranger.'

'Yeah, I guess. The police were in touch earlier, asking which computer Afan used at the café. I passed them on to Sam, my manager.' He rubbed his hip. 'It was odd, mind you, how he lied about the train.'

'What train was that?'

Hughes fingered his rainbow necklace. It was incongruously youthful against his crêpey, puckering skin. 'I was at the station. I'd just come back from visiting a friend in Tenby. I saw Afan heading onto the platform for the Cardiff service. I mentioned it next time I saw him, but he said it wasn't him, I must have been mistaken. He seemed kind of embarrassed when he denied it.' He shrugged. 'Other bits of me are flaky, man, but my eyesight's sharp. I didn't push it — none of my business if he didn't want to share and it was no biggie.'

A trip to Cardiff sounded innocuous enough, but why had Afan wanted to keep it secret? 'Do you recall when that was?'

'Sure, it was my friend's wedding anniversary. It was a Friday, beginning of June.'

When Afan was supposed to be attending Welsh class but had said he was too busy at Tir Melys. 'And you're sure it was him?'

'Oh yeah. No doubt at all. He kind of hunched forward slightly when he walked. I'd have recognised him anywhere.' Hughes sighed. 'His death is so senseless and such a waste of talent. I hope the cops get whoever did it. His bees will miss him, they'll sense his loss.'

Swift was surprised. 'Bees recognise their keepers?'

'Sure. I believe so, and lots of beekeepers reckon so too. There've been studies that show that bees recognise individual humans and use the same techniques as us to distinguish faces. Although they probably do most of their detecting from our personal odours — they have an acute sense of smell. I've read articles in scientific journals about honeybee behaviour. There's some evidence that they use mechanisms that could be employed by computer programmers for use in facial recognition. How neat is that?'

Swift imagined Afan's bees having their own mourning drone, unremarked by human ears. 'I had no idea. My knowledge of bees is sadly lacking. I like their honey, that's it. At least the bees at Tir Melys still have Bruno for continuity.'

Hughes insisted on giving Swift a jar of honey as he was leaving. It was a bit like taking coals to Newcastle and he said that there was a supply at Tir Melys, but Hughes laughed.

'You'll find that my honey has an entirely different flavour, because my bees harvest pollen from masses of dandelions in this valley. See, man, honey's a catch-all term that doesn't do this wonderful nectar justice. Each batch of honey is unique, with different aromas, colours, flavours and viscosity. Spend some time with it. Stick your nose in the jar before you eat some.' He laughed. 'Okay, okay, I can hear myself switching to bee autopilot again. Nice to meet you, swing by any time.'

Outside, Swift checked his phone and saw that he'd had a text from DI Weber, asking if they could meet at the Bridge Arms in Holybridge at around half six. Dale Toft had returned his call, saying that he didn't mind speaking about Afan. Swift rang him back.

Toft had a deep, serious tone. 'I was sad to hear about Afan. Gwyn Bowen rang me and said you'd been asking about him. I hadn't seen him for a very long time. What happened was dreadful.'

'How did you know him?'

'We were members of an outdoor activities club in Cardiff. It was called MOVE. It's gone now — there's a gym there. That was back in the mid-nineties. I knew him for a couple of years.'

'Gwyn said you seemed surprised when you found out that Afan had come back to Wales. Why was that?'

There was a pause. A painted lady butterfly landed on Swift's handlebars, flexed its wings and fluttered away.

'It's rather difficult. Delicate. I'd rather talk about it in person, if that's okay with you.'

'That's fine. I can come and see you.'

Swift agreed that he'd visit Toft in Ogmore on Sunday morning.

He cycled away into the afternoon sun, glad that he'd brought his sunglasses. The bike hummed through muddy puddles. The sides of the narrow road were thick with tree mallow and wild marjoram. The payoff for the previous climb was that most of the route back to Holybridge was downhill. Swift let the bike choose its own pace and went over what he had learned so far. There were tensions at Tir Melys, but as far as he could make out, none that centred on Afan. Dale Toft knew something that was too sensitive to discuss on the phone. The significant detail for now was that from May onwards, Afan had lied to three people — Bruno, Gwyn and Sion Hughes — about what he was doing on Fridays. Finding out why was important, but Swift suspected that it wasn't going to be easy. The train from Holybridge to Cardiff stopped at a number of stations, any of which might have been Afan's destination. Maybe Sofia Weber would have come up with something after her contact with Afan's solicitor.

CHAPTER 10

Swift was drinking a bottle of pale ale called Rockhopper, while Sofia Weber glumly circled a glass of orange juice on the table. She told him she couldn't have any alcohol in case it reacted with the strong painkillers she was taking. She hadn't bothered undoing her coat, which was still held together with an elastic band. Strands of hair had escaped from the grip at the back of her head, giving her a rakish air.

She said, 'No booze, no fun. And it's not as if the painkillers are that effective.' She was haggard, as if she was about to keel over.

'Bad day?'

'Crap — and I didn't get much sleep last night.'

'Do you want something to eat?'

'Nah, I'll grab a bite when I get home.' Her phone buzzed on the table and she reached for it.

Swift sat back and read the plaque on the wall above her head while she answered it. It informed him that the pub dated from the sixteenth century and had been a town hall, a courtroom, a market, an auction room, a coroner's court and a grain store. It was cosy, with sloping old slate floors, oak beams, antique settles and a huge open log fire. Upstairs there was guest accommodation. A group of walkers clustered around a table with maps, discussing their day's ramble and planning tomorrow's while they ate ham, eggs and chips. Nearby, two older women were deep in a game of backgammon, chatting in Welsh.

Sofia finished her call, took a long drink of orange juice and leaned forward, whispering.

'The woman over there with the badly dyed black hair and crimson lippie is telling her friend that if she was forty years younger, she wouldn't pass you over.'

Swift put a hand to his heart. 'It's good to be told I can turn heads, but she'd have to get in the queue behind Kat Glover, who seems to have taken a shine to me.'

Sofia harrumphed. 'Lucky you. She's got over Afan pretty quickly then, despite her apparent grief.'

'Maybe I'm any port in a storm, or she's transferring her emotions to me.' He smiled at the black-haired woman. She blushed and fingered the necklace at her throat.

'Rather you than me. Now, let's crack on because my eyes will close soon. I spoke to Afan's solicitor. His will is dead simple, drawn up years ago by that firm. He's left his whole estate to two anti-bullying charities. The solicitor doesn't have any financial documents, so he has no idea what Afan was worth. Given that we didn't find any either, he's going to have to start a search. We've taken the computer that Afan used at Blasus and given it to our IT people to trace his history. I'm hoping that his email account or cloud files have some information about his contacts and transactions.'

'I've emailed Amira Brodeur, who was in a relationship with Afan for a while in Lyon. She should be able to fill in some background. I haven't heard from her yet.'

'Right. I have Interpol on my to-do list for tomorrow. Call me if you hear from Ms Brodeur. Spence has run a check on everyone at Tir Melys. Guess the offender.'

'Bruno or Bryn,' he said without hesitation.

'Correct, it's Bryn,' she said, making a tick sign in the air. 'He was fined and did community service for breaking a guy's jaw in a pub fight in Cardiff when he was seventeen. Nothing since, so probably a case of raging teenage testosterone.'

'But it shows he can be violent. There's a kind of compressed energy about him and he's a loudmouth. I'd guess that Afan wouldn't have had much time for him. Where was he on Monday afternoon?'

'That brings us neatly to alibis, none of which are independently verifiable. The Merchants said that they were together for the timescale we're covering, gardening, having lunch and a rest. Guy Brinkworth was out on his bike and had handily left his phone at home, so we can't track his movements. He's given us his supposed route, which was nowhere near the coastal path. Bruno Andersen and Suki Mehta spoke briefly at 12.20 p.m. for about five minutes, when she swapped him some tomatoes for aubergines — such exciting lives those people lead. Other than that, those two, Kat Glover, Elinor Brinkworth and Bryn Price were all on their own, gardening, working, cooking and reading — or in Elinor's case, doing prep work towards adoption. They all said that they hadn't seen Afan after around half ten, when he was on the communal allotment and waved to Kat, and they were tucked up in bed when you saw your fleeting figure around midnight on Monday.'

'Have you got any forensics?'

'Still waiting on results.'

'What about the pottery left by Afan's body?'

'Everyone said that their sets are all present and correct and the numbers checked out. So, given that it's for sale, it could have come from anywhere.' Sofia yawned, and closed her eyes for a moment. 'I asked the Merchants about this rumour that they're selling. They were flustered and Jasmine got righteous. Said it wasn't my business and when I stamped on that, said it wasn't true. But I didn't buy it. When I asked them about their son, they said he was fine and dandy, raking it in in London.'

'I googled Giles Merchant. He runs a cake-making business. I'll forward you the link to it. From what I've learned, the Merchants aren't making the income they expected from their rentable rooms in the Bivium — God, I hate saying that affected word — and their income from the tenants can't be great. But the house and land must be worth a fair bit. Bryn Price knows more about it than he's willing to tell.'

'I'm going to have another word with him, lean on him more. I didn't like his cocky manner. But even if the Merchants are planning to sell, I can't see at the moment how that would connect to Afan's murder.'

Swift sipped his ale. 'I don't buy Bryn stabbing Afan, it wouldn't be his style. He could do someone damage if he got angry enough, but he'd use his fists and punch them to death. There'd be blood, mess and broken bones, not a neat stab wound.'

'I don't disagree, but he's in the queue with only his word for where he was.'

'Going back to Afan's assets,' Swift said. 'I'm fairly sure that he planned to rent out his apartment in Lyon when he moved to Brussels, and that he bought another place there. He must have done something with the proceeds from selling those properties unless he was renting them both out for income. I could ask Amira about it.'

Sofia finished her juice, cupped her left hand under her plaster and seemed to drift away into her own thoughts. They sat in a companionable silence for a couple of minutes. Swift was more relaxed than he had been for a while.

Sofia roused herself. 'Maybe Afan gave most of his money away when he took to the simple country life. The bullying charities might already have had a share.'

'He was a generous man, but he still had to pay rent.'

'True.'

Swift told her what Kat had said about Afan giving money to Caris Murray. 'Did you see Caris?'

'Didn't get much out of her. She said that she and Morgan Callender hadn't been that close, and she was more annoyed than sad about him taking off. They're both from the rough end of Holybridge, but they've not been on our radar for anything. Spence confirmed that Callender left a note, saying he was heading for London. He lived with his dad and brother and by all accounts, the brothers didn't get on. Callender's nineteen, so he was never actually filed as a missing person. Caris said she'd got on with Afan and wasn't aware of any problems. She seemed evasive, but then I find most teenage girls unfathomable. Maybe she needed a loan and Afan gave her one. I wouldn't rely too much on Kat Glover's tittle-tattle. She strikes me as a woman who always has an angle.'

Swift scratched his chin stubble. He hadn't bothered shaving for the last two mornings, because the water had been cool and Afan's bathroom mirror was the size of an envelope.

Sofia noticed. 'Are you aiming for the raggle-taggle gipsy look?'

'Not deliberately, but shaving at Afan's isn't pleasurable.'

'Hmm. Seems to me that all that was missing in his life was a hair shirt.'

He smiled at that and told her about his visit to Sion Hughes and the information concerning Afan's train journey. 'If Afan lied, and to more than one person, he must have needed to conceal something.'

'Thanks, I'll send that *dummkopf* Spence to the station tomorrow to ask at the ticket desk.' Sofia reached for her stick, swaying slightly. 'I'm bushed now and the pain's kicking in. Got to go, I've a cab due. Are you staying?'

Swift had been about to tell her about Dale Toft, but he didn't like to keep her any longer. Her eyes were washed with pain. 'I've a phone call to make.'

When Sofia had gone, he sat and finished his ale. He liked the detective, but he was aware that she wasn't operating at her best, given her injury and a sluggish sergeant. They'd missed the keys at Afan's, and she might be overlooking other details or failing to follow up on them. She was listless, and his own experience told him that injury and painkillers could lead to impaired reasoning. He didn't trust her or her sergeant to find Afan's killer.

He went out into the small, pretty garden at the back of the pub. The phone signal was strong there and it was empty, which was good, as calls to Branna involved some shouting. He rang Ruth's number. As soon as she answered, Branna seized the phone and appeared on screen. She was in her pyjamas, her hair damp from the bath.

'Daddy, Daddy, Daddy!'

'Hi, trouble, how are you?'

She laughed loudly, dancing from one foot to the other. 'Been on beach an' caught a crab!'

'Terrific!'

'An' . . . an',' she said importantly, puffing her chest out, 'Mummy an' Marcel getting married an' I'll be bridesmaid.'

She'd blindsided him, but he forced a cheerful response. 'That's amazing. Can I help you choose your outfit?'

'Yes!' she shouted. 'I want blue, like sky. You come to the wedding too. You have to be smart.'

'Well . . . Hard for me, especially when someone with a name beginning with B messes around with my clothes and gets chocolate on them.'

She jumped up and down, almost dropping the phone. 'Ha ha! That was me! Just a naughty joke! You have to wear a suit for wedding.'

'We'll see how it goes. Tell me what you had for supper.' He needed to distract her from wedding invitations, and food was always a useful topic.

'Salmon an' pasta an' ice cream.'

'Not all together, I hope. That would be peculiar.'

'Don't be silly.'

She grew tired of talking after a couple of minutes, blew an airy kiss and handed the phone to her mother. Ruth was tanned and relaxed.

'Hi, Ty. As you can see, Branna's fine and *still in the room*.'

'Good, okay. I'll talk to you about other matters when you're home. Congratulations on your wedding plans.'

'Thanks. Talk more when we're back in London. Everything okay with you? I was sorry to hear about your friend. I remember you always spoke warmly about him when you were in Lyon.'

'It's very sad. I'm making my own enquiries.'

'Hmm. Isn't it best to go home and leave it to the police?'

'No, I owe it to Afan.'

Ruth gave the slight, disapproving frown that she'd started using with him in recent months. She walked with the phone to another room with a TV flickering in the background. 'You and your strange priorities, Ty. He was hardly a close friend. You said you hadn't seen him for years. I'm not sure why you feel such an obligation. Don't forget that you have a responsibility to your daughter to stay out of trouble.'

He shouldn't say the words, but what the hell. He was fed up with Ruth's censorious tone. 'Afan was good to me after you dumped me and I was in a bad way. I haven't forgotten that.'

Ruth's lips tightened. 'Let's not do the blame game, Ty. Surely we've moved on from that, and we both have very different lives now.'

'I agree, Ruth, so maybe you could stop constantly implying that I'm to blame for doing a job that I love. Without wanting to sound rude, mind your own business. I don't judge how you run your life and work, and I don't have to conduct my life according to your, and I suspect Marcel's, standards. I'll be Branna's father on my terms, not yours.'

She made a tiny, impatient noise. 'I'd better go, it's story time and if Branna gets overtired, she takes ages to get to sleep.'

He rang off, annoyed with Ruth but glad that he'd fought his corner. The dynamic between them had shifted since she'd got together with Marcel. Swift had supported her through her difficult divorce from Emlyn, and they'd cooperated well on Branna's care. Now, Ruth frequently reproached him and had taken to quoting Marcel's views on childcare, especially where Branna's hearing was concerned. While he had a signal, he sent Ruth a brief email.

I won't attend your wedding and assume you weren't planning to invite me, so please make sure that you/Marcel don't encourage Branna to think that I might. I'll talk to her about it when I see her at home. She's got a lot to handle in the coming months and I'll deal with her in my own way about it.

That was better out of his system. He checked his calls, texts and emails in case Amira Brodeur had responded, but found no reply. There was one from Ruth.

Okay, Ty. I'll leave you to talk to B. Let's keep things on an even keel.

In the car park he unlocked Afan's bike and saw Caris Murray in the distance, talking on her phone. She seemed wired and intent, holding the phone clamped to her ear with both hands. She turned down a side street and was gone from view. He cycled after her, following her slowly once she was in his sights. She walked rapidly, criss-crossing a number of roads, each one becoming progressively more down-at-heel, the tarmac pitted and potholed. Finally, she entered a depressing, short row of shabby terraced houses that fronted the narrow, uneven pavement. It was the kind of place where lidless bins stood by front doors and the gutters were clogged with rubbish. In hot weather, it would be fly heaven.

He waited until she'd let herself in through a peeling red front door, and then cycled to the house. There was no one around, but he thought he'd better hold on to his bike. The bell was detached from its casing, with wiring showing, but it rang when he pressed it. He could see a large, wall-mounted TV through the thin net curtain of the living room and recognised Matt Damon playing Jason Bourne.

Caris answered the door still wearing her coat. She sounded apprehensive. 'What are you doing here? How did you find where I live?'

'I asked around. I just wanted to have a chat about Afan. Can I come in?'

She folded her arms. 'No. It's not convenient.'

'It won't take long.'

'Not now. I've already spoken to a policewoman today and I'm knackered.'

'DI Weber?'

'That's right. She was banging on for ages, asking me stupid questions.'

'Okay. I've got some questions of my own. Have you any idea why Afan missed Welsh lessons on Fridays, lied about the reason and got the Cardiff train?'

Caris chewed the inside of her mouth and stared over his shoulder. 'Where did you hear that?'

'Someone saw him at the station. The Afan I knew was a truthful, honest kind of person. He wouldn't have lied easily, so I'm puzzled about what made him mislead people.'

'No idea about that at all.'

Fibber. 'I thought you might, given that you were friendly.'

'Like I said, no idea.'

'Okay. Did Afan loan or give you money?'

She snapped to attention. 'Who told you that?'

'Someone I was talking to.'

Her eyes flickered while she weighed up her answer. She said defensively, 'Afan lent me some money, yeah. I had a few problems and we were friends. That's no one else's business.'

'How much did he lend you?'

She coloured up. 'That's nothing to do with you. You've no right to be asking me. I'm not the only one who tapped him for money, you know, so there!'

'Really? Who else asked him?'

She stepped back from the door. 'I'm not telling you anything else!'

He took his card from a pocket and gave it to her. 'If you fancy a chat, get in touch.'

'I won't, don't worry. You can piss off, coming here and bothering me.'

She slammed the door and the bell quivered and then dropped lower on its dangling wires. A woman with fading mousey hair peeped around the curtain at him and then vanished.

Dusk was falling, he was hungry, and he wanted to get back to Tir Melys before it was pitch dark. He cycled away fast, his head full of questions.

CHAPTER 11

It was high time he had fresh drinking water. The next morning, he took the enamel bucket and found the natural spring behind the Merchants' house, following the track behind the high beech hedges that screened their home. He heard the water before he saw it. It was in a small copse of holly and birch trees and came from a pipe set into a stony ridge with a lipped saucepan hanging beside it. He drank some from his hand. It was beautifully cold. He filled the bucket and as he walked back with it, he saw Elinor Brinkworth drive away in the Land Rover with Frankie curled up in the back window. Dr Brinkworth might be at home, polishing his PhD.

He placed the bucket by the sink and made his way over to Cuddfan, the Brinkworths' house. There was no answer when he knocked at the door, so he followed the brick herringbone path around the side of the house to an egg-shaped timber building with a mossy green roof and full-length windows, painted a sunny orange. He could see Guy Brinkworth inside, seated at a bench. He was wearing an LED headband and goggles, his head bent over his work. Swift had prepared his excuse for visiting and tapped gently on a window. Guy looked up, removed the headband, pushed the goggles to the top of his head and opened the door.

He said discouragingly, 'Can I help you?'

'I hope so. I'd like to buy Joyce, my stepmother, a piece of jewellery for Christmas, and it would be good to get her one from an individual jeweller, rather than something mass-produced. So, as I'm here and you make jewellery . . .'

'Oh, I see, a paying customer. Well, you'd better step in.'

Inside, the studio was bright with natural light and furnished with two identical workbenches and height-adjustable upholstered chairs, one black and one red, at either side of the room. The walls were covered with fitted drawers in graduated sizes, racks of tools, organiser boxes and flexible lamps. Glass-fronted display cabinets contained a wide selection of bracelets, rings, necklaces, earrings, pendants and brooches. They gleamed and winked in the light.

Guy stood staring down his nose, with his usual peevish expression. He wore a twisted silver torc around his neck.

Swift smiled. 'I'm so sorry to interrupt your work. I must be a nuisance. It seemed too good an opportunity to pass up, given that I'm not sure how long I'll be here.'

Guy was just a tad more gracious, even if he still sounded grudging. 'Of course. I was working, and consultations are usually by appointment, but you're here now. What did you have in mind?'

Swift hadn't a clue. He pictured Joyce, his stepmother, who liked gaudy, floral outfits and brightly coloured accessories. 'My stepmother likes wearing brooches. Do you make those?'

'I can make anything you like. Your heart's desire, as they say. Here, take a seat.' He pulled a chair out. 'My jewellery ethos is based on the Bauhaus style — beauty and practicality.' He gestured at a plain gold circle on his workbench. 'I'm working on a gold and diamond bangle at the moment. It's a wedding anniversary gift. It's simple and strong, like the lady who's going to wear it.'

Swift nodded enthusiastically. Anything to keep Guy engaged. 'That sounds good to me.'

'I presume your stepmother doesn't live around here?'

'No, she's in London.'

'I can't meet her, then, and get a sense of the person. In that situation, I usually find that it's best to have a brainstorm and take it from there. I presume we're talking about a mature lady?'

'That's right.'

Guy picked up a pen and notepad. 'Let's look at metals. Silver, gold, copper, pewter, stainless steel or platinum? There are others, but they're the most popular.'

Swift hadn't a clue. 'Gold.'

'Okay. Now some of the most popular stones — agate, jade, garnet, moonstone, sapphire, pearl, diamond, ruby?'

'I've seen her wearing red stones,' Swift said. He seemed to be wandering into uncertain territory.

'Garnet or ruby, then. Garnet is more economical, depending on your budget and how fond you are of her.' Guy gave a sly grin. 'Is she a wicked stepmother?'

'Not at all. Infuriating and overwhelming at times, but she means well.'

Guy sneered. 'That's damning with faint praise. It's the kind of sentiment Elinor comes out with. Heaven save me from people who *mean well*.'

'Really? Surely good intentions help to make the world go round. It would be a worse place without them.' Although even as he said it, he knew that Guy had touched a sore spot and he was being a hypocrite where Joyce was concerned. He'd never quite forgiven her for replacing his dead mother and outliving his father, and he didn't visit her as often as he should. Her questions about his love life were intrusive, and she made it clear that she found his odd career change puzzling. After half an hour of her company, he was always desperate to escape.

Guy laughed. 'You're more sophisticated than you pretend. There's a quote from Margaret Thatcher: "No one would remember the Good Samaritan if he'd only had good intentions. He had money as well." Now, what shape brooch would your stepmother like? I can make geometric, circular, oval, square, bird-shaped, lozenge, trefoil — or perhaps an animal?'

It was the first time that Swift had seen Guy unwind. He, on the other hand, was bewildered. 'Can I think about that?' He clutched at a passing idea. 'She likes otters. She has one in stone, sitting by her garden pond.'

Guy rolled his eyes. 'Rather an otter than a gnome with a fishing rod, anyway.' He tapped the pad. 'That's an idea to start with. Tell you what, I'll show you a few design pages. If you don't like anything you see, I can do some illustrations, based on what you've given me. I'm sure we can make something that she'll love.'

'Sounds good, thanks. How much does a piece like that cost?'

'Depends on the carat and the stones. You can go all out Burton and Taylor with twenty-four carat gold, but I'd recommend nine carat yellow gold. It's strong and durable, suited to a brooch. If we went with that and a garnet surround, it would be around £150.'

That was a lot more than Swift usually paid for a gift for Joyce, but it would assuage his guilt at avoiding her as much as possible and for not having seen her since Easter. 'That's fine.'

Guy opened a deep drawer and removed a ring binder. He leafed through, and extracted several clear cellophane pockets, handing them to Swift. 'Have a look at these. They'll give you a general idea and then we can go into it in more detail.'

Swift started flicking through the designs while Guy reached for a pencil and drew in a notebook. He waited a few moments and then said, 'This is a lovely part of the world. You must be content in this community.'

'Content is too strong a word,' Guy answered. 'We're here now and settled. It's a beautiful area and I love being near the sea. I like it for the peace and quiet and being able to work in this studio, but I can take or leave most of the people here — preferably leave. I avoid them, stick to my work, gardening and cycling.'

'They're not your cup of tea?'

Guy laughed. 'Suki's okay, if a tad wishy-washy. Bryn's an arrogant fool, Kat's emotionally retarded, Bruno's in a world of his own most of the time, and as for the Merchants! Where to begin? Jasmine's a pompous bitch. She wears the trousers and Peter's her doormat. They could do a lot more with this place, bring in more interest and income and it would benefit us all. We get by okay but Tir Melys is a tad stagnant.'

Swift had heard this kind of comment several times now. 'Why don't they do more?'

'No idea. Status quo, I suppose. People have made various suggestions at the colloquy. Kat wanted to set up foraging groups and dawn chorus walks, Bryn was keen on running a course on sustainable smallholding and Suki fancied setting up classes on Shamanism. Jasmine's always batted them away.'

'Must be frustrating.'

'I suppose. I don't get involved. I've no wish to conduct extracurricular activities. This business keeps us going nicely, so I don't pay much attention to any of them. I eat supper with them all once a week to keep things sweet, which is pure purgatory. The quality of their conversation makes me yawn. Sometimes, I struggle to stay awake. Elinor spends more time at the Bivium and goes visiting, but then she's keen on what she regards as stimulating dialogue.'

Swift shook his head. 'I couldn't live among people I thought so little of.'

Guy held his pad up and away from him, regarding it. 'Like I said, the environment here suits me.'

'Do you ever wonder about their opinion of you?'

'No. I'm not interested in other people's opinions about me, especially when they're not my intellectual equals.'

Swift had to stifle a laugh. 'The people here might not drive me away, but the not-quite-hot-enough water would. Why is the shower always tepid?'

'That's the air source heat pump. It extracts heat from the air outside. We're used to the water temperature, but it can come as a bit of a shock when you've been used to traditional gas or electric heating. Visitors always comment on it. The upside is that you're benefiting the planet.'

Swift supposed he'd just have to accept his water-induced goose pimples in a good cause. He got up and studied the display cases. 'Did Afan ever buy any of your jewellery?'

Guy's pencil slowed. 'Can't recall that he did, unless he got something from Elinor. He was a favourite with the ladies here, with his oh-so-gentle ways.'

'You didn't like him either, despite the fact that he was highly intelligent? He had a Master's in criminal law. Surely you'd have found him someone you could converse with. An intellectual equal.'

If Guy clocked the sarcasm, he didn't react. 'Did he have a Master's? He never mentioned it. I can't say I noticed his brains and no, I didn't like him much. I'm sure the ladies found him *emotionally* intelligent. I didn't have much to do with him. He was one of those weak, colourless men who hide their feebleness with a grave expression.'

'You don't mince your words, do you? He was my friend. I didn't find him hollow.'

Guy glanced up and said pointedly, 'You asked me if I liked him. DI Weber asked me the same question and I gave her the same answer. I can't be bothered skirting around social niceties, and I'm not one of those people who think that you have to speak well of the dead, no matter what they were actually like. Afan didn't care for me much either, so he was an unlikely customer. He didn't seem the jewellery type. I never saw him wear any, not even a watch.'

'How did you get into making jewellery?'

'Through Elinor. She was doing a diploma in silversmithing when I was studying for my doctorate. I tried my hand at it and found I had a real aptitude. I was planning to have an academic career, but I changed my mind when I discovered this unexpected flair. Elinor says I'm more talented than she is, and I believe I agree. She doesn't have my concentration. Certainly, I sell a lot more than she does.'

'I suppose Elinor won't have so much time for working once you adopt. Unless you're planning to co-parent fifty-fifty, that is.'

Swift had tried to keep his tone neutral but Guy sounded suspicious. 'I'll leave the day-to-day childcare to Elinor. One of us has to make a living, and I'm best suited to that. That's if the adoption ever actually happens.'

'Oh? Why wouldn't it?'

Guy was off on his favourite topic. 'The social worker doesn't like me. You can tell poor old Terry's got a chip on his shoulder about my academic success, and he doesn't like the way I refuse to tick all his little boxes. He expects us to toe the line and be grateful. Elinor does — she sucks up to him, gives him coffee and cake and does all her homework like a good girl, but I question and challenge him. Once bureaucratic idiots like that take against you, you're done for.' Guy smirked. 'Terry sits there with his mouth opening and closing like a goldfish.'

Swift could almost taste his dislike of this arrogant man. 'It has to be a rigorous process, surely. The social worker has a big responsibility.'

'Yes, which is why I'd expect to be visited by someone who's literate and articulate, rather than a guy who's educationally challenged.' He stared through his pale lashes. 'Now, I'm a busy man and I need to make the most of Elinor's absence. Once she's back, her stream of consciousness will no doubt resume. I have ear defenders for when she's at work, but somehow, her verbal onslaught still distracts me and *Fwankie* always has to join us. Sometimes I come to work and find that she's entertaining Caris and her friend Gwyn. Her coven of gossips. Much as I'm enjoying this chat, have you seen anything you like?'

Swift pointed at random to a garnet brooch. 'Could you make that, but in an otter shape?'

'Certainly. I assume you're leaving us soon, so you'd need to pay up front before you do and give me your details. There's no great rush, as it's a Christmas gift. I'll make sure you have it by the beginning of December.'

'I might not be leaving that soon. Afan had no next of kin, so I'd like to do what I can regarding his death and the aftermath.'

Guy picked up his LED headband. 'Please yourself. Can you make sure the door's closed properly on your way out? It sticks sometimes.'

Swift went back to Afan's. He found a note from Suki slipped under the door.

DI Weber rang the landline and said can you contact her.

He made a coffee, mulling over his conversation with Guy. The encounter had made him want to have a wash. The man interested him in an appalled kind of way. He appeared to dislike his wife intensely, and most of the people he lived among. He didn't even like his wife's dog and the way he had mimicked Elinor's use of *Fwankie* was vindictive. Swift suspected that he felt deeply inadequate, and his sneering was a form of defence. He hid his fears by bullying and undermining his wife, and claiming intellectual superiority and artistic talent.

He finished his coffee and decided to drive to find a phone signal. He didn't want anyone at the Bivium overhearing his phone conversation with Sofia Weber. He drove to the nearest headland where he'd noticed a small car park and saw that he had a reasonable signal. Sofia answered and said she'd ring him back in a few minutes. He took his binoculars from the glove compartment and watched the sea, but there were no seals or dolphins visible today. The wind was high, buffeting the waves restlessly. He pointed his phone at the sky, took a photo of the delicate, wispy shreds of cloud chasing across the deep blue and emailed it to Ruth for Branna.

Lovely, silky cirrus clouds. The whitest cloud in the sky, which rhymes with you're the apple of my eye.

When Sofia rang back, she said, 'Sorry about that. I was talking to Spence and I needed to get rid of him. He came up with something useful, though. He's a local, so he has handy contacts, which occasionally compensates for his lack of initiative.' She groaned. 'Sorry, had to move my sling. Spence had a chat with a mate of his who's on ticket sales at the station. The sales guy remembered Afan buying a return to Cardiff on two occasions recently. He couldn't recall what day of the week. He asked a couple of his colleagues as well, and one of them was certain that she'd at least twice sold Afan tickets to Cardiff. She remembered it was on Fridays because she was doing the weekly shop after work. Also, she mentioned that Caris Murray had travelled on the Cardiff train on one of those evenings. She knows Caris from school. They had a brief chat and Caris said she was going to spend the weekend with an aunt.'

'It could be a coincidence that they were on the same train, except that there's no such thing.'

'I agree. I'm going to talk to Caris again. I'll give her a sweet invite to come to the station, see if I can rattle her.'

'I saw her after you left last night, and I followed her on my bike to where she lives.'

Sofia laughed. 'I'm not sure you should be telling me that you stalk women on a bike.'

'I don't do it habitually, so you needn't bring me in for questioning. It didn't do me much good. I asked Caris about Afan going to Cardiff, and she said she knew nothing about it. Then she told me to mind my own business about the loan he gave her. I had a slightly more useful encounter with Guy Brinkworth this morning. He made it clear that he disliked Afan, although he extends that antipathy to most people at Tir Melys.'

'Yeah, including his wife.'

'He's very wound up about the adoption. He seems to resent the intrusiveness of the process, and he's doing his best to sabotage it. There's something about his behaviour that puzzles me.'

'I sensed there was something else under the surface too,' Sofia said. 'Given that he dictates to his wife about most subjects, why not just put his foot down and say he doesn't want a child?'

'A couple of people have commented that Guy was wary of Afan, who openly criticised him for bullying Elinor.

Maybe Guy was jealous of the fact that Afan was supportive to Elinor, and his spite and annoyance boiled over. He was out and about that afternoon, he had opportunity.'

'It's a scenario. But just conjecture for now. I wish the bloody forensics would come back to me. There's a gastric bug going around the lab, so everything's been delayed.'

She rang off, saying that she had to get checked out at the hospital and might be there for hours. Swift watched the wind teasing and driving the sea for a while longer. It was congenial, working alongside Sofia, even if he had concerns about how pain was affecting her. That cut and thrust, the exchange of ideas and information with a colleague was the one thing he sometimes missed now he was working alone. His thoughts snaked back to Guy Brinkworth. If he had stabbed Afan, he'd have placed the grave goods around him with scorn. It was just the kind of supercilious act that would appeal to him — *aren't I clever?*

CHAPTER 12

Bruno had asked Swift if he'd lend a hand with the bees. Swift had been uncertain, pointing out that he knew nothing about beekeeping. He was also somewhat alarmed at the prospect. He wished he'd never watched *Swarm*, the film about killer bees invading Texas. Bruno had reassured him that he needn't do anything with the hives. When he arrived, Bruno was chatting to Bryn Price, the two of them leaning close. They were like conspirators, moving apart as he approached. Bryn said he'd leave them to get stung to death.

'Ignore him,' Bruno said. 'He's a wind-up artist. Trapping wasps can be your job today. Afan used to do it every autumn.' He smiled. 'He called it the "Waspathon". Wasps are sugar junkies, and they're busy this time of year because aphids and other pests that they eat have died out. That's why they're always bothering picnickers, and worker wasps head for the hives. If one gets in, it'll bite a bee in half and carry the abdomen away to feed to its colony as well as stealing the honey. Wear Afan's protective gear, you need to whenever you're working around an apiary.'

The sun was mild and warm. They worked for a while in companionable silence. As he carried out the job that used to be Afan's, wearing his hooded jacket and gloves, Swift experienced again that strange sense of tracing his footsteps. Bruno was carefully removing the last of the honey before treating the hives for the winter ahead. Swift followed his instructions and set about organising wasp traps. He filled empty glass and plastic bottles with small amounts of beer and placed them around — but not too near — the hives. When Bruno had completed the work on one hive and was taking a break, Swift decided to broach the subject of Afan's trips to Cardiff. He explained what Gwyn Bowen and Sion Hughes had told him.

Bruno shrugged. 'I've no idea. Afan used to cycle to town around three every Friday. He said he went to Welsh classes. He never mentioned Cardiff.'

'Did he come back home on Friday nights?'

'Haven't a clue. I assumed he did. He was entitled to do whatever he liked. I just don't understand why he'd need to lie about it.'

'Did Afan get on well with Caris Murray?'

'Yeah, they were friendly. Caris is okay, and she works hard.'

'Some people think that Morgan Callender was her boyfriend, but she says they were more like mates. What did you make of them?'

Bruno said cannily, 'You're sounding like a cop now. Bryn told us at supper last night that you're a private investigator these days. You kept that quiet.'

Damn Bryn and his nosiness. Swift held his hands up. 'Asking questions is a habit, hard to break.'

'I guess, but people don't always like being quizzed. I hardly knew Morgan. He was a skinny, furtive guy. Afan used to talk to him, seemed to find him okay, but generally he was seen as unreliable. Can't help you with what went on between him and Caris. Sometimes at that age, you don't even understand what's going on yourself.' Bruno's tone had changed, and he'd become less friendly. 'So, do we need to watch what we say around you now?'

'I hope not. I don't make any secret of the fact that I want whoever murdered my friend to be caught. If I can do anything to make sure that happens, I will.'

'Sure, okay, can't argue with that. But bear in mind that we're used to minding our own business here and living real quietly. We've already talked to the police, given statements and had fingerprints taken. That's a big deal for people.'

Swift said sharply, 'So is murder. Afan's lying in cold storage while his killer enjoys the sun and air. All of your lives here are going to be affected for a long time, so you'd better get used to it.'

Bruno sounded petulant. 'Maybe we'll get used to it, but we don't have to like it. Thanks for the help today, much appreciated.'

Swift could tell that he was being dismissed. He walked back to Afan's, hung up his protective gear and found his phone. The lack of a signal was beginning to grate. He wouldn't have minded if he'd been on holiday, but now that he was working, it was a real hindrance. He wondered if he might be better off getting a room at the Bridge Arms, especially if the rest of the community were going to react to the news of his job in the same way as Bruno had. He pictured steaming hot water, a deep bath and one of those power showerheads like a dish. But if he wasn't staying at Tir Melys, he couldn't observe and listen, and Sofia might cancel their deal.

He met the Merchants heading to the Land Rover as he was wheeling the bike out. Today, Jasmine's yoga clothes were in blue and red stripes and she wore a matching scarf tied in turban fashion on her head. She resembled a tube of toothpaste and she seemed fatigued. Peter wore an old tweed jacket, patched at the elbows, and flannel trousers.

'Where are you off to?' Peter asked.

'In search of a phone signal. How about you?'

Jasmine replied. 'I have a GP appointment. Just a routine check-up, to get my meds tweaked.' She attempted a smile. 'Are you comfortable in the cottage, Ty, got everything you need?'

'Yes, thank you.'

'Keeping occupied? Do ask me if you're at a loose end, I'll have no trouble finding work for you.'

'I haven't been bored. I've been giving Bruno a hand.'

'Yes, you don't strike me as the kind of man who'd ever lack something to do. Are you staying into next week?'

'If that's okay. It's good to be around the place and people Afan knew.'

'Of course. Your work doesn't need your attention? We hear that you're a private investigator in London.'

'That's right. I run my own agency. There's nothing that can't wait for now.'

'Well . . . An interesting career. You must have some fascinating stories to tell. Maybe you can regale us with some over supper.'

He couldn't tell from her bland expression if she was being sarcastic. 'I have worked on some intriguing cases but I tend not to use them as party pieces. In the end, they're about people's losses and grief.'

Peter piped up. 'I guessed you'd be principled about it.' There was a definite hint of sarcasm there.

Jasmine reached out and touched one of the bike's handlebars. 'It's strange, seeing you with that bike, instead of Afan. We all miss him.'

'I'm sure.'

'He had a calm, reassuring presence that uplifted the community and he was that rarity, a good listener. I found him easy to talk to. He's much missed, isn't he, Peter?'

'Oh yes,' Peter echoed, 'very much so.'

She gave a watery smile. 'Are you coming to my little concert on Sunday? I wondered if I should cancel it because of Afan's death, but then I decided to carry on and hold it in his memory. He loved listening to traditional Welsh airs, so it will be a way of honouring him. "The Ash Grove" was one of his favourites, so I'll play that at the end. We've sold thirty tickets and it's always an enjoyable evening.'

He'd better curry some favour and he appreciated her gesture to Afan. 'Of course I'll come, thanks.'

'Lovely. See you then, if not before. Don't be a stranger at supper.'

'We'd better get going or you'll be late for your appointment,' Peter told her.

He watched them walk away. Jasmine had a hand to her brow, shielding her eyes from the sun. *I found him easy to talk to.* Had Jasmine confided in Afan about her and Peter's financial troubles? Maybe that was what Caris had meant when she'd said she hadn't been the only one asking him for money.

He cycled to the point near where Kat had stopped the Land Rover on Monday night, and saw an overgrown track leading to a field of lavender. He bumped the bike along the track and laid it at the base of a hedgerow of blackthorn and spindle. He sat on the warm ground and stretched his legs out. The lavender had been harvested and pruned but he could still smell its rich scent.

When he checked his phone, he saw that he'd had an email and a missed call from Amira Brodeur.

Dear Ty, of course I remember you. This is terrible news about Afan and I am so sad. Why would anyone want to kill him? Was it to do with the person he was trying to help? There was something difficult going on. I tried to call you. Here is my phone number. Ring me any time.

It was almost one o'clock, so nearly two in Lyon. Amira might be taking a lunch break. He called the number she'd given.

'Hi, Amira. It's Ty Swift. I got your email. Is this a good time to call?'

'Hello, Ty. Yes, it's okay. Let me just close my door.' He heard footsteps and then she picked up again. 'This is the most awful news. What happened?'

He explained the circumstances. 'Afan was stabbed in the chest. I found him when I went for a walk on the coast path.'

'So you didn't get to meet with him?'

'No. We hadn't spoken for many years.'

'My God, I still can't believe this. What do the police think?'

'It's early in the investigation. I'm helping them as much as I can. They're still waiting for forensics. When did you last have contact with him?'

'About eight weeks ago. We weren't in touch regularly — perhaps a couple of times a year on the phone, and then occasional emails in between. Afan told me all about his bee-keeping and making mead. It sounded wonderful and I was so pleased for him. He'd found peace and a way of living that meant a great deal to him.'

'Yet you said in your email that there was something difficult going on.'

'The last time we spoke, Afan said that he was helping someone who was in a very problematic situation. He said . . .' She paused. 'He said that it was a bit cloak-and-dagger and it had to be, because of possible consequences for the person concerned.'

'Did he give you any indication of who this person was? Male or female? Someone at Tir Melys?'

'I'm so sorry, no. He was being very circumspect, but he hoped that he'd helped this person to find a way out of a problem. Then we went on to talk of other things. Was that the difficulty he wanted to talk to you about?'

'Possibly. Cloak-and-dagger doesn't sound like Afan.'

'It doesn't. I was surprised. But he said that secrecy was crucial regarding this situation. He said that it was a relief just to mention it to me, but he couldn't talk about any details.'

'And he definitely said that it was a person, singular?'

'Yes, I'm sure of that. Ty, Afan had no family. Who will take care of his things?'

'There's a solicitor in Cardiff who's his executor. The police have been in touch with him. He had very little at his cottage here. Amira, do you know if Afan sold his apartments in Lyon and Brussels?'

'I think he did.'

'Afan's will leaves his estate to charities against bullying. Did he tell you that?'

She took a breath. 'No, but it doesn't surprise me, because of his childhood.'

This was the first route he'd found into Afan's past. 'What did he confide in you?'

'Not a great deal. One of the reasons why we didn't stay together was because he was so closed off. He told me so little. But he did say that his parents' marriage was very unhappy. He was an only child, and both his parents took their misery out on him and bullied him. His father was the worst, very mean and spiteful to him. When his father died, his mother sent him to a boarding school, couldn't wait to get rid of him. She died soon after. I believe that he was often sad as a child.'

'I'm not surprised. He never told me any of this.'

'No. As I said, he was a clam. He formed that habit in childhood to protect himself and he could never escape it. It's hard to share your life with a clam. The shell is too hard. When I heard what happened in Brussels, I was very worried about him, and so relieved when they agreed that he could retire on grounds of ill health.'

'I heard that he suffered stress in his job. Was it linked to bullying?'

'Afan loved that Brussels job and had settled in so well there. Then he had a new manager who was impossible, always pushing and criticising him and making veiled threats. In the end, Afan filed a grievance about bullying and harassment, and he was sick with the stress. It was a horrible, drawn-out affair. You could say that finally, they paid him to go away and get rid of the problem. It happens quite often, to avoid tribunals and hassle. You've seen how it goes.' She sounded sad, resigned.

'What you've told me joins a lot of dots about Afan and explains why he settled at a place like Tir Melys. Did he move here soon after he left Brussels?'

'Yes, he'd been in contact with the community and moved straight there. He was content there, happy, grounded. It seemed like the last place where you'd find violence, murder. This is so hard to understand.'

'I'm sorry, Amira.'

She sighed. 'I realise that it was terrible for you, but I'm glad that it was you who found Afan. Someone he was fond of, not just a passer-by. You understand?'

'I understand. Could you do something for me? Could you send me an email with all the information you've just given me about Afan? I'll pass it to the police.'

'Of course. I'll do it this afternoon. I want to come to Afan's funeral. When will it be?'

'There's no date yet. I'll talk to the police and his solicitor and inform you.'

'Thank you. We had some lovely evenings, didn't we, by the Rhône? Wine, music and laughter.'

'We did.'

'I have to go to a meeting. I will email later. It's good to talk to you about Afan.'

Swift stretched out on the ground, hands behind his head, and gazed at the sky. Afan had realised profits from property sales and he'd have had a hefty payoff from Interpol, given his seniority and years of service. Perhaps the money was sitting in savings accounts. He reflected on what Amira had told him. Who could Afan have been helping with cloak-and-dagger methods? It seemed to have been one person. Perhaps it had been Elinor, who was certainly in a pickle, sandwiched between the adoption service and her bullying husband. What were the trips to Cardiff about and were they linked to her situation?

His phone pinged. He sat up and saw that he'd had a text from Sofia.

Forensics back. Nothing, except one of Kat's hairs on collar of Afan's jacket. She said he let her wear it once when they were foraging and it started pouring. Rings true, given that he was a gent. No trace of anyone unknown in his house, just Kat, Suki and Bruno, who all admit visiting him, and of course yourself. Giles M in deep financial waters. Creditors have filed statutory demands for payments of debts. He could be bankrupt if he doesn't negotiate payment. Could be something or nothing in terms of Afan.

He replied, giving her the bones of his conversation with Amira, and adding that the details would be in an email. He added, *Could Jasmine or Peter have asked Afan for a loan? If so, they'd hardly have killed their benefactor.*

He was wheeling the bike back to the road when his phone rang, caller withheld.

'Hello, is that Mr Swift who was here the other night?' A woman's voice, thin and wheezy.

'I'm Tyrone Swift. What do you mean, the other night?'

'You were talking to my Caris at the door. I heard what you were saying.'

He recalled the face at the window. 'Are you Caris's mum?'

'That's right. Caris threw your card in the bin and I found it. I can't stay on the phone long. Can you come and see me tonight? Caris won't be here.'

'Okay. What time? About seven?'

'That'll be all right, yes. I'll have had my dinner. Make sure you knock loud, in case I have the telly on.'

He mounted the bike, planning to microwave some soup and take the car into Holybridge later. Suddenly, he remembered that Kat had invited him to dinner tonight, and he'd forgotten to make an excuse. He was relieved to have a reason for being absent from Tir Melys and not having to spend a solitary evening with her. He saw that it was almost five o'clock and sped back, cursing the lack of phone signal there. This was exactly the kind of situation that called for an arm's length, apologetic text message.

* * *

Kat's small hexagonal house was called Cartref Melys, and painted bubblegum pink with a corrugated roof. The wooden steps up to the door were lined with her woodcarvings. A huge ginger cat lay on top of the roof of her wood store, enjoying the evening sun. Swift knocked at the door and was relieved when there was no answer. He'd just stuck a note under the door when Kat popped out from a nearby polytunnel. She was perspiring, wearing denim shorts with a sleeveless vest.

'Hi, I'm sorry to disturb you. I just wanted to say that I can't make it for a meal tonight.'

Her bottom lip curled down. 'Oh, that's a disappointment. I've already made a strawberry trifle and I was just picking leaves and herbs for a salad. You might have said earlier.'

'I apologise for not telling you. I've been busy today and I lost track of time.'

'Busy? Really? What can you have been doing?' She limped closer to him and he could see the sweat on her forehead.

He resented the assumption in her question. 'Various things.'

'And what's so important that you can't come tonight?'

'I have to attend to some work,' he said truthfully.

'Work? On a Friday night?' Clearly, she didn't believe him.

'My kind of work isn't nine-to-five. Things happen and I have to respond.'

She stared at him and said doggedly, 'So, what will you be doing tonight that's more important than eating the lovely meal I've prepared? Where do you have to go?'

'I can't go into that, it's a confidential matter.'

She stepped right into his space. Her hands were caked with soil. He saw a hair dangling from her bottom lip. She sounded truculent. 'Oh, like that, is it? I can see I'd better mind my own business.' Her voice changed to a wheedling tone. 'Well, come for dinner another night. I could really do with the company and we hit it off so well. I'd love to get to know you better. I keep missing Afan really badly and the nights are sad and empty. How about tomorrow?'

'I don't want to make an arrangement I might not be able to keep, that would really be bad manners. I've put you out enough as it is.'

She clicked her fingers. 'Let's go foraging early one morning. I bet you'd enjoy it. I could show you the places I went with Afan.'

'Maybe, Kat. Let's leave it there for now. I have to get on.'

He turned the bike and she followed him onto the path, touching his arm.

'Are you coming to Jasmine's concert Sunday night?'

'Yes, I expect I'll see you there.'

'I can come and call for you if you like, and we can go together.'

'That's okay. I'll see you in there. Have a good evening.'

He walked away quickly, before she could attempt another delaying tactic. He sensed her gaze on him until he turned off the path and was screened by trees. She was one of the creepiest women he'd ever met.

CHAPTER 13

'Have a seat, love, thanks for coming. I can't offer you tea or anything. I'm a bit whacked this time of evening. Just about all I can do to wash up my dinner plate and take my tablets.'

'That's fine.' Swift sat near Ms Murray, in the corduroy-covered armchair of a three-piece suite. Her chair was positioned beside a grey oxygen cylinder and a mask attached to it lay in her lap. The back room was tiny, with faded embossed wallpaper and a three-bar gas fire inset to a tiled fireplace. Half a dozen houseplants cheered the restricted space. The back window had been replaced with French doors. They stood open onto a small square patch of paved yard, bounded by a pocked, frost-damaged brick wall. The yard was crammed with tubs of bright flowers: dahlias, pinks, zinnias, cosmos and love-in-a-mist. An empty washing line stretched across the yard and a rabbit stared disconsolately from a hutch by the back wall.

'So, Ms Murray, why did you want to see me?'

She was a woman who'd once been well-built but had shrunk with age and illness. She must have been in her late fifties, but her face was a worn seventy. Her skirt and short-sleeved blouse were much too big, with the shoulder seams drooping down her arms, where flaps of skin hung. She had a kindly expression. She'd have been a buxom, pretty young woman. Caris had inherited her cheekbones. She raised her mask to her face and took a puff of oxygen.

'Call me Lori. I don't like going behind my Caris's back, but truth is I'm ever so worried about her.' Her voice was listless and faint.

'If I can help, I will. You said that you heard me at the door the other night, asking about Afan Griffith.'

'That's right, and I heard Caris being downright rude to you,' she said apologetically. 'I didn't bring her up to behave like that.'

'I'm used to it. You'll have seen from my card that I'm a private investigator. People often dislike my questions and it's a difficult time for anyone associated with Tir Melys. It struck me that Caris is stressed out.'

'She is, that's true, but that doesn't mean she shouldn't mind her manners. Caris was very fond of Mr Griffith. She was crying here when she heard he'd been found dead. She's been on edge all week.'

'Afan was my friend. I'd come here to visit him. I heard from people at Tir Melys that he and Caris got on well.'

'They did. I was thrilled when she volunteered there and got so interested in gardening. We've nowhere to grow things here, although she does wonders with the little space we've got, and I love the tubs.' She gestured to the back yard. 'It was good for her, going there and meeting new people, learning new things. And she gets to bring home loads of lovely fresh fruit and veg. Eggs, too and sometimes cuts of lamb or chicken. That's a real help, what with me being on benefits now. I can cook if I sit on a stool in the kitchen and take my time. I make big soups and stews. I might be a bit buggered, but I can still cook up a storm when I put my mind to it!' She paused, swallowed and continued. 'Caris could only get a part-time job at a warehouse when she left school and she doesn't have much of a life, stuck here with me. She's my youngest and the others have all moved away, got their own families. I'm glad of her help but I don't want to hold her back. She's only eighteen, she should be having some fun. Anyway, Tir Melys was good for her until Morgan Callender, her boyfriend, started tagging along there with her.' She shook her head and took a sip of water from a glass on the small table beside her.

'You didn't like Morgan?'

Before she could reply, there was a huge cheer and Abba's 'Dancing Queen' burst into the evening air, accompanied by a loud chorus of voices.

'Oh God,' Lori said. 'That's next door, having a karaoke evening. I can't complain, 'cause I used to go in there regular when I had a voice. Could you close the doors, love?'

Swift closed the doors. The music was still audible, but slightly muffled.

'Ta. I miss my karaoke. My favourites were "I Will Survive" and "Don't Go Breaking My Heart". They still invite me in sometimes, but I couldn't even hum now and no point in being a party pooper. I've got heart failure, see. Had to give up work five years back and I don't get out much now. Actually, it might be nice to die belting out Gloria Gaynor, instead of parked in my chair, staring at the rabbit, both of us bored stiff. Do you like karaoke?'

'I have a dim memory of a bar in Soho a long time ago and singing "Space Oddity". I was very drunk, so I'm sure it was awful.'

They both laughed and Lori said, 'Doesn't matter, it's the fun that's important. Where was I?'

'It sounded as if you didn't like Morgan Callender.'

She paused for a moment. 'It wasn't so much that I didn't like him. I was sorry for him — you had to be, with his family — but he'd latched onto Caris and he dragged her down. She was always worrying about him, texting him to ask if he was all right. He was *ling di long* — lacked direction in life. Caris is no go-getter, but she's a lovely girl, got a spark to her and she gets stuck into things. I never understood the attraction. Morgan's nothing much, and I reckon Caris could have had her pick of what little talent there is in this place. Morgan just used to hang around her. I knew a chap like that when I was young. He sort of sucked up other people's energy, the way I suck oxygen out of this canister, God help me.'

Lori had a good turn of phrase and he filed *ling di long* for future use. He considered how to put his next question. 'Were Caris and Morgan more than friends?'

Lori grinned, showing a set of startling white dentures. 'Judging by the noises that used to come from upstairs now and again, I reckon so. I'm no prude, but let's just say that I used to turn the telly up.'

Swift smiled back. 'Caris told me that she and Morgan were just mates.'

'Really? That's an understatement. When I saw them together, they seemed very lovey-dovey. She was moping about here after he legged it. She really misses him, I can tell, but she won't talk about it.'

'Tell me what Caris said about Morgan's disappearance.'

Lori sucked in oxygen, taking slow breaths. 'Summer Nights' belted out from next door — *tell me more, tell me more* — and Swift saw a cigarette butt fly over Lori's wall and land on top of the rabbit hutch.

'Not much,' Lori said at last. 'She said that Morgan had had enough of his brother and he'd gone to London for good. When I asked her if they were staying in touch, she said no and went quiet on me, so I didn't push it. I'm enough of a pain to her without nagging. She's entitled to her own life, but I don't like to see her fretting. To be honest with you, I was glad that Morgan was off the scene. I thought she'd get over him and find herself someone with a bit more to offer apart from a sad story.'

Lori still hadn't told him why she'd wanted to see him, other than being worried about her daughter. He was interested in why Caris had lied to him and the police about her relationship with Morgan. It might be best to stick with the thread that led to Callender for now. 'Tell me about Morgan's family.'

'Where to start? Rough as sandpaper, the Callenders. The mother died, leaving the father, Terfel, with the two boys. Terfel's weak and hopeless, always out of work — Morgan takes after him. The older boy Calvin's always been a nasty item. Big fellow, handsome and a charmer when he wants, but rotten through and through. People round here have always known that he terrorised Morgan and the father did nothing to stop him. Don't ask me why Calvin's that way, he was just born bad. A rotten bully, he is. I've noticed Morgan all cut and bruised sometimes, and that's just the damage you could see.' She paused for a puff of oxygen. 'Morgan's weedy and skinny, no match for his brother even if he'd wanted to put up a fight. He stayed over here a lot, just to have somewhere safe to lay his head, even before he and Caris were an item. I used to worry that Calvin would kill him one day and I'd tell him that he needed to get away, but I never thought he'd have the bottle to do it. I'm glad he did, but sorry for Caris. She might have gone with Morgan if it wasn't for me tying her down. As it is, she says they're not in touch because Morgan needed a clean break from here. Too many bad memories. And now Mr Griffith's dead, another friend of hers has gone and she's so unhappy.'

There it was again, the theme of bullying. It ran through this investigation like a refrain. 'Are you worried about Caris because she's depressed?' He couldn't imagine why Lori would want to talk to him about that.

'Sorry, I'm going round the houses. I'll try and get to the point. It's not just that Caris is upset about Morgan and now Mr Griffith. I'm worried about what she's up to. She's been away a lot of weekends for months now since Morgan left. Leaving on Friday, not back till Sunday usually, depending on her shifts at work. She took off late this afternoon. Spence rang from the police earlier, wanting to talk to her but she'd already gone.'

Sofia would have got him to call as the good cop to bring Caris in. 'You know DS Spencer?'

'His mam lives at the end of this road. He went to school with my eldest. He's a nice lad, always willing to lend a hand.

Takes his mam out every Sunday to the carvery for a roast dinner. She's a friend so I get to hear all about it! He's got a good heart, has Spence.'

Lori seemed far away, so he said, 'You were telling me about Caris going away at weekends.'

'That's right. She told me that she's visiting her aunty Becca in Cardiff, said that she's not well and she's helping her out. Becca's on her dad's side and we've never had much to do with each other. She's a bank manager and a bit up herself, so I was surprised when Caris said they were in touch. When I asked what was wrong with Becca, she said something vague about her having an operation. It sounded funny but Becca's on her own, so I reckoned she must have asked Caris to give her a hand. Anyway, Becca rang me week before last, when it was my husband's anniversary — he died eight years back. She asked how Caris was doing, said she hadn't seen her for ages. She sounded fine and dandy, said she'd just been on holiday to Lanzarote.' She gasped, rested her head back and used her face mask.

Swift waited until she had recovered. He listened to 'Billie Jean' being hollered on the other side of the wall. 'Did you speak to Caris about Becca's phone call?'

She shook her head. 'I was going to, but in the end, I felt really awkward and I flunked it. I was a bit gobsmacked, to be honest. I mean, Caris has never lied to me, not about important things anyway. What if she's caught up in drugs or doing something illegal? I can't think of any other reason why she'd fib. And where's she staying, if she's not at Becca's? Who's she got mixed up with? When I heard you asking her why she'd borrowed money from Mr Griffith, I thought it must be for drugs. That's what you hear, don't you — that people beg, borrow and steal to feed their habit. I've read about the big drug problem they have in Cardiff, and how easy is it to buy them there. And that might be why she's been so moody too, if she's taking those awful things. When I saw on your card that you're an investigator, I reckoned you might help me find out what she's doing. Whatever you charge, I'll pay you if it buys me peace of mind. I can't sleep at night, wondering what's going on.'

The obvious reason for Caris's lie didn't seem to have occurred to her. It couldn't be easy, sitting here all day, worrying and imagining the worst. 'Have you considered that maybe Morgan is in Cardiff and Caris goes there to see him? It seems odd that her trips away started after he left home.'

Lori's eyes turned to saucers. 'But he's in London. Caris said he went to London and she's not in touch with him.'

'Maybe London's a red herring. If Morgan wanted to put his family off the scent and make sure that his brother left him alone, he could have said London but headed to Cardiff.' Swift was sure that whatever was going on involved Cardiff, and he now believed that Afan had been part of it.

Lori was having a little surge of energy and her pale cheeks were slightly flushed. It would be down to the relief of sharing what had been on her mind.

She said, 'Oh, like a double bluff. You could be right. Listen, I always go through pockets before I do a wash. I found this in Caris's jeans pocket when I was putting them in the machine. I'm not that familiar with Cardiff, so I googled the road. It's in an area called Roath. Nowhere near where Becca lives, but that's no surprise now.'

She handed Swift a Co-op receipt for a shop on Ninian Road, Roath. It was dated a fortnight ago and listed the sale of sliced ham, cheddar cheese, milk, teabags and a chicken biryani.

'This tells us that Caris does go to Cardiff. Whether or not to see Morgan is another question,' Swift said.

Lori's face had drained of colour again. 'Hang on, if she's seeing Morgan, why wouldn't she just tell me, instead of making up stories? I don't understand. I can keep a secret. I wouldn't tell a soul. Who is there to tell these days anyway, except Reg?'

'Reg?'

'The rabbit.'

Swift looked out. Reg had vanished, presumably to curl up and ignore the flying fag butts from next door. He turned back to Lori. 'I can see you're exhausted. All this worry is bad for you.'

She shook her head. 'Oh, Mr Swift, that's not all of it. I found something else and it baffled me. There was a note signed by Afan in another of Caris's pockets — this one was in the old trousers she wears to Tir Melys. I read it, put it back, and left the trousers in her laundry bin. I didn't want her to know I'd seen it. I popped into her room again just before you arrived. The trousers are still there, but no note.'

'Can you remember what it said?'

'It wasn't a long note. He said he was disappointed, and this wasn't what he'd expected when he'd offered help. He said they needed to meet and sort out the situation. He hoped that the arrangement could continue, but he was doubtful. Something along those lines. I do remember one bit where he said, "It's not how friends behave towards each other." That upset me, because it was sort of sad, and I wondered what Caris could have done to make him write that, especially when she spoke so fondly of him.'

Swift was wondering too. 'Was the note dated?'

'No.'

'When is Caris due back?'

'Sunday lunchtime. She said she'll make me dinner and then she wants to go to the harp concert at Tir Melys. She enjoys those. She's going with Gwyn, her friend who runs the bookshop. Will you try and find out what's going on?'

'I'll try, but I don't want your money and you need to ask Caris yourself. Have an honest conversation with her when she gets back and tell her that you found the shopping list and the note. There's no other solution, really. In the meantime, if I hear anything that might throw some light on the situation, I'll contact you. Does that help?'

'Yes, I suppose it makes sense. Otherwise I'll just be worrying myself sick.'

'Is it okay if I keep this receipt?'

'It's not doing me any good, love.'

'One last thing, have you got a photo of Caris, or even better, one of Caris with Morgan that I can have?'

She got up slowly and shuffled out of the room. There was a crash from next door, hoots of laughter and the party struck up 'Delilah'.

Lori came back with a small photo in a light Perspex frame. 'Here. I took that of both of them out in the yard last year.' She sank down and swayed in her chair, tapping the fingers of one hand on her knee and moving the other in time with the music. 'You can't beat Tom Jones for a belting song. My mam went to school with his sister.'

'Can I do anything for you before I go?'

'No, you've been ever so kind, coming here and listening to me going on. And on a Friday night. I'm sure you've better things to do.'

He pictured supper chez Kat. 'Nothing better, believe me.'

She smiled faintly. 'I've forgotten my manners too, what with my stupid worrying. I'm very sorry about Mr Griffith. From what Caris told me, he sounded such a nice man. It's hard, losing friends.'

'Thank you. I'll see myself out.'

'I'll stay up for a while, listen to the music and sing along in my head. Not much point trying to sleep, is there?'

Swift smiled. 'Not unless you've got earplugs.'

He sat in the car and checked trains to Cardiff the next morning. He debated whether to call or text Sofia. It was gone nine and he didn't like to disturb her. It could wait. He hoped that she was at home with her feet up, getting some rest. He could contact her from the train tomorrow.

He drove back to Tir Melys past fields of sheep. They were blurred, ghostly shapes in the dark. He'd moved Afan's keys, tucking them behind a stack of tins at the back of the dresser. Maybe they unlocked a secret in Cardiff.

CHAPTER 14

The train to Cardiff was packed, standing room only by the time it left Holybridge. Swift's carriage contained a group of about thirty excited girls, all teenagers who'd swarmed from the valleys, heading for the weekend delights of the capital. Swift just managed to get a seat and was jammed in next to an odoriferous toilet with the door hanging open and paper strewn on the floor. He sat, overwhelmed by cheap scent, wishing that he'd chosen to drive. It was a warm, sunny day and the girls yelled and laughed, tottering up and down the carriage on strappy sandals and spiky heels. They flicked their long hair, flirted with three boys who sat in a nervous huddle, and swapped cola, chewing gum and lipstick. They were all dressed in skimpy outfits that revealed acres of glowing skin. Swift listened to their carefree chatter, feeling ancient.

'I never told him that, that's a lie an' he's no right sayin' it!'

'I don't like this colour, Daisy, haven't you got somethin' else?'

'My dad said I've got to be back by midnight. I said why, d'you reckon I'm gonna turn into a pumpkin?'

'I'm dyin' to see this virtual reality place! I'm gonna go in the horror movie mansion.'

'I'm 'avin' a great big burger as soon as we get there, I don't care if it gives me a fat belly!'

He'd never been a light-hearted teenager. He'd gone straight from relief at not developing spots, like most of his school friends, to shouldering grief. His mother had died when he was fifteen, and her illness and loss had cast a shadow that he'd tried to ease by rowing his boat on the Thames. From what he'd seen and heard, he couldn't imagine that Caris had ever been like one of these happy-go-lucky girls. She'd spent her adolescence concerned about Morgan and her mother.

He realised that there was no chance of talking to Sofia Weber in this din and if he left his seat, he'd never get back to it, so he texted her instead, to explain that he was on a crowded train and what he was doing. He asked her to check Calvin Callender on the PNC. She replied within minutes.

Okay, I'm at the station for a while today, so keep me posted. Spence left a message on Caris's phone yesterday when he couldn't raise her, but she hasn't replied. Have had some interesting info back from Canadian police about Bruno. Talk later.

By the time the train meandered into Cardiff, Swift was desperate to flee from his forced immersion in the teenage world. The voluble girl called Betsy sitting next him had held court to her friends when she wasn't slinking up and down the aisle. He now knew far more than he needed to about Gareth and Daisy's love life, which was a rollercoaster of arguing, splitting up and getting back together. He'd also been educated in the thrills of Laser Quest and Storm Disco. Then there was Bellissima, the makeover and photo shoot shop, where Betsy was going to have her lashes dyed. She'd also benefit from an expert cosmetic consultation with skin tone matching and free samples — 'An' I don't care what my mam says, I'm gettin' a skin peel.'

He stepped from the train like an escapee from a life sentence and checked the map on his phone while screeching girls raced past him to the ticket barrier. Roath was about a forty-minute walk. He bought a coffee on the station concourse and set off, glad to be on the move.

Ninian Road was wide and tree-lined, opposite a huge park. The small Co-op was on a corner and busy with customers. Swift leafed through magazines, waiting for a chance to talk to one of the assistants at the counter. When the queue had dwindled, he took out the photo of Caris and Morgan and approached a woman who was free.

'Hi, I wonder if you can help me. I said I'd drop by on some friends when I was in town, but I've lost their address and they're not answering their phones. They live on this street. They're called Caris and Morgan. Caris has mentioned that she shops in here. Would you recognise them from this photo?'

He wouldn't have believed his story, but the woman was friendly and eager to help. He got the impression that having something different to talk about had brightened up her day. She studied the photo carefully but shook her head.

'They don't ring any bells. There's loads of flats on this street with lots of coming and going, especially with Airbnb. We get so many people in and out of here, it's hard to remember them.' She showed the photo to the young man at the next till, but he also shook his head.

Swift was about to leave it there when he paused. He took the photo of himself and Afan from his pocket and passed it to her. 'How about the man with me in this photo?'

She nodded immediately, tapping it. 'I recognise him. Haven't seen him in a long while now, but he used to pop in to get a sandwich. He was friendly, very polite. I remember him because he asked me about the area. He was looking at houses to buy. You're a bit younger here!'

'Don't remind me. You wouldn't know which house he was visiting?'

She smiled, her cheeks creasing into deep dimples. 'Not the number, no. The reason he sticks in my mind is because we had a laugh. He'd seen a house he liked, and it had a pink stone pig outside on the wall by the steps. That tickled him, and he said that he might create a family crest with a pig rampant. I can't say if that's the place he bought, mind, or even if he bought anything around here at all, because I didn't see him again after a while.'

'How long ago was that?'

'You've got me there. I've worked here for ever. At least five years ago, probably more. Sorry, but there's people waiting.'

Swift set off along the street. The houses were Victorian, large and handsome, and in good condition. He could see from the numbers of bins and doorbells that most of them were multiple occupancy and unless he spied a pink pig, finding Morgan and Caris would be difficult. He'd have to do a property search online or wait for Sofia to come up with information. He walked for a good ten minutes, crossing busy intersections. The park opposite was teeming with runners, cyclists, sunbathers, dog walkers and a football game. The houses grew larger and were set back further from the road. Then he saw it — a large, fat pig curled on top of a stone pillar by a set of steep steps, its snout in the air. It was blue now, but still amusing, with a kind of porcine dignity.

The house was three-storey and imposing, with two tall brick chimneys. It was set on a steep incline, built of grey and cream granite. The deep bay windows were edged with inset geometric designs on the first two storeys. The path to the front door bisected a well-kept lawn. Six black bins stood in a neat row inside white iron railings. Swift could see that it would make a good investment. Perhaps this was where Afan had found a home for some of his money.

He climbed the eight steps to the solid front door, patting the pig's head on the way. The stone was warm and rough. None of the six doorbells indicated a Griffith or Callender. He reached into his pocket for the set of keys he'd brought from Afan's cottage, the ones labelled FD. They opened the door, confirming his hunch that he'd found what lay behind Afan's 'cloak-and-dagger' comment to Amira. He closed the door quietly, locked it again, and pressed one bell randomly. There was no intercom, but after a short wait the door opened, revealing a tiny Japanese woman in a red minidress, with a slice of toast in her hand.

'I'm so sorry to disturb you, but I'm calling on Morgan Callender and I can't remember which number he lives at. He is expecting me.'

'Number six, top floor,' she said, turning away and vanishing down the hall, leaving him to close the door.

So much for home security. Swift stepped into a white-painted hall with cream and blue mosaic floor tiles. A noticeboard on the left-hand wall had information about bin collections and recycling. There was a post rack below it. A large fire extinguisher hung further down the hallway, beyond the brown-carpeted stairs.

Swift climbed the stairs. The house was well maintained with no tell-tale scuffmarks on the carpet or the white walls, and there were metal stands containing houseplants on the landings. Each flat had a different-coloured front door and through the arched landing windows he saw a small, lawned back garden with an apple tree hung with bird feeders in the centre. If he'd known that Afan was a landlord, this was the kind of handsome property that Swift would have expected him to own.

Flat six had a bottle-green front door. He rang the bell and the young man in the photo opened it.

'Hi, are you Morgan Callender?'

The slight youth blinked rapidly. He wore blue flip-flops, jeans and a thin vest. 'Who let you in?'

'My name's Ty Swift, I'm a friend of Afan's. I wanted to speak to you. I expect Caris is here. We met at Tir Melys.'

Caris appeared behind Morgan, eyes wide. 'What are you doing here?'

'If you let me come in, I'll tell you. I'm not here to cause you any trouble. You should hear me out.'

Morgan turned towards her. 'Caz?'

She hesitated and then shrugged. 'You'd better come in then.'

It was a studio flat, built into the eaves. Just one good-sized room, painted cream with skylight windows. There was a mattress on a platform in the far corner and a fitted kitchen area with glossy white cupboards. Swift spotted jars of Tir Melys honey and a couple of bottles of home-made wine on the worktop. The living space was furnished with a small glass-topped table and two chairs, and two sofas covered in batik throws. Caris sat on one of the sofas, her legs tucked beneath her. She glared at Swift. He sat on the other sofa. It sagged beneath him.

'Well, Caris. The police have been trying to contact you. Have you responded to DS Spencer's message?'

'Not yet.'

'Don't you think you should?'

She ignored the question and asked, 'How did you find us?'

'Through a shopping list. I visited your mum last night and she gave it to me.'

She sat up straighter. 'What do you mean, a shopping list?'

'A receipt from the Co-op on the corner of this road. Your mum found it. I took things from there and asked around.'

Caris picked up a cushion covered in jewelled mirrors and squeezed it. 'Sod it. I forgot she goes through my laundry. You'd no right, going to see my mam and bothering her.'

'Actually, *she* phoned *me* and asked me to visit. She found the card I'd given you in the rubbish bin. Let's face it, you're not very good at covering your tracks. I wouldn't apply to join MI5 any time soon.' He smiled, keeping it friendly.

'I don't believe you. My mam wouldn't have called you,' she said, but she sounded uncertain.

'Why would I lie about it? Not everyone tells as many fibs as you do. Phone your mum now if you like and ask her.'

Morgan had perched beside her. He was better-looking than his photo suggested, if you liked the nervy, emaciated type. His large eyes were arresting, a deep, shining brown. He muttered, 'What's going on, Caz?'

'This is the guy I was telling you about who was asking questions. He found Afan's body. I expect he charmed my mam into blabbing. She gets so desperate for company she'd give Jack the Ripper a cuppa if he called by.'

'She doesn't know much, though, does she?' Swift said. 'She's worried about you and imagining all kinds of things.'

Caris scowled at him. 'Now you've found us, what do you want?' She was wearing a short floral dress with an elasticated neck that sat just below her shoulders. Now and again she fingered a silver necklace with an oval emerald pendant that nestled against her creamy skin.

Swift shrugged his jacket off. It was warm at the top of the house and no windows were open. The flat was tidy but smelled of bodies and cooked breakfast. He wasn't sure what these two were up to, but they were on edge and he didn't want them to throw him out. 'I'm honestly not here to pry into your lives. I don't care what you're doing, unless it has something to do with Afan's death.'

Morgan relaxed a little but Caris eyed him and said, 'Go on.'

Morgan was an easier target, so Swift focused on him. 'I assume that Afan owned this house, and that's why you were anxious to find out about what would happen to his estate after he died.'

'That's right,' Morgan said.

'Did he come to an arrangement with you when he found out you wanted to get away from home? I understand you were tormented by your brother, Calvin.'

Morgan put out a hand and rested it on Caris's knee, rubbing the tiny yellow flowers on her dress hem. He turned to her, an unspoken question, and she nodded.

He said, 'Afan knew what my life was like back in Holybridge with that vicious bastard. Caz and me were talking to him one day and I said I was thinking of going to London, try to get any kind of work and a place to doss. I'd been on the internet and I'd seen that there were squats and stuff. Caz was really upset, but I couldn't see any other way out, and it had to be better than living with Calvin. I was at my wits' end. Caz couldn't come to London 'cause of her mam. Next time we saw Afan, he told us he owned this house in Cardiff and he needed a caretaker, someone to keep an eye on the place, do odd jobs for the tenants and liaise with the managing agent. He said this flat had just been vacated and I could have it rent-free if I paid my own bills and kept an eye on the house. I'm fairly handy with DIY stuff and it sounded like a dream. I nearly bit his hand off, I can tell you.'

He was intense, sitting on the edge of the sofa, trembling slightly and blinking hard. He had the vigilant gaze of the abused. He'd have spent his life until now watching his back and dodging the blows. After his own experiences, no wonder Afan had empathised with his predicament and wanted to help him escape. Swift doubted that Afan had needed a caretaker — usually, the agent would be responsible for repairs or other matters that needed attention in a rented property. He'd created the job to give Morgan a safe place and to allow two young people to find a life together. Caris placed a protective hand against Morgan's back.

'Did you ever consider reporting your brother's behaviour to the police?' Swift asked.

Morgan grimaced. 'You're joking. If I'd done that, he'd have beaten me senseless. He told me if I ever went whinging to anyone, he'd make sure I needed a nurse for the rest of my life.'

'And your dad never stood up for you?'

Caris answered for him. 'He's on tranquillisers, hardly gets what day of the week it is. He never stuck up for Morgan and he let Calvin rule the roost.'

'Your mum's worried sick about where you're going at weekends,' Swift told her. 'She's imagining all kinds of awful things. She's found out you're not seeing your aunt.'

Caris put her head in her hands. 'Bloody hell! Did you tell her?'

Swift shook his head. 'Not me. I've told you, I'm not here to interfere in your lives for the sake of it. Let your mum tell you herself. I've suggested that she needs to have an honest conversation with you. I understand why you've been lying to her, but that needs to stop, especially now that Afan's dead and your future here is uncertain.'

Caris rallied. 'What's any of this got to do with you anyway? Why are you poking your nose into our lives and following me around? Us being here is all above board.'

'I'm angry that my friend's dead. If you'd been honest with me and the police about your relationship with Morgan, if this arrangement with Afan was as you describe it, I wouldn't have needed to talk to your mum or come here.'

Morgan cracked his finger joints. 'Don't you get it? Caz couldn't tell you or her mam the truth. She hasn't even told Gwyn, her best friend, about me being here. We don't want Calvin to find out where I am!'

'I understand that. There's no reason why he should.'

Caris snorted. 'You reckon? Once the cops get wind, it'll be out there. Everyone's got their ears to the ground in Holybridge and Calvin's like that bloody Bryn Price. He's got his fingers on the pulse.'

'It's been so amazing being here,' Morgan whispered. He folded his arms across his chest. 'I've been safe for the first time since my mam died. It's really secure, being up the top of this house with a lock on my door. Calvin bought the story that I'd gone to London, so I could go for a run over in the park without having to check around me. We were hoping that in a while, Caz might be able to work something out with her mam and move in here with me. She could get a better job in Cardiff. I knew it was too good to last, and when Caz told me Afan was dead, I reckoned I'd probably get chucked out of here — if Calvin doesn't find me first. Then I'll have to go to London, and that means me and Caz will hardly see each other.'

Caris bit her lip and put her arm around him. They were so young, so desperate and struggling. Afan had handed them an unexpected gift that had been snatched away. This house would be sold in due course, once probate was granted. Swift didn't enjoy pressing them more, but it had to be done because although they were young, they weren't innocent. They were still concealing something.

'Caris, why did Afan write you a note saying that he was disappointed in you and that it wasn't how friends behaved?'

He expected that she'd question how he'd come by the information. Instead, her eyes brimmed with tears and Morgan stared at the waxed floorboards.

Swift waited. 'Did you steal from him?'

'No! I'd never do that!'

Swift hazarded another guess. 'Did something happen here, something that Afan found out about?'

Caris went to speak, but Morgan shook his head. He moved closer to her and stammered, 'That was my stupid fault. Maybe Calvin's right after all and I am a waste of space.'

Swift left a couple of beats and kept his tone soft. 'What happened? Can you tell me?'

Morgan grabbed Caris's hand. 'I met a guy called Mikey at the café up the road. We'd both been running, and we got chatting. Some days we ran together, had competitions. It was nice to have a bit of company. He told me he had to move out of his flat because the rent was going up. He'd found somewhere else, but there were a couple of days between him leaving where he was and starting his new rental. I knew that number three downstairs was empty, waiting for the new tenants. I've got keys to all the flats, so I told him he could stay for a couple of days. He did, and he threw a massive party. Stuff got trashed, windows broken, someone sprayed graffiti all over the walls. Maya on the ground floor called the police. They contacted the agent, who told Afan what had happened. He came here and I had to admit it was my fault. He got a terrible shock when he saw the place. I could tell he was fed up.' He leaned his head on Caris's shoulder.

'Afan was really dicked off,' Caris said. 'The flat had only just been redecorated for the new tenants. We promised it'd never happen again, but I could see he was having second thoughts. Then he got the estimate for all the damage and that was when he left me that note.'

'When did all of this happen?'

'About two weeks ago,' Morgan muttered.

'Afan left me the note the Friday before he died,' Caris said. 'I never got a chance to talk to him about it. He was good to us and we didn't mean to let him down.'

Morgan said miserably, 'That guy Mikey seemed on the level. I haven't seen him around here since. I really liked him. I was such a fuckwit and I've messed everything up.'

The timescale meant that this wasn't the troubling matter that Afan had contacted him about. Morgan had rested his cheek on Caris's shoulder. Abused people were rarely good judges of character, their perceptions were skewed, and they were often self-sabotaging. Morgan struck him as the kind of needy person who attracts trouble, a gullible young man who wasn't used to shouldering any responsibility. Reports of his time at Tir Melys indicated that he was unreliable, and Swift doubted his self-proclaimed DIY skills. He understood why Lori Murray had said her daughter could do better for herself. Afan had no doubt been moved by Morgan and Caris's problems, but he must have wondered what he'd let himself in for after the incident in the flat below. If he hadn't died, he'd probably have asked Morgan to move out. Morgan and Caris must have realised this, and Swift supposed that one of them might have stabbed Afan to buy themselves time. It was a thin motive, but people had killed for less if they were scared, and these two were certainly highly anxious and muddled. But he couldn't see either of them having the wit or the gumption to commit murder. The police would check their alibis for Monday, but he asked anyway.

'I was at work,' Caris said, 'on a ten to six shift.'

Morgan pointed at the floor. 'I was in flat three all afternoon, helping with the cleaning. They said I didn't have to, but I wanted to give a hand. Anything to try and make things okay again.'

He'd probably thought it might earn him brownie points with Afan, but by then it didn't matter. 'Do either of you know of anything else that was worrying Afan? Something that was on his mind?' He focused on Caris, because Afan had liked her enough to tell her personal details that he hadn't shared with anyone else at Tir Melys. Swift could see why. Although she'd lied to him, she'd done it to protect Morgan and there was a sense of decency about her. He'd got the same feeling about her mother. Two sincere women, struggling against huge odds. 'Caris, you mentioned that someone else had asked Afan for money. Who?'

'No idea. He said that he might give someone a loan, but he needed to mull it over.' Caris turned to give Morgan a reassuring kiss on the temple.

Swift decided to leave it there. Caris followed him out to the hall, pulling the door to, as if they were the grownups, not talking in front of the child in the room behind them. She stroked the shining emerald at her throat.

'That's a lovely necklace,' Swift said.

'Thanks. Elinor gave it to me. I helped her prepare and freeze a load of veg. Was . . . Was my mam okay when you saw her? Was she very upset?'

'Yes, she was, but bewildered as well. She's been worrying about what you might be involved in.'

Pain crossed her face. 'I haven't liked lying to her, it's been a nightmare. I didn't know what else to do, and I had to protect Morgan. I love my mam and I do trust her, but the less I told her, the better.'

'You will talk to her about all of this when you get back?'

'Yes, I'll have to.' She glanced behind her and lowered her voice. 'What will happen now, about Morgan being here?'

'The police will interview you and Morgan. You need to ring DS Spencer.'

'I will, later on. Will Morgan be able to stay here for now?'

'I expect so. But from what you said, he might be wiser to move on as soon as he can. Would his brother really come to Cardiff to find him?'

She blinked tears away. 'Persecuting Morgan was Calvin's favourite hobby. He'd go miles to torment him.'

He was moved by her plight, sandwiched between her clingy boyfriend and her sick mother. 'Morgan could search around Cardiff. There will be opportunities. Maybe he'll find a job with accommodation, they do exist. There are other cities nearer than London, if he wants to put more miles between him and his brother. Bristol or Birmingham would be near enough for you to see each other.' Even as he said it, he knew that Morgan lacked the wherewithal to fend for himself. He'd squandered the opportunity handed to him on a plate. If he'd gone to London, he wouldn't have survived. He saw the same understanding in Caris's eyes and the droop of her shoulders. She was the one who always had to be in charge. He wanted to urge her to go to Bellissima's or Storm Disco and have some fun.

'I'd better get back to Morgan, make sure he's okay.' She hesitated, and then stepped closer. He could smell her lemony shampoo. 'What you asked about Afan having any other worries. There was a strange situation at Tir Melys — a bit of a nightmare that I got trapped in. I wish now that I'd not got involved and told Afan about it. I've really regretted it, and I've started trying to put it right.'

'What kind of nightmare?'

She licked her lips nervously. 'It's hard, because it concerns other people. I never meant it to . . .' A phone rang and Morgan called, 'It's yours, Caz.' She turned away. 'I'd better get that, in case it's my mam. I'll be back tomorrow to see her, and I'll be at the concert later. I'll talk to you then.'

On the way back down, he saw that the door of flat three was open. A woman dressed in overalls, carrying a can of paint, was just going in. She glanced at him.

'Redecorating?' Swift asked.

'And some! We've almost finished now, but the place was in a right state. Yobs throwing a party, apparently. If I was the owner, I'd be spitting hot coals!'

Swift sat on the steps outside the house, just below the pig. He was frustrated by Caris's last remarks, indicating some other problem at Tir Melys. He rang Sofia Weber. 'I found Morgan Callender. Caris is with him.' He ran through what he'd discovered and gave her Morgan's address. 'They both have what sound like solid alibis. Caris promised that she'll ring Spencer this afternoon.'

'I won't hold my breath. That's all really helpful. Sounds like Afan thought they were star-crossed young lovers. He must have realised he'd saddled himself with a real problem when he heard about the damage. I'll contact the solicitor now.'

'Morgan won't have to move immediately, will he?'

'I don't see why he should.'

'His big fear is that his brother will come after him if he gets wind of where he is.'

Her voice was low, drained of energy. 'Well . . . that's another problem and not one for me. I've enough on my plate. I can issue an "on pain of death" instruction around the station that nobody's to breathe a word, but I get what Caris means about the grapevine in Holybridge. I've looked Calvin up and there's no record. I asked Spence about him. He's got a reputation for being a lout and a big mouth, and he definitely dabbles in the drugs scene, but he's never been fingered for anything.'

'What did you find out about Bruno?'

'Ah yes, Bruno the bee man. He did two and a half years in jail in Alberta for theft, came out nine years ago and headed to the UK soon after. It was all horse-related crime. He worked at a vast stables and was helping to relieve the owners of equipment — trailers, tack and the like. Expensive stuff. I suppose that Afan might have found out somehow.'

'Even if he had, that would hardly be a reason to kill him. Would anyone at Tir Melys be that bothered if they knew about Bruno?'

'Possibly not, my Lone Ranger, but not everyone likes the idea that a thief is living among them. Bruno might believe that it would disturb them. Are you going to delve into the fleshpots of Cardiff for the rest of the day?'

'I might indulge in a little culture, Inspector.'

'Ha! Fill your boots. I'm a bit chilly today, despite the sunshine. Maybe the weather's about to turn and I'm feeling it in my bones.'

Before he left the steps, he sent a text message to Lori Murray.

I've seen Caris. She's fine and with Morgan. Please keep that to yourself. I'm sure she'll explain it all to you tomorrow.

He gave the pig a final pat and set off to find a Welsh-themed present for Branna.

* * *

He had an interesting chat with Bryn Price later that night. He headed to the kitchen when he arrived back to fetch milk and Bryn was in there, slugging wine, chopping tomatoes for chutney and chucking them sloppily into a huge stainless-steel pot. He had earbuds in and was executing little dance steps but took them out when he saw Swift.

'I like late-night cooking sometimes,' he said. 'I'm a bad sleeper and it relaxes me. Glass of chateau loganberry?' Bryn waved the bottle. He was well oiled and a little unsteady on his feet. The tomato chunks were hit and miss, and Swift eyed the sharp knife, hoping that Bryn didn't slice his finger.

'I will, thanks. You'll be here until the early hours, doing that.'

'Nah. I'll leave it all marinating overnight. Gives it a great flavour. Then I'll cook it up tomorrow. Bruno's going to give me a hand filling the jars.'

Swift took a slice of underripe tomato, followed by a sip of wine. His palate tingled. 'I wonder if he ever misses Canada. Wales must seem very small-scale.'

Bryn took another gulp of his wine. Some dribbled down his chin, but he didn't notice. 'He doesn't mention it. Anyway, the boy's come back to his roots, hasn't he? The valleys called to him across the cold Atlantic.' He sang through a hiccup, waving the knife around. 'Come home again, come home again, they call through the oceans of time.'

'Bruno told me his mother came from around here.'

Bryn laughed. 'Good old Bruno. That's an understatement.'

'What do you mean?'

Bryn haphazardly sliced a huge green tomato in half and glanced slyly at him. 'Hmm . . . That would be telling and I'm not sure I should. Careless talk and all that.' He mixed the ingredients in the pot with a wooden spoon. 'Oh, what the hell . . . doesn't matter if I tell you now, when we're almost there. Bruno's great-uncle Davey used to own this farm. He sold it to the Merchants at a knock-down price, three months before he died. He couldn't manage the place, it was getting run down and he had no kids, so he decided to offload it. There was talk around here, because some people reckoned old Davey was a bit doolally and didn't really understand what he was doing, but the sale went through very fast. Davey went into the old people's home in town, then pegged out. Bruno's mam used to stay here a fair bit when she was a child and help with the lambing. So it's in his blood, you might say.'

'Have other people here heard that story? Do the Merchants have any inkling about Bruno's family connection?'

Bryn laughed again. 'You're the man with the questions. I wouldn't be surprised if Bruno'd told Afan, although we'd agreed that he shouldn't let on to anyone. But old Afan was a bit of a father confessor, people opened up to him when they'd have done better to keep their gobs shut.'

'Which people are you talking about and why wouldn't you and Bruno want anyone to be aware of his connection to this place?' He was hoping that the wine would lead Bryn into further disclosures, but he was disappointed.

'Patience now, Mr Magnum PI. I'm pissed, but not that pissed. Sometimes, you have to watch and wait. I expect you've done that, lurking in dark corners with the collar of your trench coat turned up. All will be revealed, very soon. Just stick around.' He threw dark brown sugar into the pot, spattering some on the cooker, repeating with a laugh, 'Yes, there'll be a big reveal.'

CHAPTER 15

Swift walked to the chapel early the next morning. He sat for a while in the chill silence, focusing on nothing in particular but feeling remorseful about his dead friend. He recalled golden evening light, a pavement café, glasses of absinthe and listening to a torch singer with Afan.

'Need your love so badly, I love you oh so madly
But I don't stand a ghost of a chance with you.
I thought at last I'd found you but other loves surround you
And I don't stand a ghost of a chance with you.'

'Funny how things turn out,' Nora had said to him when they'd last spoken. She'd phoned him to say she was sorry that she'd seen Fitz Blackmore behind his back. 'I didn't mean to fall for him. I didn't mean to cheat on you. Things weren't right with us and it just happened. We never know what's round the corner waiting for us, do we?'

Swift rose, went to the hermit's chamber and stood inside for a few minutes. He was sure that Afan would have entered the secret space when he needed peace.

Who were you going to meet on the coast path, Afan?
Me in your bed, you in the morgue.
Funny how things turn out.

On the way back, he heard the Land Rover behind him and stepped to the side. Suki slowed and stopped. 'Lift?'

He'd wanted the walk, but needed the opportunity to speak to her alone, so he climbed in. A box holding a few pieces of her pottery lay on the back seat.

Suki gestured to it. 'There's an early market in Holybridge on Sunday mornings. Just in the summer season. A stallholder sells my stuff for me, so I've been in, replenishing his supply.'

'Do you sell much?'

'It varies, but not bad. How are you doing?'

'Fine, thanks.'

'Have the police made any progress with their investigation?' She handled the vehicle confidently, an elbow propped on the open window.

'I'm not sure. I hope things are progressing. Did you talk to the Merchants about the future here?'

'No, I spoke to Bryn and he told me to hang on. He said we'd all hear more very soon. So I decided to wait for a while,' she said.

'There was something else I wanted to ask you.'

'Oh yes? Go ahead.' She smiled at him. Her teeth were tiny and even.

'Someone mentioned that you had an argument with Afan, back in the spring.'

'Really? Who is this "someone"? One of the community?'

'I'd rather not say.'

Her grip on the wheel had tightened. 'That's not very pleasant, an anonymous allegation.'

'Allegation's a bit strong. It was just a passing remark.'

'Indeed. And where was this argument supposed to have taken place?'

'In Blasus.'

'Blasus! An argument in Blasus . . .' She tapped the wheel. 'I rarely saw Afan in there. We did have a bite to eat earlier in the year. I don't remember an argument. We never argued, neither of us was the type. We did discuss the possibility of developing more activities at Tir Melys. We'd throw ideas around now and again, but never come to any decisions. Afan sat on the fence about it. I might have been trying to persuade him that we should branch out a bit.' She pulled into the parking area and turned to him. Her voice hardened. 'Then again, I might well have been telling Afan that he needed to stand up to Kat and stop her invading his space. I used to get quite upset about that sometimes. The way he let her bug him. I'm sure neither of us realised we were being monitored. We probably had a friendly discussion, maybe a bit lively at times. Does that answer your question?'

'Thanks, yes. I hope you didn't mind me raising it.'

She took the keys from the ignition and adopted a milder tone. 'That's okay. You've lost your friend. So have I. It's hard. I just wish that people wouldn't make spiteful comments. It doesn't help deal with the grief. I expect it was Kat, with her big wooden spoon, or maybe vindictive Guy.'

'It doesn't matter who mentioned it. It's not important. See you later, at the concert.'

He left her sorting through the box in the back and went on to the cottage. He hadn't handled that well. Suki had flinched at the memory of a lunch that, by her reckoning, had been a friendly discussion. Perhaps she'd just been uncomfortable because someone had been talking about her.

* * *

Swift drove into Ogmore-by-Sea late morning, following the line of the estuary. A thin, misty rain dimpled the River Ogmore. Dale Toft's detached house was on a corner plot, built of brick and stone, with a sea view and a first-floor balcony.

Toft led him into a long, narrow sitting room. It was busy with ornate rugs and crammed with faux antique furniture. It was hard to move without tripping over occasional tables and standard lamps. The low ceiling was textured in whorls of plaster and the striped sofas were huge, with carved wooden arms and tassels. Large photos, converted into framed paintings, dominated the walls. They showed a hearty family. Two of the children had their father's broad, squashy nose.

'Coffee for you?' Toft asked.

'Please.'

It was ready in a silver pot on a tray and he poured it into a china cup with a daisy pattern. When Swift sniffed it, he could tell it was going to be instant and terrible, despite the posh trappings. He took a sip gamely and blinked. It tasted strongly of chicory, like the bottled coffee that his great-aunt Lily had used in cakes. He couldn't recall the name, but the label had featured a scene from the British Raj: a seated man in a kilt and a pith helmet, with a tent in the background and a turbaned Indian servant standing by.

Toft checked his watch. 'We've got an hour. The family's at church.'

'You don't go?'

'They're RC. I'm Baptist. Different paths to the same God.'

He was in his forties with a ruddy complexion, one of those men who'd been fit in youth but become a bit paunchy. He must have still liked the outdoors, as his arms and neck had a healthy glow. Swift had spotted walking poles in the porch.

He shifted his perch on the plump, over-stuffed sofa. It was the kind of punishing furniture that resisted you. 'I'm interested to hear what you can tell me about Afan Griffith. It sounded as if something difficult happened back when you knew him.'

Toft had sensibly passed on coffee and was drinking a glass of orange squash. 'It was a nasty episode. It's not easy to talk about it. I suppose Afan had his reasons for not telling you. I can understand that.'

'Whatever it is, it can't hurt him now.'

'No, even so . . .'

Swift said, 'I understand your reluctance. I'm a private investigator as well as Afan's friend. I'm doing my best to help the police with their investigation into Afan's background. The police might well be in touch with you soon.'

Toft pinched the bridge of his fleshy nose. 'I can't see what relevance it would have to what happened to him. This was years ago.'

'It's possible, that's all,' Swift said.

'Well, then, if it might help . . . As I said to you, I met Afan through a club that offered all kinds of outdoor activities. Our main interest was bouldering. There are some great spots for it in Wales, including around here. I'd been to the East Cliffs here with Afan a couple of times, just the two of us. We were skilled, so now and again we took out small groups of people who wanted more experience. Have you ever climbed or been bouldering? Do you know about the role of the spotter?'

'I've got a boat and I row as often as I can, but I've never climbed. Bouldering is climbing short distances without ropes or harnesses, isn't it?'

'That's right,' Toft replied. 'It's more about technique and power than endurance. Some people like it because you don't have to heave lots of equipment around. Basically, you need a crash mat and a chalk bag, to keep your hands dry. The spotter is the person who stands below the climber, by the crash mat, ready to guide them safely back down to the mat if they slip. The aim is to break their fall and protect their head from an impact. It's an essential part of bouldering outdoors.'

'Sounds like a hugely responsible role.' Swift had a sinking feeling that he could predict the ending of this story.

'It is. Crucial. One Saturday, Afan and I took a small group of four, two men and two women, just by Southerndown beach and the East Cliffs here. They had different levels of experience, so I went to one group of rocks and Afan was further along. We'd been there for almost an hour when I heard awful screaming. It seemed to go on for minutes. I couldn't move, because I was spotting one of the group. I got him back down as quickly as I could and ran to where Afan was. The woman in his group had fallen and hit her head. It was a terrible sight. Lots of blood and she was just, well . . . crumpled. She was taken to hospital, but sadly she died a couple of days later from head trauma.' He finished his orange squash, patted his chest and let out a deep breath. 'Even now, it chokes me up.'

'I'm sorry, that sounds terrible. How did it happen?'

'Afan said — and the other climber, the man who was with him, confirmed it — that he'd been distracted for a split second. There were some teenagers fooling around on the shore nearby, just past an outcrop of rock. One of them started yelling with pain because he'd trodden on a sharp shell and cut his foot open. They were out of sight, but the shout was enough to distract Afan and — Sod's Law — in that moment, the woman who was climbing lost her footing and fell. She missed the crash mat and landed on rocks.'

Swift was shocked. He pictured the scene — the sea behind, the sun and breeze, the woman poised on the rocks above, young people larking about on the shore. Then, in seconds, a broken body. It was a trauma that would slice deep and stay with you.

Toft stood, walked around the sofa and adjusted a vase of flowers on a table. Then he perched on the sofa arm. 'I was so sorry for Afan. He was in bits about it. There was an investigation and an inquest, of course, and the verdict was accidental death. Up to that fall, Afan had done everything right and by the book. Conditions were dry and chilly, which meant that the friction between hands, feet and rock was at its best. Bouldering in good conditions is equivalent to cycling with the wind at your back, and the rocks were medium difficult, suited to what Afan knew of his group's abilities.'

It sounded as if Afan had gauged the conditions well, paying the same attention to environment and weather as Swift did to wind forces and tides before he launched his boat. It was what Swift would have expected of him. 'It sounds like really bad luck. That can happen when you take any physical risks.'

'True, but there's understanding that and the emotional impact of a death on your watch. Also, we discovered during the investigation that the woman who died had exaggerated her levels of experience. She'd done some indoor bouldering but almost none outdoors. That was very foolish of her, because there's a lot more to anticipate and contend with in outdoor work. Indoors, you have colours and markers to guide you. Outdoors, holds and footholds are far less obvious, and you have to think much harder, coordinate your breath and movements. In a way, you have to learn a whole new set of skills. If Afan had been aware of that, he'd have given her an easy route. There are plenty around here.'

'Did that help Afan? He'd acted properly but she'd misinformed him. It wasn't his fault.'

'It didn't seem to. In the end, he'd altered his stance and been distracted, even if the reason for that was beyond his control. A good spotter gives the climber the confidence to focus one hundred per cent on the moves, and that's how Afan usually was, utterly reliable. We'd spotted for each other and I had complete trust in him. He should have been focused and ready with outstretched arms to guide the student to the pad and away from hazards. And he was, but for that bloody stupid teenager yelling his head off. Worst of all, if that wasn't bad enough, we found out that the woman who died was a single parent with a ten-month-old baby.' Toft leaned forward, hands clasped between his knees. 'Afan was gutted. He left the club, never came back and later I heard that he'd gone abroad to work. That's why I said I was surprised that he'd come back here, with those awful memories. I was pretty shaken up by it, I can tell you. These things leave their mark. I left the club too. I've never climbed since or taken responsibility for any group activity. I swim and walk.'

'Who was the woman who died?'

'Her name was Dru Knight. She'd moved back to Cardiff from London to live with her mam while she was pregnant.

The grandmother minded the baby while she worked. She was employed in a carpet shop.'

'Do you remember the names of the other members of the two groups?'

Toft rubbed his forehead and glanced at his watch. 'It's more than twenty years ago. I recall a Jimmy. That's all, I'm afraid. It was a busy club and lots of people came and went — students from the university, all sorts from all over. I've tried not to dwell on it down the years. It's painful talking about it, even now. I have to fetch the family from church, if that's all.'

Swift drove to a car park near the beach, bought a hot dog from a stand and sat on a wall, catching mustard on his finger as he ate. A dense sea mist had drifted in, bathing everything in a swirling grey vapour. He didn't mind the warm, light drizzle it carried. The little pulses of rain on his face were refreshing. A woman appeared from the mist, walking with her hands in her pockets. She passed in front of him, glanced in his direction and smiled. For a moment, he almost exclaimed *Ruth!* The same tawny hair and hazel eyes. Same delicate beauty. She carried on, walking away from him and within seconds, she'd vanished into the grey. He wanted to follow her, talk to her, find out if she was anything like the woman he missed. The impulse was strong. He resisted it and closed his eyes, disturbed. The emotions were still there, damped down like embers that might flame up if they were sparked. He waited until his breathing quietened. When he opened his eyes, the mist seemed to have thickened and the world was utterly silent. Perhaps he'd imagined the woman. He rubbed his eyes, went back to the car and forced himself to reflect on the matters queuing in his head.

There was Caris. He was impatient to learn about the other dilemma at Tir Melys that had trapped her, and that she'd shared with Afan.

Someone had been into the cottage when he'd returned last night. There'd been no sign of a break-in, so whoever it was must have a key. Nothing had been taken, but the drawer in the kitchen table hadn't been quite closed and he was sure he'd shut it firmly because it stuck easily.

He returned to Bryn's teasing crumbs of information from the night before. He'd been drunk and talkative, but Swift reckoned that Bryn had only told him exactly what he'd wanted to. It had cast Bruno in a new light. He hadn't just washed up at Tir Melys, as he'd implied. What must it be like for him, living in a place that had once belonged to his family and had changed hands in what sounded like a dubious transaction? And what was his motive for taking up a tenancy there — was it really what he'd called *hiraeth*? Had Bruno confided in Afan and then turned against him for some reason — maybe because Afan had challenged his motives and the big reveal that Bryn had mentioned? Bruno might have decided to silence Afan. It seemed a flimsy motive, but perhaps not to a man who was under pressure.

The Merchants must be planning to get rid of Tir Melys. That was why they hadn't agreed to any suggestions for new ventures. If Afan had got caught in that web, he might have been a threat to someone.

This information about Afan and the bouldering accident might be vital. In Lyon, Afan had been a keen walker, just as he'd been at Tir Melys. He'd never mentioned an interest in any other outdoor activity and would have had even more of a reason than Dale Toft for giving up climbing. The accident must have weighed on him down the years. Had it, or a person associated with it, come back to haunt him?

Swift was staring out to sea when Lori Murray rang him. He heard the tension in her voice.

'I'm sorry to bother you again. It's just that Caris isn't home yet, and she's not answering her phone. I've still got a number for Morgan but when I rang, it said it's no longer in use.'

Swift saw that it was two thirty. 'What time were you expecting her?'

'No later than one. I rang the station and they said there's no train disruption.'

'Maybe she's been delayed in Cardiff.'

Lori sounded dubious. 'Maybe, but she's very good about ringing if she's going to be late. Was she okay when you saw her?'

'She was fine. You didn't call her yesterday?'

'Me? No. I've done the potatoes all ready for her to roast. I always prep the veg for her.'

'She's only a bit late. I expect she's on her way. I'll check in with you in a while.'

Back in the car, he hoped that Lori Murray was just being an overanxious mother. Then he took his phone from his pocket and searched for Dru Knight. There were a number of hits. The first he selected was from a report in the *South Wales Echo*:

WOMAN INJURED IN CLIMBING FALL

Drusilla Knight, 25, from Splott, Cardiff, was badly injured on Saturday afternoon. She was bouldering with companions from the MOVE club when she fell from a rock, injuring her head as well as sustaining other fractures. Ms Knight is in intensive care in Cardiff Royal Infirmary. There has been no comment from the police or MOVE. Ms Knight lives with her mother and has a baby son.

The article was accompanied by a photo, the kind of head-and-shoulders shot taken in a booth, of a young, dark-haired woman with a cheeky grin.

Later that week, the same paper carried the story that Dru Knight had died. A month later, the *Western Mail* had a summary of the inquest. It repeated the information that Dale Toft had given him, including a verdict of accidental death. It also listed the names of the three other climbers who'd been present, all of whom had been questioned by the police. One name stood out as Swift scanned them:

James Khalil

Katrina Glover

Norman Hunter

Kat Glover, who'd subsequently taken up residence at Tir Melys and who'd had a marked interest in Afan Griffith. Perhaps she'd been driven by more than romantic yearnings.

He'd been speculating as to why Afan had been so long-suffering with Kat. Now maybe he'd found the reason.

* * *

Swift stopped the car fifteen minutes from Tir Melys, while he still had a signal, and phoned Lori. It was almost four thirty.

'Still no sign of her and I can't raise her on her phone,' Lori said. 'I rang Gwyn, because she's supposed to pick Caris up here at half six. She hasn't heard from her either. I'm beside myself with worry.'

'I can call the detective who's investigating Afan's death. Let me have a word with her. Maybe she can ask the Cardiff police to call on Morgan, in case Caris is still there. Perhaps she's been taken ill.'

He phoned Sofia Weber and was relieved when she picked up, sounding woolly. 'Sorry to disturb your Sunday.'

'It's okay. I'm at the hospital, being poked about and waiting to have a blood test, so it's nice to have a distraction.'

'What's wrong?'

'Dunno. I've got a temperature. I keep coming over a bit odd and sleeping the sleep of the dead, so they decided they needed to stick needles in me.'

'On a Sunday?'

'Yeah, I'm in A & E. They must be having a slow day. They were keen for me to come in. What have you got?'

He explained about Caris. 'Four hours or so isn't a long time, but her mother says it's unusual for her to be so late without ringing. Caris was supposed to be back to cook lunch for her mum, and she was planning to attend a concert at Tir Melys this evening. I don't understand why she's not answering her phone. She needed to talk to her mother today about the situation with Morgan.'

'She called Spence yesterday afternoon and agreed to come into the station first thing Monday morning. Maybe she and Morgan talked it all over last night and decided to do a runner together, given that there was a chance that his bolthole would be blown. They might have caught a train to London, or anywhere else for that matter.'

'She wouldn't do that to her mother, not without giving her some explanation or at the very least phoning her. She cares about her.'

Sofia sounded cynical. 'She didn't mind pulling the wool over her mam's eyes for months.'

'True, but she had a good reason for doing that and she fretted about it. It's been hard for her. Divided loyalties. I've got a strange feeling about this. She and Morgan have a direct and close connection to Afan.'

'You don't have a current phone number for Morgan Callender?'

'No. I expect he changed it once he left home, so his brother wouldn't find him. One of the few sensible things he's done.'

'Okay, I agree that it's odd. I'll call Cardiff and ask some uniforms to call at Morgan's. Are you going to be at Tir Melys tonight?'

'Yes, so no phone signal. I'll call you from the landline later. Do you want me to ring Ms Murray back?'

'No. I'll speak to her and get this underway. I might be able to rouse Spence. I agree that this seems out of character, but teenagers can be erratic, especially when they're lovelorn and confused. Ring me if Caris rocks up for the concert wondering what all the fuss is about.'

He started the car and drove to Tir Melys, anxious and disturbed. Caris knew something about the community that was weighing on her. He was concerned that she might have forced someone's hand by attempting to put a nightmare situation right.

CHAPTER 16

The Bivium was busy with people arriving for the concert. Elinor was on the door and told Swift that they'd sold all the tickets. He wondered if some of the audience were rubber-neckers, titillated by the proximity to murder. He asked if Caris had arrived, but Elinor said she hadn't seen her. Bruno and Suki were on kitchen duty, preparing trays of finger foods — sandwiches, crackers with toppings, tiny sausage rolls, savoury pastries, miniature quiches and individual fruit tarts. Kat was arranging glasses with bottles of Tir Melys wine and mead. The concert would last for an hour, and then the guests would help themselves to food at the dining table and drinks at the kitchen counter. Another table had been set up with a selection of community produce for sale — honey, wine, mead, preserves, willow baskets, woodcarvings, jewellery and pottery.

Swift just had time for a shower and a change of clothes. He headed to the Parley with minutes to spare and saw Gwyn Bowen sitting at the end of a full row. He leaned down to speak to her.

'Have you heard from Caris?'

'No, nothing. Her mam rang me and said she hadn't come home, so I didn't call by for her. Maybe she's come down with something. I've tried her phone but she's not answering, and she hasn't texted me, which is a bit weird.'

'This is unusual, isn't it?'

'Yeah. She doesn't let people down. I mean, she's been a bit distracted recently, but if she makes an arrangement, she generally sticks to it. I haven't actually seen her since Afan died, just texted and one quick call.' Gwyn plucked at her sleeve. 'She's been kind of elusive. Her mam's really worried. I'm hoping she'll turn up, although I don't think she'll come here now. She'd have to cycle, so it'd hardly be worth her while.'

'Contact me if you hear from her.'

'Sure.' Gwyn's eyes were huge behind her glasses. She was dressed attractively in a turquoise shirt and jeans, her hair curling softly around her shoulders. 'Ms Murray said that you saw Caris yesterday. I suppose you were asking her about Afan. Was that in town?'

'We met up briefly,' he confirmed.

He had the impression she wanted to ask more, but she said, 'Oh, okay.' She tucked her hair behind the pretty earrings she wore. 'Did you have any luck contacting Dale Toft?'

'I saw him this morning.'

'That's good. Did he tell you anything useful about Afan?'

'We discussed what had happened back when they knew each other. It was interesting.'

'I wonder if the police—' Gwyn started to say.

There was a sharp tap on Swift's shoulder, and he turned to see a bright-eyed Kat.

'I've saved you a seat beside me. Better sit down, it's going to start any minute.'

She wore a white, calf-length cotton dress. It had lace frills around the neck and armholes, and she'd attached white roses to her pigtails. She was a bizarre version of a little girl. He followed her to a seat towards the back of the room. Bryn was passing and whispered to him, 'Here comes the bride!'

Kat gazed at him. 'How come you're pally with Gwyn Bowen?'

'Why do you ask?'

'She's very up herself, trying to be glamorous.'

'She is very stylish tonight,' he said to annoy her.

'Really? She needn't put on airs, because her bookshop hardly makes any profit, and she has to give Welsh lessons to make ends meet. People get their books online these days, don't they? She's tried organising literary events to drum up interest, but they haven't taken off. She might have to give up the shop and move out.'

'That would be a shame. The bookshop is well stocked, and she clearly cares about it. Why do you say that she might have to give it up?'

'Bryn told me. One of his uncle's friends owns the place and rents it out to her. I wouldn't have thought she'd be the type to interest you.'

'People interest me, full stop.'

She smiled coyly. 'Do I?' She'd done something strange with her eyebrows. They seemed dense and a bit startling.

'Where were you living before you came here?' he asked.

'I was in Cardiff.'

'Did you know Afan before you moved here?'

She reached for a pigtail and said sulkily, 'Strange question. Why are you asking me that?'

'You asked me if I was interested in you. Now you don't seem to like a friendly enquiry.'

'Jasmine's about to start,' she said with obvious relief, sticking the pigtail end between her lips.

Jasmine was wearing a long green velvet dress edged with blue and laced across the bodice. It was fitted at the waist and flowed down in panels. The sleeves billowed as she walked up the side of the packed room. Very Lady Guinevere, Swift thought, joining in the applause. Jasmine stood at the front, next to her harp, her hands joined in front of her waist.

'Thank you all so much for coming tonight. Wales has an unbroken tradition of harp playing and I'm proud to continue that here at Tir Melys. I play the triple harp, which is considered to be Wales's national instrument. It has a unique, shimmering voice. I'll be playing traditional ballads and dances for you.' Her smile turned to a solemn gaze. 'This concert is dedicated to Afan Griffith, who was a member of our warm, close community here at Tir Melys. He was found brutally murdered last Tuesday. We all mourn Afan in our own ways, but I hope that the music tonight will help us to celebrate his life and honour his memory. You can drink to him afterwards also, with a glass of his wonderful mead. The final piece tonight will be "The Ash Grove", which Afan was fond of. Thank you.'

She sat at the harp, shifted her stool, rested her hands on the instrument, lowered her head for a few moments and started playing. She was a good musician with a sure touch. Swift scanned the room. All the members of the community were present, most of them in the front row. Peter Merchant sat directly in front of his wife. Guy Brinkworth was staring up at the ceiling, his arms folded, his body language expressing boredom. Swift closed his eyes, relaxing into the rippling strings. Memories of the woman he'd seen in the mist at Ogmore returned and he pictured her again, appearing and disappearing like an entrancing wraith. He was aware of Kat beside him, watchful and tense, chewing on her hair, and resented her presence. After several pieces, all of which received hearty applause, Jasmine announced that she would now accompany Bryn Price singing the beautiful lullaby, Suo Gân. Bryn got up from the front row. Unlike Jasmine, he'd made no special effort with his appearance and was wearing jeans and a creased red T-shirt. He sang confidently, legs apart, his right hand over his heart.

'Sleep my darling, on my bosom,
Harm will never come to you;
Mother's arms enfold you safely,
Mother's heart is ever true.
As you sleep there's naught to scare you,
Naught to wake you from your rest;

Close those eyelids, little angel,
Sleep upon your mother's breast.'

The big, brawny man singing the tender lyrics held the audience. Swift noted the door edging open and hoped that Caris was about to appear but saw that it was a flushed and awkward DS Spencer. There were no spare chairs, so he sat on the floor with his back to the wall, wriggling uncomfortably in his constricting suit and loosening his tie.

Jasmine played four more airs. After final warm applause, she stood, beaming, and invited everyone to have refreshments. Before anyone could move, Bryn got up again and stood beside her. His eyes sparked with excitement and malice.

'Just before the nibbles, I'd like to inform everyone here of some news. Quite a few of you have been attending these concerts for a while now, and you've become our friends. Jasmine told you that we're a warm, close community. We all work hard here, tending the land, and although we're tenants, we put our hearts and souls into this place. Sad to say, Jasmine doesn't mean her sweet-sounding words. There won't be many more concerts. You see, Jasmine and Peter Merchant have had Tir Melys valued, and they're planning to put it on the market next week. They're selling out from under us and we'll be given notice. This is reliable information, confirmed yesterday by my contact at the estate agents in Haverfordwest. I suppose you took your business there, Jasmine, rather than Holybridge, in the hope that we wouldn't find out before you decided to inform us, when it would be too late for us to do anything.'

A gasp ran through the room. There were a few muttered *Nos*! Chairs shifted. Kat burst into tears and grasped the opportunity to clutch at Swift's arm. Jasmine was white with shock. Peter Merchant slumped down in his seat.

'Is this true?' Elinor had shot up. She stood, gripping the back of her chair, staring at Jasmine.

Jasmine croaked, 'This isn't the time or the place . . .'

Bruno challenged her. 'Oh, come on, Jasmine, just spit it out, there's nowhere left to hide.'

'Yeah, no more porky pies.' Bryn smiled widely, enjoying himself.

Jasmine gazed at her husband but there was no help from that quarter. She stared over the heads of the audience and swallowed, as if she was about to fold to the floor, but she made a brave effort to hold her ground. 'This isn't the way we wanted to break this news, and I'm saddened that Bryn has chosen to mar our wonderful commemoration of Afan. Sadly, because of personal circumstances, we've had to take the very difficult decision to sell Tir Melys.' There were more gasps. 'We will consult our tenants fully.'

'Yeah, after the event!' Bryn shook his head.

Kat wailed, 'But this is my *home*! You can't do this to us! I can't leave my lovely home!'

Heads turned, mouths open. Jasmine sank down onto her stool. Her husband finally roused himself to get up and go to her. He put a hand on her shoulder. She shook him off.

Bryn took charge. 'Right, everyone. It's been a shock but better that it's out in the open. Let's have those refreshments. We could all do with a bracer at this point, and the redcurrant wine is particularly fortifying.'

Swift extricated himself from Kat. 'Go and get a drink, Kat. I need to speak to someone.'

Kat dabbed at her eyes, the picture of misery. Swift drew DS Spencer aside as the audience filtered through to the refreshments.

'Are you here on duty?'

His heavy-lidded eyes were sleepier than ever. 'Yeah. The boss asked me to come and make sure Caris Murray hadn't turned up.'

'I spoke to Gwyn Bowen. She hasn't heard from Caris. Any news of her?'

Spencer shook his head and ran a finger around his tight collar. 'She's not in Cardiff. Morgan Callender said she left just before nine this morning, to catch the train. He said she always texts him to confirm she's home and when he didn't hear from her, he rang her but she's not answering.'

He scratched his neck. 'Morgan Callender in Cardiff! He's a sly one all right, pulled a blinder there, leaving that note about going to London.'

Swift thought about Spencer's local connections and his boss's opinion of his abilities. 'You do understand that you mustn't mention Morgan's whereabouts to anyone? He's terrified that his brother might track him down.'

Spencer sounded wounded. 'Yeah, the boss said to keep my lip zipped. I do know when I'm not supposed to say stuff! How come you managed to find that house in Cardiff?'

'I asked around. It's called detective work. Have you spoken to Ms Murray?'

'I called in to her just before I came here. She's in a terrible state, bawling her eyes out. My mam's in with her.'

'Is Caris a missing person?'

'Not as such. We're checking the hospitals for now. Boss said we'll give her till ten o'clock, see if she appears. Bloody hell, it's warm in here! I'm parched, I could do with a glass of water, and I need to go around everyone and ask if anyone's heard from Caris today. Boss wants me to report back by nine thirty.'

'Is DI Weber still in hospital?'

'No, she's back home with medication. I hope it improves her mood. She nearly chewed my ear off earlier.'

In the refec, Swift grabbed a slice of quiche and a bottle of beer. The Merchants were nowhere to be seen. There was a babble of excited conversation as people discussed Bryn's revelation. Elinor had been home to fetch Frankie and came through the door cradling him. She was ashen and tearful. Bryn was in the middle of a group, talking animatedly. Bruno stood alone by a window, sipping a glass of wine. Swift joined him.

'Hello, Bruno. Quite an evening.'

Bruno glanced at him and went back to window gazing.

'Bryn told me last night that there was going to be a big reveal soon. It was dramatic in there. I'd guess that was Bryn's idea, making the news into headlines.'

Bruno's mood seemed flat, his face immobile. 'We decided to tell people tonight so that the Merchants had nowhere to hide. Force their hands. They've been planning this behind our backs. Bryn said he'd told you about Uncle Davey.'

'Did Afan know that this farm used to be in your family?'

'I told him not long ago,' Bruno said, 'and about our suspicions regarding the Merchants. I asked him if he'd loan Bryn and me some money if the place went up for sale. We plan to buy Tir Melys — and at a knock-down price, the way the Merchants got it from Davey. What goes around comes around, ain't that the truth?'

'What makes you think they'll sell it to you at less than market value?'

Bruno looked out at the hazy shadows of the gathering dusk. He pressed his palm to the window. 'We've been doing our homework behind the scenes. The Merchants aren't the only ones who can conceal their plans. They're desperate to sell. Their son's in deep financial doodoo. We want to keep the community going. If people want to chip in financially, they can, but we wanted to be in a position to buy it anyway. We outed the Merchants tonight so that they'd face as much embarrassment and hassle as possible, from both the tenants and the local community. Bryn's got the local news onto it tomorrow. We're going to put a deal to them tonight. No putting it on the market, a fast sale to us and we'll call off the dogs. Good news story, people get to keep their homes and the community stays intact.'

It might well work. 'And you get your old homestead back.'

'Not mine, but near enough.'

'Did Afan agree to lend you money?'

Bruno traced a pattern on the moisture his hand had left on the glass. 'He hadn't decided, he said he'd let me know. We plan to get people to buy their houses where they can afford it, so that we have a community of owners, not tenants. So I told him we'd be able to repay him pretty quickly.

It wasn't the money that bothered him. He wasn't sure about our tactics regarding the Merchants. Him and his high principles. He didn't like us being underhand and said we should all have an open discussion about it.'

'Can you afford to do it without Afan's loan?'

Bruno grew tetchy. 'Enough, now. I'm fed up of your constant questions.'

Bryn waltzed up, brimming with energy, threw an arm around Bruno and placed a smacking kiss on his head. 'Nearly there, my friend.' He winked at Swift. 'I saw you were chatting up the lovely Gwyn and Kat didn't like it.'

'You don't miss much.'

'You're right there. I was hoping to talk to Gwyn myself, but she's already gone. She might be interested in moving here if everything works out. She could cut her losses and leave that hopeless bookshop. Time she had a lucky break.'

'Has she been unlucky?'

'Well, her dad's buggered and in a nursing home. She was seen as a high-flier when she was at school. Top-class brain. But she lost the plot at some point and flunked out. Terrible waste of talent if you ask me, and now she struggles to find the rent on those premises. So, did you like my reveal? I did promise you one!'

'Pure theatre. Jasmine suffered publicly, as you intended.'

Bryn laughed. 'Just deserts. We've got big plans for this place. The house will be a crafts centre, for starters. And it will be a proper community of owners, not a feudal domain. I've told the others we'll have a meeting here at ten in the morning without Jasmine and Peter, where we can go through everything. Come on, Bruno the bear, we've work to do at the big house with Jasmine and Peter while they're still licking their wounds. Let's see them squirm while they accept our proposal.'

Swift decided to call it a night and finished his beer. Elinor intercepted him as he headed for the door, staring anxiously into his face. Her breath was sour.

'What on earth are we all going to do? This is unbelievable.'

'Bruno and Bryn seem to have a plan. Talk to them about it. Where's Guy?'

'He said he's had enough for one night. He's hiding in the studio. What will happen about the adoption now, with this hiatus? Everything just thrown up in the air. Fwankie's all upset too, he senses something's wrong.'

She swayed as she spoke, and Swift held her elbow for a moment, worried that she might keel over. 'You should go home, Elinor. You're not well.'

'Home. Where is that going to be, I wonder?' She shivered.

Swift was relieved when Suki came over and gave Elinor a glass of mead. He said goodnight and stopped at the phone on the veranda. He rang Sofia Weber.

'No news of Caris,' he said. 'I caught up with DS Spencer. He's asking around the people here. There's been major drama tonight.' He filled her in on Bryn's reveal and Bruno's connection to the farm. 'Also, I've got some news for you about Afan's past. He was involved in a serious accident. I've spoken to someone who was there.'

'Oh, okay. I need to get the ball rolling on Caris tonight. Can we catch up properly tomorrow?'

He could hear that she was running on empty. 'Of course.'

'Make it the afternoon. I've got to go back to the hospital in the morning for a few more tests.'

'I hope everything's okay.'

'Oh, hospitals . . . They like to give you more to worry about. Once they decide to process you through the system, they take pleasure in practising on you. I'm sure it was a ten-year-old who stuck a needle in me earlier. Talk tomorrow.'

Swift glanced through the open door behind him. He saw DS Spencer making notes while Elinor talked at him and Frankie pawed at his jacket. He stepped out into the cool, slightly smoky air, glad to leave the feverish atmosphere of the Bivium behind. It was time to put pressure on Kat and explore her earlier discomfort. At the cottage, he wrote her a note.

I'll take you up on your offer to go foraging. I'll call for you at 6.30 a.m. tomorrow. Then you'll be back in good time for your meeting about the future of Tir Melys.

He went to her house and slipped the note under the door. He had the feeling she was going to regret issuing the invitation when she read it. Sometimes it was good to turn the tables. Back outside the cottage, he stood and regarded the crops, silvery and shadowy in the moonlight. A quick breeze chilled his scalp. To the newcomer, this place would seem appealing, tranquil, but something about it made him melancholy and fearful. Perhaps he was projecting his own loss and anxieties onto the landscape. He longed suddenly for the noise and bustle of London.

* * *

It was a clear, dry morning with a fresh wind blowing straight off the sea. Kat was huddled into a bulky grey parka jacket with the hood up. She said she hadn't slept much, which was probably true of the community as a whole. Bryn's big reveal would have caused broken, panicky dreams. She acted friendly but he sensed the strain within. Her limp seemed more pronounced. They walked towards the meadow and he asked her how long she'd been foraging.

'I started when I came here. I'd watched a TV programme about it, that's what set me thinking, and once I was settled here, I taught myself. I forage throughout the year. The winter months have thinner pickings but there's still plenty to collect — acorns, beechnuts, chestnuts and sloes. I made sloe gin for Christmas gifts last year.'

She stopped, flexed her injured foot and made a little gasping sound, like an airbed deflating. It sounded phoney and he made no comment. She glanced at him to check his reaction and then carried on. She was such a player. At least her hair was tucked into her hood, so she couldn't have a nibble.

He asked, 'What are we looking for today?'

‘Whatever we see, really. There’s no particular plan with foraging. The major finds at this time of year are blackberries, elderberries and crab apples. You might be interested in seeing the less common plants.’

In the meadow, she led him along the hedgerow and pointed to an area of low-growing plants with broad, oval leaves and purple spiked flowers.

‘There you are. Greater plantain.’

‘Isn’t that a weed?’

‘It is, but it’s also okay to eat. The young leaves are best. I use them in salads. They were in the salad you missed the other night, when you blew me off for supper. Here.’ She nipped a small leaf from the plant and gave it to him.

It was slightly tart, rather like Kat. ‘Not sure I’m that keen.’

‘It grows on you. Afan didn’t like it at first either.’ She took a cloth bag from her pocket, knelt down and opened it out. ‘I’ll pick from this plant if you do another.’ She added despondently, ‘Better make the most of this while I can. I might be homeless soon.’

‘Bryn and Bruno are hopeful that the Merchants will sell to them. They were going to discuss it with them last night.’

‘Yeah, maybe. We’ll see. It’s been a crap week, that’s all I can say. Everything coming apart at the seams.’

‘Where will you go if you do have to leave?’

‘I’m not sure yet.’

They picked in silence and then carried on along the edge of the meadow. Swift noted that her limp had improved. Kat gave an informative commentary on the riches of the hedgerow and the uses of flowers, nuts and berries. Sharing her learning seemed to lift her mood. She was much better at this than at woodcarving.

She commented briefly on the hazelnuts they gathered. ‘Best to pick them now, when they’re still green. The shelled nuts make tasty nibbles, or you can roast them in the oven, or make hazelnut butter. If you wait till later in the year, they’ll probably all have been taken by squirrels.’ When they moved on to rowanberries she told him that they were once planted to protect farm cottages from roaming witches. 'You can't eat them raw, but they make great jams and jellies. You can make schnapps with them. I was planning to ask Afan if he wanted to try making schnapps with me this autumn. Best laid plans. He's gone and I'll probably be gone too.'

'If you do stay, you can organise foraging expeditions for the public. I understand that people here have lots of ideas about developing Tir Melys and branching out.'

'Maybe. Just can't see it working, somehow.'

'Well . . . you're good at this foraging business. You have skills you should share. You'd get people to come along if you publicised it.'

'Really? You mean that?'

'Of course.'

'Thanks. Thanks a lot.' She smiled, her eyes locked on him, brightening.

He did mean it, but he was deliberately softening her up. He disliked her so much that he couldn't bother sparing her feelings. He bent, cracked two hazelnuts on a stone and handed her one of the nuts. She had a child's plaster on one of her fingers, decorated with Elsa from *Frozen*.

'I've found out about the bouldering group and what happened to Afan at Ogmore,' he said. 'You were there in another group when Dru Knight fell.'

She rolled the nut in her hand. 'Did Afan tell you about that?'

'Never mind. Were you in touch with him in the years since then?'

She rolled the nut with the tip of a finger. 'Not as such.'

She can never manage a simple yes or no. 'Did you realise that Afan was living here when you arranged to move in?'

'I might have done.'

'I'll take that as a yes. Let's see. Was your decision to move here anything to do with that knowledge of the Ogmore incident and a desire to revisit it with Afan?'

She pulled a mulish face. 'You can mind your own business. You're not the slightest bit interested in my company or foraging, are you?'

'I might be, having tried it. Foraging, that is. Did you fancy Afan back then, when you were a member of MOVE? Were you following up an old flame or was there more to it?'

'What are you on about?' She seemed rooted to the spot and her hands were clasped tight around the hazelnut.

'I'll tell you, Kat. Afan must have spent years trying to get over what happened to Dru Knight. He found peace here and then you turned up. I can't imagine what that must have been like for him.' In fact, he could, only too well. Demanding, predatory Kat had arrived and lurked across the way, hungry for Afan's attention and affection, a constant reminder of the awful event. 'Did you blackmail Afan? Did he pay you to keep quiet about Dru Knight?'

She threw the hazelnut into the hedge. Her expression was peevish. 'I'm not talking to you. You're so nasty. I can't imagine why Afan was friends with you. He was nice. He was sorry that I'd suffered my own trauma back then at Ogmore, seeing that woman with her head split open. Brains and blood all over the place. I never got over it, actually, and when I had my own injury, it brought it all back.'

'I'm sure it did. And you decided a trauma could be exploited, in more ways than one.'

'I hate you!' She seized the foraging bag and swung it at him, catching him on the arm. It bounced off. Leaves and nuts weren't much use as weapons. She stomped away, back along the meadow, barely limping.

He picked, cracked and chewed a couple of hazelnuts and walked on towards the coast path. He needed to see the horizon, scent the salt air. His phone picked up a signal. He had a missed call from Sofia.

'Aren't you supposed to be at the hospital this morning?' Swift said when she answered.

'I am. I'm hanging around. Hospitals are ninety-nine per cent waiting, one per cent treatment. I wish they'd make up their minds about what's wrong with me. I'm nauseous all the time now, as well as knackered. There's been no contact from Caris. We've CCTV of her on the platform at Holybridge at noon yesterday, so she caught her train home. Last sighting of her was at 12.10 p.m., on camera when she crossed the bridge into town. After that, nothing. Her phone's been switched off since one o'clock Sunday.'

He filled her in on his visit to Dale Toft and his meeting with Kat. 'I've been puzzled as to why Afan tolerated Kat's encroachments into his life to such a degree, and that explains it. Have you got any information yet about Afan's finances?'

'Hang on. I've got something from our techies but haven't had a chance to go through it all yet. They found various online folders and they've confirmed that he had very substantial savings, stocks and shares. Let's say he was a rich man living a frugal life.' There was a pause. 'Okay, I'm into what they've highlighted in Afan's current account. He had a monthly payment to Haskin Estates in Cardiff — that's the management company that rents out the flats for him. One to the Merchants for his rent, payment for his phone and until February this year, a standing order for three hundred a month to a T Wright. Have to follow that up. Oh, here we go, another current standing order to Ms K Glover for one hundred a month. Not big blackmail bucks, but a steady trickle of extra income.'

'I'm not sure that it was blackmail as such, but I believe that there was emotional coercion.'

'Not quite with you.'

'Afan was nothing if not conscientious to a fault. If Kat turned up here and piled on the pressure about her enduring trauma from Ogmore and her subsequent leg injury, he might have decided that he owed her. He probably pitied her. If payment ensured that she didn't publicise what had happened at Ogmore, so much the better.'

'Yeah, I see. And if she was benefiting financially, she'd have no reason to kill him.'

'It makes her an unlikely suspect.' He heard voices in the background, one a low male rumble.

'Got to go, keep lone ranging.' Sofia rang off.

He walked back to the cottage. Afan had been generous with his money and property, funding Kat and bailing out Morgan. He might have felt pressured when Bruno also asked him for a loan. It was one thing to be open-handed, quite another to be treated like the local bank. And who was T Wright? He couldn't make sense of any of it.

CHAPTER 17

Swift was a couple of miles off the coast, sculling through moderate waves in a fresh breeze. White horses foamed along the side of the boat. Tall cliffs framed the coastline to his left. The sun was fitful, but the sky was bright, all blue and white patches. He'd needed to clear his mind while he waited for a call back, so he'd hired the *Seastar* just outside Holybridge and launched her off the slipway there. It was a solo boat, made from glass-reinforced plastic. He liked its lightness, the way it handled and cut through the water at a pace.

It was a while since he'd navigated open waters and he was still adjusting, trying not to resist the wind. After half an hour, he was starting to relax, getting the rhythm of the currents and letting the boat follow the waves. He remembered the golden rule — don't fight the sea. He'd read that rowing on rivers was like road biking, while coastal rowing could be compared to mountain biking, and his muscles were confirming that. He positioned his blades to make sure that he caught the deep face of each wave. The concentration and heightened state of awareness was bliss, as was that moment when the boat started to glide across the air bubbles trapped beneath. Razorbills and guillemots were whirring overhead, fellow travellers across the waves.

After nearly an hour, he saw St Madoc's cove. He was aiming for the caves there and steered the boat inwards. The waves grew gentler as he neared the shelter of the narrow gap into the caves. He passed under a low roof and steered through the channel. Shards of light penetrated from above, reflecting on emerald-green water that reminded him of Caris's pendant. He wondered if she was wearing it now, wherever she was. He feared that she was dead and that it might be adorning her corpse.

He allowed the boat to rock gently through a series of hollows in the rock, dipping an oar now and again to keep his course. The caves smelled of the sea and damp, rotting matter. After the rush of the waves and bird calls, this underworld was silent and cool. There were dark streaks of red oxide in some of the jagged walls and strangely shaped fissures above his head. He reached out to touch a boulder. It was slimy and smooth. He let the boat drift through caverns for some time, aware of the stillness. The weight of rock above him was like a secure shield. He was perturbed, convinced that Caris's disappearance must be linked to Afan's death. He was aware, too, of other vague disquiets that he couldn't name.

A sliver of light spilled in through a gap at the end of a channel. He spotted the small sandy strip of beach he'd noted on a map. He headed for it, pulled the boat up and took the bottle of water and cheese roll that he'd brought with him onto the sand. He was hungry, his appetite whetted by exercise, and he ate his picnic in solitude, listening to the meditative hiss of the sea.

His phone rang. DS Spencer stumbled over his words. The signal was weak and crackling. Swift had to tell him to take a breath and start again.

'The boss left . . . text message. She's . . . into hospital and they've . . . turn her phone off . . . bone infection. Osteomyelitis . . . said to tell you . . . carry on being "Lone Ranger". Make sense?'

'I understand. Any news about Caris Murray?'

‘Nothing . . . asking around the streets . . . CCTV . . . nobody saw anything. Quiet . . . there . . . Sunday.’

‘Is someone taking over from DI Weber?’

‘The boss? Waiting to hear.’ He sounded lost, his voice a little boy’s. ‘Concentrating . . . Caris.’

‘Could you call me if you hear any updates about DI Weber?’

The signal powered in momentarily. ‘Yeah, okay. I rang just now but they said she was having treatment and couldn’t speak to anyone. Her brother’s at the hospital.’

Swift rang off. He wanted to call the hospital, but they wouldn’t tell him anything. Spencer would be directionless without Sofia, a little lamb seeking its mother. He had no faith in the sergeant’s ability to find Caris without his boss at his side. He finished his water. He’d planned to spend longer in the cave system, but now he’d need to up the pace of his own investigation. He was apprehensive about the person who was moving silently around Tir Melys, slipping unseen into Afan’s cottage. Their behaviour suggested unfinished business.

He dragged the boat into the sea and started rowing back to Holybridge in choppier conditions. His muscles had stiffened a little but soon warmed and relaxed as he found a rhythm. To his relief, one of the staff gave him a hand with the boat up the slipway. He stopped at the café attached to the hire shop for a mug of tea and a slab of fruitcake to up his energy level. When he checked his phone, he saw that he’d had the call he’d hoped for, from Joanna Knight, Dru Knight’s mother. There was only a handful of Knights listed around Splott and he’d done a trawl of them, eliminating two young women and an older man. He’d left a message for Ms Knight, keeping his fingers crossed that he’d struck lucky. He listened to the voicemail. A cold, cautious tone.

Hello, is that Mr Swift? I got your message. Not sure how I can help you about Dru. Seems a bit strange after all this time, but I suppose I don’t mind if you want to call me back.

He washed down a mouthful of the rich cake and rang Ms Knight.

‘Thanks so much for coming back to me.’ He explained who he was. ‘I’m sorry if my contact brings back sad memories, but my friend, Afan Griffith, was murdered recently. You might have seen it on the news.’

‘No, I avoid the news, too depressing. That name’s familiar, though. I’ll never forget it. I suppose it’s the same man who caused my daughter’s death.’

‘It’s the same man who was bouldering with her at Ogmore. I’ve heard about the accident, how your daughter was injured.’

She sounded as if her teeth were clenched. ‘Accident. Yes, that’s what they said it was. It should have been manslaughter. Griffith should have gone to prison for what he did. I’m glad he got what was coming to him in the end.’

He could hear that her pain was as raw as if her daughter had died yesterday. ‘I’m sorry.’

‘Why should you be sorry? You don’t know me.’

‘True, but I realise it must have been very hard for you.’

‘Hard? I’ll say! Dru had got herself knocked up by some man in London and came back here with her tail between her legs. Took it for granted, of course, that I’d bail her out. She’d no right to be off climbing up rocks when she had a child. Completely irresponsible. Next thing, I was on my tod with a baby. Thank goodness I’d nagged Dru into taking out life insurance. I’d have gone under without that.’

‘Was Afan in touch with you after your daughter died?’

‘No, he bloody well wasn’t.’

‘I wondered if he’d offered you and your grandchild financial help.’

She laughed. ‘You’re joking. He sent flowers for the funeral and I binned them. If he’d offered blood money, I’d have thrown it back in his face.’

‘Does your grandchild still live with you?’

‘Trevor? Why are you asking about him?’

‘Is his surname Wright?’

‘Yes.’

‘Does he still live with you?’

'No, he's in Penarth.' She paused. 'Why do you want this information? What are you after?'

He'd got what he needed. He wished he hadn't upset her. 'I'm just checking on a few things. I'm sorry to have bothered you.'

'So you should be. I don't like getting phoned up like this. Oh, hang on — this money angle — did Griffith's conscience bother him? Did he leave Trev something?'

Maybe she was one of those people who watched programmes like *Heir Hunters* and hoped for the letter revealing an unexpected windfall. He didn't like to raise false hopes but it had to be done. 'I'm not sure. But wouldn't you regard that as blood money?'

'That'd be different,' she said. 'Like Griffith paying his dues.'

Swift let that pass. 'I'd like to speak to Trevor. Could you give me his number?' He expected her to refuse, but she rattled it off. Despite her anger, the lure of an inheritance was a strong one. 'Was Trevor expecting to benefit from Afan's will?'

'I'd have thought that . . .' She checked herself. 'I can't be doing this anymore. Trev's headstrong, just like his mother. Never listens to me. He can deal with his own affairs. Bugger off.'

It was always good to be told where you stood. Her denial concerning financial help had been genuine. Trevor had been dealing with his own affairs and accepting money from Afan without her knowledge. Why had the regular payment stopped, and had Trevor thought that he would benefit from Afan's death?

Swift had forgotten to take the teabag from his mug. The tea was stewed but he drank it anyway while he rang Trevor's number and listened to his cheery recording. *Hi, Trev's voicemail is broken. This is his fridge. Leave a message and I'll stick it to myself with a magnet.* He left a message and stood by the door of the café. The sun was setting, burnishing the sea red-gold. More boats were coming back on the evening tide. Weary rowers sat by the water's edge, talking quietly. A cluster of windsurfers stood on the shingle, sipping coffee and sharing a packet of biscuits. There was the sense of a peaceful end of a day well spent. Once again, he thought that Afan should have been here to share the pleasure of the moment.

* * *

Swift was back in Cardiff, this time transported by an uncrowded mid-morning train. He sat with Trevor Wright in a noodle bar in Castle Arcade, near the wine shop where the young man worked. It was on the first floor, next to a balustraded walkway. Wright had a bland expression, a round, soft face and a brash manner. He was making his way speedily through a bowl of teriyaki beef, as if he was worried that someone might snatch it away. Swift had opted for a pumpkin katsu curry.

'Nan told me you'd called her,' Wright said. 'I bet she roughed you up. That's her style. She was getting on my case about finding out if Mr Griffith left me any money.' He mimicked his grandmother: '*You need to make sure you follow up on that, and don't put it off like you usually do with things.*'

'Were you expecting him to leave you anything?'

'He won't have.'

'Do you say that because you were in contact with him?'

'I might have been. What's it to you?'

Swift ignored him. 'Your nan's unaware of the standing order Mr Griffith had made to you.'

Wright speared a sliver of beef. 'How come you know about it?'

'I find things out.'

'I suppose I should thank you for not dobbing me in with my nan about that.'

Swift took a sip from his Tiger beer. 'Thanks aren't needed. But I'm interested in how the standing order came about and why it ended.'

The greenish light from the oriel windows in the arcade roof gave Wright a sallow complexion. His red and white

T-shirt stated, *Partners in Wine*. He scratched his chest above the lettering. 'Why are you poking your nose in?'

'Filling in the blanks.'

Wright pointed with a chopstick and said flippantly, 'You think I might have murdered him.'

'Did you?'

'As if!'

'That's not an answer.'

Looking startled, Wright paused with a portion of peppers and onion halfway to his mouth. 'Course I didn't!'

'Can you prove where you were when Mr Griffith was murdered?'

'I can. Work. All. Day. Long.'

'Okay. Let's say I accept that. It's helpful to hear about your contact with Afan Griffith.'

'I suppose it's no skin off my nose.' Wright finished his food, burped and pushed the bowl away. 'Afan Griffith contacted me on Facebook when I was sixteen. He told me who he was, and how he'd always regretted what happened to my mum. He said he'd like to offer me some financial help. At first, I worried he was some kinky perv coming on to me. Then I read some press cuttings my nan kept in the sideboard and saw that he'd been there when my mum had the accident. I thought, why not? If he reckoned he owed me and had the dosh to spare, I wasn't going to refuse.'

Swift imagined what that must have been like for a sixteen-year-old. What teenager wouldn't like the idea of money arriving in their account every month as if by magic? 'That's when the standing order was set up.'

'Yeah. Griffith said I should use the money however I wanted, but he encouraged me to put it towards my education.'

Swift doubted that Wright had put the money to that use. Working in a wine shop didn't demand qualifications. Rain was falling. Swift could hear it on the high windows, like a distant percussion. 'Why did the money stop?'

Wright tensed. 'I told Griffith to cancel it. I'd always been told that my mum had died in an accident. I didn't read the full inquest report until early this year. I'd never understood exactly what had happened, how much Griffith was at fault. Nan never told me. Griffith should have done his job properly and broken my mum's fall. Then I'd have had her in my life, instead of a cranky battleaxe of a nan.'

'What made you read the inquest report?' Swift asked.

'I got to wondering . . . My girlfriend's pregnant. I'm going to be a dad. Baby's due any minute now. I was thinking about my mum a lot. Dreaming about her. I've no memories of her. I wanted to find out more about what had happened. When I read about it, all the details, I was furious with Griffith. He'd been trying to make amends with his money, and I'd betrayed my mum by accepting it. I sent him a message saying I didn't want his payments anymore.'

'You never met Afan Griffith in person?'

Wright picked up his chopsticks and tapped them sharply on the edge of his bowl. 'Nope. And tell you what, I'm glad he's dead. Makes me happy. I've got to get back to work.'

Swift watched him lope away, hands shoved in his pockets. He'd have had a strong motive for killing Afan. Swift didn't want to contact DS Spencer, but Wright's alibi needed to be checked through formal channels. He thought about how to pitch it without mentioning his arrangement with Sofia and rang the sergeant.

'Any news of DI Weber?'

'Not good,' Spencer said mournfully. 'She's got a really bad infection and a fever. She's not responding as they'd hoped to the antibiotics. Should I send her flowers — or maybe chocolates, do you think?'

'Nice idea, but probably not for now. Has someone else taken over the Griffith investigation?'

'Not yet. No one available. I've got to plough on.'

'Anything on Caris?'

Spencer sounded as if he was struggling to stay awake. 'No. It's like a UFO beamed her up. Her mam's in bits, keeps phoning me. So does Morgan. I've nothing to tell them.'

Swift could only hope that Spencer hadn't mentioned UFOs to Ms Murray. 'Could you do something for me?'

Spencer sounded panicky. 'Me? What?'

'It's nothing complicated. I followed up some information that Gwyn Bowen gave me. Afan Griffith was involved in a climbing accident years ago. A woman died. I met her son today. He told me that Afan had been paying him money for years by standing order, by way of making up for the loss of his mother. His name's Trevor Wright. He discovered the full details of the accident earlier this year and stopped the payments. He admitted that he was angry with Afan. He told me he was working the day Afan died, but you need to check his alibi.'

'This guy turned down the money?'

'He accepted it for some time, but yes, he did. I suppose if you have information on Afan's bank account, you'll see that's the case.'

'Why would anyone turn down money? Doesn't add up to me.'

Spencer was clearly stuck. 'That's not the issue. Wright's resentment is. You need to check him out.'

'Okay. What's his name again?'

He could hear Spencer's brain lurching into low gear. 'Trevor Wright. His mum was called Drusilla Knight. You can google her. Have you got those names?'

'Hang on. Yeah.'

'Wright works in Cardiff, at Castle Wines. You need to verify that he was there when Afan died. I suggest you get onto it straightaway. Could you text me the outcome?'

Spencer sounded cautious. 'Am I allowed to do that?'

'Why not? Tell you what, do a thumbs up emoji if the alibi checks out, thumbs down if it doesn't.'

Spencer repeated the instruction. Swift pictured him drawing a thumb and shook his head as he ended the call. He'd arranged to call in on Morgan Callender, in the hope that he might have information about the nightmare situation at Tir Melys that Caris had alluded to. He retraced his route to Roath. He was alarmed at the news about Sofia Weber. He'd read that osteomyelitis was a rare, serious condition and could be fatal. He'd only just met her, but she was an ally and she'd become a friend.

* * *

Morgan Callender was wan and sickly. The blinds were still down in the flat and the air smelled unpleasantly sweet. The small space was untidy, strewn with clothes and dirty dishes. The young man couldn't sit still and paced up and down while they talked.

'Something's happened to Caz. I could tell the police thought that too when they came round. How could she go missing on a Sunday morning?'

'Did Caris get any phone calls before she left here on Sunday?'

'No. No one phoned her.'

'What about the call she took as I was leaving?'

'That was her work, asking if she could do an extra shift this week.'

'Did she seem worried about anything?'

'No.' He leaned against a wall. 'If anything, she was happier than she'd been in a while. We talked for ages after you left on Saturday, and we were both more cheerful. We agreed that I needed to leave here as soon as possible, and we'd find somewhere to live together in Bristol, like you suggested. That way, Caz wouldn't be too far from her mam. Caz was going to tell her mam the truth when she got home. We said we'd start looking for jobs and a flat this week.' He sank to the floor and put his head in his hands. 'What am I going to do now?'

Swift went to the mucky sink and poured a glass of water. He took it across to Morgan. 'Here, drink this. I need you to help me, if you can.'

Tears flowed down Morgan's cheeks. He took the glass. 'How can I help, stuck here?'

Swift sat on a dining chair and pushed aside the remains of a takeaway Chinese meal on the table. 'When I was leaving here on Saturday, Caris mentioned a problem at Tir Melys. She said that she wished she hadn't got Afan involved in it. Have you any idea what she was referring to?'

Morgan said, 'No. The only thing we ever talked about concerning Afan was this place.'

'What about the other people in the community? Did Caris ever have arguments with any of them?'

Morgan sipped water. 'The police asked me that. I couldn't think of anything. She liked some of them better than others. She got on with Bruno and Suki . . . and Afan, of course.' He started crying again.

Swift gave him time. He cleared the table and other surfaces of dirty mugs and dishes, put them in the sink and filled it with hot water. He found a cloth and wiped the table clean.

Morgan said dully, 'You don't have to do that.'

'I hate mess. Indulge me. Go back to those times you went to Tir Melys with Caris. Did she clash with anyone?'

'You reckon someone there has done something to her?'

'No idea, but it's worth considering. So try and remember. And could you open a window while you're doing that?'

Morgan stood up and opened a skylight. Cool, clean air washed in. He perched on the arm of the sofa. 'Caz sort of kept to her work when she was there. She didn't like Kat, because she was always pestering Afan. The only other person she didn't have much time for was Guy Brinkworth. Once when I was there, she'd been in their house, talking to Elinor. She said Guy was an out-and-out shit, far more than anyone realised.' He rubbed his eyes. 'That's it. That's all. Should I come back to Holybridge and help look for Caz?'

'Doesn't sound like a good idea, given your brother's behaviour.'

'I've been worried about him. I had a couple of weird calls yesterday, unknown number. Just a silence, then the calls ended. I bet it's him. It's the kind of thing that'd be his idea of fun. That means someone's told him my number and he might have this address.'

'Where would you stay if you came back to Holybridge?'

'I could ask Caz's mum.'

Swift shook his head. 'Calvin would find out and then Ms Murray would have even more trouble at her door. It wouldn't be fair on her.'

Morgan gave a sob. 'What am I going to do, not knowing what's happened to Caz?'

Swift doubted that he had the resources to act on his own. But he had to start learning, especially if Caris wasn't coming back. 'Tidy this place up, for a start. Then search for a job and somewhere to live. Hopefully, Caris will turn up and then at least she'll come back to positive news.'

'I'm not sure if I can do that, manage this stuff on my own.'

'What's the alternative, Morgan? Wait until you're out on the street with no money coming in? It's up to you, but I know which I'd rather do in your circumstances.'

'You think I can do it on my own?'

'I've every faith in you,' Swift lied.

CHAPTER 18

The heavens opened as Swift cycled back to Tir Melys from the station. He'd stopped at the Bridge Arms for an evening meal. The cottage pie had been delicious, but now he regretted delaying in town. It was gone nine, the light obliterated by heavy cloud. His headlight just about picked out the road. All he could hear was the roaring rain as it pounded him, streaming into his eyes. He crouched lower and pedalled on. He was beginning to wonder if he'd been seeing Tir Melys from the wrong angle. It was like studying a photograph or a painting in a gallery. You could get too close, absorbed in the detail and intensity. If you altered your stance, you could find a different perspective, see aspects you hadn't noticed before. He pondered the financial problems, the concert audience, the Brinkworths' studio, random comments and the things that Caris had chosen to reveal and conceal.

Half a mile from the turning to Tir Melys, he could barely see where he was going. He'd decided to stop and wipe his face when an engine roared close behind him. He half turned, and then he was flying through the air and rolling on the ground. He landed on his back in a soggy ditch. He twisted, gasping with pain, and tried to identify the car but all he could glimpse were blurred tail lights, vanishing into the obscuring deluge. He lay still, catching his breath and moving his limbs cautiously. Everything seemed to be working. His back throbbed and he could taste blood on his tongue, salty and sharp.

He hauled himself up, staggered to the road and found his bike. It had been thrown along the verge. Miraculously, the lights were still working but the back wheel was buckled, and the front one had bent spokes. He got on and tried riding it, but the damaged spokes kept catching the brake. He dismounted and pushed it with difficulty for a couple of metres. He gave up on the seizing brake, tucked the bike into the hedgerow behind a tall oak tree and continued on foot. His legs were like jelly, his face burned and ached. He plodded on, head down.

He fell through the door of the cottage and collapsed into a chair. He sat for minutes, without the strength even to remove his sodden clothing. Then he roused himself and drank a large glass of mead. It warmed him instantly. *Thanks, Afan.* The stove was still glowing. He stacked it with wood, groaning as his back pulled. He rested with his hands on the warm top, noting that they were covered in grazes, and then straightened up slowly. In the bathroom, he stripped off. The tiny mirror reflected his lacerated face and a fat bottom lip. He stood under the shower, longing for it to be hotter. The stove was blazing by the time he was dressed in dry jeans and a jumper. He poured another glass of mead and sat close to it, shivering despite the warmth.

Someone had tried to kill him. He was sure that the accident had been intentional. The engine's sudden roar and the vanishing vehicle told him that. They had accelerated. He got up and checked that he'd locked the door. He'd finished the mead and was slumped in a light doze when someone hammered at the door and he heard Elinor shout his name.

She burst in and stood trembling by the table. Her yellow oil slicker dripped on to the floor. Frankie was tucked inside her coat, peeping out from below the collar. 'Ty, you must come. It's awful. Please, you must come.'

'What is it?'

She opened her mouth, but no sound came out. Then she gulped and whimpered, 'Caris. It's Caris. I found her. She's dead.'

'Where?'

'In the chapel. I was out in the Land Rover and I just stopped in to say a prayer. Please, please help.'

He was fuzzy from shock and the mead. He shook his head and reached for his waxed jacket. 'Elinor, I've had a few drinks. Can you take me there in the Land Rover?'

'Yes, of course.' She was staring at him. 'What's happened to your face?'

'It's nothing. Have you told anyone else?'

'No. I came straight to you.'

'Good. I want you to fetch the Land Rover and drive it down to the Bivium. I'm heading there now to ring the police. I won't be long.'

She was trembling, leaning against the table for support, but she roused herself and left the cottage. He put a torch in his pocket, locked up and hurried to the Bivium. He was stiff and his back hurt like hell. By the time he'd finished his call, Elinor was waiting outside in the Land Rover with Frankie asleep in the back. They drove to the chapel in silence. Swift had never been privy to a mute Elinor before. The rain was still full force and the windscreen wipers swished ineffectually. Swift wondered what she'd been doing in the chapel late on such a night. It was an unusual time to pray. He also wondered if she'd tried to run him down earlier.

'It's best if you stay here, in the Land Rover,' he said. 'It reduces contamination of the crime scene.' *And if you killed Caris, it doesn't give you the chance to cover any traces.* 'Are you okay with that, Elinor? The police won't be long. Keep the doors locked.'

Elinor whispered, 'Caris . . . she's in the hermit's hidey-hole. Sort of scrunched up. It's horrible.'

Swift slipped gloves on and opened the chapel door. He lit his way with the torch to the hermit's hidden chamber and stood at the entrance. Caris was on the floor in a dark pool of blood, curled up with one leg bent, her hair falling over her face. She wore a denim jacket over a T-shirt and jeans. He approached her carefully and checked that there was no pulse. When he played the torch beam around her neck there was no gleam of an emerald. There was a lack of ritual to this death, no grave goods. She'd been concealed, dumped, not displayed. Perhaps there were two killers at work here. He was bitterly angry, even more so than at Afan's death. Caris had been so young, so burdened with responsibilities, and he now believed that she'd got out of her depth with someone in this community.

He stepped back into the body of the chapel. The cold snaked beneath his clothing. Morgan would despair when he heard this news. He went back to the door to check that Elinor was okay. She was sitting with the engine running, her eyes closed. He envied her the warmth in the vehicle.

He was numb with cold and shock by the time the police arrived — DS Spencer, bleary-eyed, with two uniforms.

Swift explained what had happened. 'Do you mind if Elinor and I go home? I can't see that we can contribute anything else right now.'

'That's okay,' Spencer said. 'I've got to wait for the crime scene manager anyway. Have you been in a punch-up?'

'Someone ran me off the road earlier. How's DI Weber?'

'Bad, apparently. That's all they'll say. I can't believe it. One minute she had a broken arm and now she's . . .' He sounded tearful.

Swift went back to the Land Rover. Moving was an immense effort. Elinor still had her eyes closed. He walked around the vehicle, shining the torch on the front and left side. There was no obvious damage.

'Did you see her?' Elinor whispered when he climbed in. Frankie was on her lap, his eyelids flickering.

'Yes. We can head back now.'

Elinor put a hand on the gear lever. 'I had a row with Guy after supper. He'd written another sarcastic letter to social services behind my back. I was so upset I just took off for a drive around the coast. Then on the way back, I decided to visit the chapel.'

Swift put his hands in front of the warm air vent. 'What made you go into the small chamber?'

She hesitated. 'This is embarrassing.'

'You don't have to tell me, but the police will ask.'

'I was thinking . . . maybe I could hide in there. Guy would worry and he wouldn't be able to find me. If I hid until tomorrow, he'd be so frightened, he'd stop all this destructive behaviour. But then I realised that I couldn't do that tonight, because Fwankie was with me and it wouldn't be fair on him. I could come back on my own another day and hide, so I stepped in to see how it might feel . . .' She glanced at him. 'I suppose you're sitting there worrying that I'm completely mad. Unhinged.'

He wasn't sure what to make of her. He said nothing for a while. The rain thudded and the engine purred. He drifted sleepily, and then forced himself to stay alert.

'You're sad and desperate, Elinor. Let's go back.'

* * *

He invited Elinor to have cocoa with him and she accepted readily. He was exhausted and didn't want her company, but she was at a low ebb and he needed to exploit that.

He asked, 'Do you want to tell Guy where you are?'

'No. I expect he's fast asleep. Nothing ever disturbs Guy's sleep. Anyway, I don't care if he's not and sitting up worrying. I hope he is. He deserves to be.'

'I've not heard you speak in that way about Guy before.' *You're usually busy making excuses for him.*

She stared at the floor. 'No . . . well . . . every worm turns, or so they say.'

They sat by the stove with mugs of cocoa and biscuits, in a soft pool of light from one lamp. Frankie was cocooned in one of Elinor's arms, accepting bits of shortbread. She was in the armchair and rocked him like a baby. Swift had given her a towel and she'd draped it around her shoulders. Her hair straggled down in damp curls. The wind had risen and was snapping at the windows.

'The late fruit will rot,' Elinor said glumly. 'And no . . . no Caris to help pick it.'

'No, no Caris.'

'Do you think the same person killed Afan and Caris?'

The hot cocoa stung his lip and he winced. 'Can't say.'

'It's terrible. Unbelievable. Why would anyone leave a body in a holy place?'

'Maybe it was just convenient.'

'How can you be so calm?' She put a hand to her mouth and turned to him. 'Shouldn't we tell the others what's happened?'

'It's gone one in the morning. There's no point in waking everyone up, and we should leave it to the police.'

'I suppose, yes.' She took a shuddering breath. 'I don't want to stay here now. The Merchants have agreed to sell to us, but I don't want to carry on. Everything's spoiled. All our plans built on shifting sands. To think of the sacrifices I've . . . Oh, Fwankie, what are we going to do?'

Swift's head was aching. He swallowed a couple of painkillers. 'You've had a dreadful shock. You were very fond of Caris. She told me.'

She shifted. 'Did she?'

'You gave her a lovely emerald pendant.'

'Yes.'

'Very generous.'

'Well . . . she was helpful with our produce.'

'Maybe she was, but I've been wondering if you gave her the pendant and other jewellery for a different reason. Not a good one.'

She winced, bent and kissed Frankie's head, then stared into her cocoa.

Swift reached into the tin of biscuits and took a digestive. He was ambushed by another memory of Ruth, of lunching with her after she'd married. One of those wistful, strange meetings they used to have in London. She'd pushed aside the complimentary shortbread. *Neither of us likes shortbread, we never eat it.* He was burdened by thoughts of her, and wished he'd never seen the woman at Ogmore. The fire's warmth had made him sluggish and he fought through inertia. It was as if the constant rain and damp here had seeped into his brain and numbed it. He forced himself to straighten up, aware that he was nearer to a resolution of these crimes. He spoke quietly.

'Elinor, I'm certain now that Caris, and possibly someone else, had you between a rock and a hard place. Tell me about it.'

She caressed the dog's head. 'Listen to that storm building. I hope there's no damage to our roof. It's cosy in here, isn't it?'

'Yes. And safe. Two people have died, Elinor. This has to stop.'

She sighed. 'I haven't felt safe for ages, have I, Fwankie?' She turned to Swift, a look of appeal and despair. 'I've been frightened of saying or doing the wrong thing. Like I've been fighting on so many fronts I can never win. I want a baby so much.'

'Yes. But that can't be at any price. I've seen the jewellery you've been giving away.'

'But that's not the only cost you're talking about.'

'No.'

'Ah, if you only knew. If you had any notion of what I've been through. I wonder if you can spend your soul. The stories say you can sell it to the devil, so why not spend it too?' She held her mug out to him. 'Can I have another?'

He made fresh drinks, coffee for himself to try to stay alert, and sat back beside her, stifling yawns. Elinor shared another shortbread with Frankie. Her chair creaked faintly as she rocked. Then she started talking. Swift surreptitiously pressed record on his phone. It was a long, rambling and anguished story with much backtracking and pauses for bouts of tears. She was in a pitiful state. He listened intently, holding exhaustion at bay. He was hearing a blend of truth and lies, and he wasn't sure how to sift one from the other. The more he heard, the more he realised how burdened Afan had been with other people's dilemmas. The man must have been overwhelmed at times.

It was almost 2 a.m. when Elinor went home. Swift was anxious as he watched her walk away. Should he let her go? She was highly volatile, and her husband would do nothing to ease her unpredictability. Her monologue had calmed her for now. He wished that he could ring Sofia and discuss his suspicions. There was nothing more that he could do tonight. He fell onto the bed fully clothed, his head full of the complex yarn Elinor had spun him. He fell asleep instantly.

CHAPTER 19

A thunderstorm woke Swift at just gone seven. He'd slept deeply. The air was humid, and his clothes were sticking to his body. He made coffee and stood at the open window, studying the turbulent sky. A trellis of runner beans had collapsed, and the gutters were streaming. He felt better this morning than he'd expected. He was stiff and his back ached, but it could have been worse.

His reflection in the bathroom mirror wasn't pretty, with the grazes now a livid red. He decided to leave well alone and not to shave. In fact, he'd grow a beard until he got home to the luxury of hot water. He showered and ate bread and cheese while he played back Elinor's voice, then made a copy of the recording with edits. It was hard to gauge how much of what she'd said was misdirection. He had an idea why these murders had been committed, but he was unsure about who was involved and hesitated over his next steps. This place, with its strange brew of seething emotions, seemed to be draining his energy and befuddling him. He poured another mug of coffee, mulling over what he needed to do and the best way to achieve it.

First, he drove just far enough to get a phone signal, noting that the chapel had been cordoned off and a heavy-duty padlock fitted to the door. There were no police cars around. When his phone came to life, he saw that DS Spencer had texted him a thumbs up about Trevor Wright. He called the hospital, enquired about Sofia and was given the neutral response of 'Ms Weber is comfortable'. Next, he phoned Spencer. 'Thanks for the alibi confirmation.'

'That's okay. We've removed Caris's body. We're on our way back to Tir Melys to talk to everyone, including you.'

'How did Caris die?'

'Stabbed in the back. That's all I can tell you.'

'Time of death?'

Spencer spoke as if he was reading from a crib sheet. 'I can't share that information with you. Enquiries are ongoing.'

Not going very far with you in charge. 'I wondered if you're going to have to include all the people who came to the concert in your questioning.'

'What I said before,' Spencer said in a robotic voice.

He'd better not push the sergeant's limited skill set. 'Okay. Have you informed anyone about Caris's death yet? Other than her mother, that is.'

'Just her mam and Morgan.'

Good. 'I'm sending you the recording of a conversation I had with Elinor Brinkworth in the early hours of this morning. It's significant. Can you speak to me first when you arrive? I'll be at the cottage.'

Spencer agreed. Swift made one more call, a crucial one, and left a voicemail saying he'd visit during the morning. He drove to where he'd left Afan's bike, managed to wedge it in the boot of the car and took it back, where he stored it in the shed. He retreated to the cottage, made coffee and stayed there until Spencer arrived. He didn't want to mix with any of the others until they'd been questioned.

He gave Spencer a coffee, watching as he stirred in four sugars.

'Thanks for this — I haven't slept. The boss has made a tiny bit of improvement,' Spencer said, holding a forefinger and thumb up a centimetre apart.

'That's good. Let's hope she continues to fight back. It would be welcome news for her to hear that this killer, or killers, are in custody. Probably do her as much good as the medical treatment.'

'Yeah.' Spencer didn't sound optimistic.

Swift shoved the biscuit tin to him and went through an account of the previous night.

'You should report that someone tried to run you down,' Spencer said, focusing on the least important issue.

'Maybe I will. Have you listened to the recording I sent you?'

Spencer dunked a biscuit in his coffee. His colour was high. 'Not yet, I had to get other stuff organised.'

Swift saw that he was flustered and unsure. He said impatiently, 'You need to, and talk to Elinor Brinkworth next. She has vital information about Caris and Gwyn Bowen.'

'Okay. I hope there's going to be some forensics back on Caris's body, something to give us a steer. Her mam's in bits. My mam's taken her and Morgan into her house.'

'Morgan's here?'

'Yeah. He turned up early this morning. He's all over the place. My mam's letting him stay with her so he can keep his head down, out of Calvin's way.'

'He'll need to.'

He said wistfully, 'My mam'll be good with him. She likes having someone to organise and boss, she'll be in her element. She'll do his laundry and make him humongous dinners.'

'You're used to having a strong woman in your life, DS Spencer.'

'Oh . . . yeah, that's right. You can call me Spence by the way, everyone does.'

'If you're needing a steer, here's one for you,' Swift said as Spencer finished his coffee. 'Think of those grave goods. Why did someone put them by Afan and come back here for the book to place on his body?'

Spencer rubbed his forehead. 'The book? Oh, yeah. Is that important?'

'I'll leave it with you.'

* * *

In the bookshop, Swift perused the local history section while Gwyn Bowen answered a phone query. The shop was empty as usual. When she'd finished, he went to the desk. He was about to wing it, but it wouldn't be the first time. She wore black jeans and a grey T-shirt. Her hair was tied back in a red cotton scarf and draped across one shoulder.

When she saw his face she said, 'Have you been in an accident?'

'Sort of. It's not that bad.'

'I got your message,' she said. 'Something about Caris?'

'That's right.'

'I've been out of my mind with worry. Is there any news?' She was pallid, the usual peach bloom on her cheeks dimmed.

He'd thought that the Holybridge bush telegraph might already have informed her and was relieved that she hadn't heard. 'Can we talk somewhere less public?'

'Okay. We can go upstairs to my flat. I'll just lock the door.'

He watched her slip the sign to *Closed* and turn the key in the door. She was light on her feet, in flat shoes decorated with little silvery bows. He followed her up narrow, creaking stairs.

'Watch your head at the top here,' she called. 'You'll need to duck.'

He bent under the lintel and through the low doorway. She led him into a spacious sitting room with a deep bay window jutting over the narrow street. The furniture was old and shabby, the walls were painted off-white. The slanting floorboards gleamed warmly with wax and she'd added colour with batik throws similar to the ones he'd seen in Morgan's flat.

'Have a seat. That armchair's the comfiest. Tea or coffee?'

'No thanks. Have you heard from Bryn Price?'

She sat opposite him and frowned. 'Bryn? No.'

'He was hoping to talk to you after the concert on Sunday night, but you'd gone.'

'I was tired and worried about Caris. I wanted to get back, call in to see her mam. Bryn has my number.'

'The Merchants have agreed to sell to the community, which is good news. He thinks you might be interested in getting rid of the bookshop and buying into Tir Melys. I understand the shop isn't doing that well and you're struggling.'

She was offended. 'Oh, I see. I'm not sure that's anyone's business but mine.'

'I've found that Bryn makes everything his business. I expect he'll be in touch. That was quite an evening on Sunday, wasn't it?'

She shifted in the seat. 'I thought you'd come about Caris?'

He'd been cruel, keeping the news from her, but he'd wanted to confuse her, and he suspected her of her own heartless acts. 'That's right. I'm afraid I have bad news about her.'

'Oh.'

'She's dead. Her body's been found.'

Tears spilled down her cheeks. 'Oh, God, no! Where?'

'In the chapel at Tir Melys.'

'Was she murdered?'

'I'm afraid so.'

'Poor, poor Caris. And her mam. It'll destroy her mam.'

'Yes.' Her shock appeared genuine. He waited while she cried, removed her glasses and wiped her eyes.

'When was she found?'

'Last night. Elinor found her.'

Something changed in her expression. She retreated into herself. It was as if she'd pulled on a mask. She said, 'I can't believe this. Afan and Caris both dead.'

He hoped she'd put her glasses back on. She looked vulnerable without them and he didn't want to think of her in that way, or gaze into her lovely eyes. 'Is this the room where Afan had his Welsh lessons?'

'What? Yes. Why do you ask?'

'Just wondered. I seem to have been retracing his steps everywhere I go. It's strange but somehow right.'

She pressed a tissue to her eyes again. 'Do the police have any idea why Caris was in the chapel?'

'I'm not sure. Will you be able to tell them anything?'

She stared at him. 'You believe I know something about Caris's murder?'

'Honestly? At the moment, I'm not sure.'

She cleared her throat. 'All I can say is that I was expecting to meet Caris at her mam's on Sunday to take her to the concert, but she didn't come back.'

Swift wasn't sure of his ground. This young woman had come up with a way to distract him and had sent him off course to Ogmore. Time to switch tracks on her. He gestured to the throws. 'You and Caris had the same tastes. She had these pretty throws in Morgan Callender's flat in Cardiff. Did you buy them together?'

Her lips parted in surprise. He watched as she struggled to digest the comment.

'Cardiff? I don't understand. Morgan's in London.'

'No. He's never been in London. He went to Cardiff when he left town, and Caris spent weekends there with him.'

'How could he be in Cardiff? He wanted to be far away from his brother. I don't get it.'

Swift touched the weave of the throw. It was soft and fine. 'No. But then, you and Caris had grown apart of late, hadn't you? Not quite the close friends you once were. You told me that you hadn't seen that much of her recently. She kept a major part of her life from you. You fell out, of course, about what you were up to with Elinor Brinkworth. That's the problem with getting involved in tangles with people. It can backfire.'

Those eyes like pale grey moonstones stared at him. To his relief, she put her glasses back on. 'I'm not sure what you mean.'

He'd keep it light and conversational. 'Well, Gwyn, I've been puzzled about two young women who visited Elinor and owned her expensive jewellery. I saw the price tags when I was in her studio. Caris can't have been earning big money at a warehouse. I've heard that you're in financial trouble with this shop and like Caris, you have responsibility for a sick parent. Yet you could both wear beautiful, exclusive pieces. I had a long chat with Elinor last night. Very cosy, in front of Afan's stove. The story she told me wasn't a cosy one, though. It was sad and desperate. What you experienced when you were at school was terrible and I'm sorry for you. No child should undergo that, carry the memory of it through life.'

The silence stretched. A tourist coach rumbled past outside. Swift saw a boy in a baseball cap with his nose pressed to the window.

Gwyn found her voice. 'What did Elinor tell you?'

'A lot.' *I wish I was more certain about how to decipher it.* 'I can understand that you hate Guy after what he did, or rather failed to do. Bryn Price mentioned that you didn't achieve your potential at school. Now I understand why.'

She said in a frosty tone, 'I don't want to talk about that. It's my private business, no one else's.'

'Gwyn, you've made it other people's business through your actions. There's no privacy after murder.'

She clasped her hands together. 'I haven't murdered anyone!'

'Maybe not, but what you've done has contributed to someone deciding to commit murder. You have to talk about what happened to you at school. To the police, if not to me. For now, though, if it will help you make up your mind, I'll play you what Elinor told me about your experience.'

He found the edited section on his phone and played it. She listened to the tear-laden voice, staring at the phone as if it was alive.

Gwyn came here for the first time with Caris last January. I'd ordered a design book, and she delivered it because she was interested in seeing the studio. She didn't stay long, and I thought it was odd, the way she took off suddenly. Caris came to see me a week later and asked if I'd meet her and Gwyn at the bookshop. It was all a bit mysterious, something about Gwyn needing to talk to me. I went and had a coffee with them in Gwyn's flat. Gwyn told me that she'd recognised Guy, and that was why she'd left the studio in a hurry. He'd been a supply teacher for a while when he was studying for his PhD, before we moved here. He did a fortnight at a school in Holybridge, where Gwyn was a pupil. Gwyn said that she'd been molested by a boy in the playground one day. Guy was on duty and she told him what had happened. She said he made light of it, told her it was just a bit of horseplay and to forget about it. She never did forget, but she never told anyone. She said that after that, she lost all confidence. It blighted her school life. Guy left the school just days after it happened, and she never saw him again. She hardly knew him and didn't remember his name. Of course, when she walked into the studio, she recognised him. I'd chatted to Caris about our plans for adoption and she'd told Gwyn. Gwyn said that if she told the authorities about Guy's behaviour towards her, we'd never be allowed to adopt. I begged them both not to say anything. I thought I'd go mad. I offered them jewellery to keep quiet. I gave them expensive pieces regularly, much more to Gwyn than Caris. I could tell that Caris wasn't comfortable about it and a month or so ago, she told me that she wouldn't take anything else from me. In fact, she gave me back a couple of pieces, but I insisted that she keep an emerald. I appreciated her silence. I must have given Gwyn stuff worth thousands. Guy leaves the accounts to me, but I've been terrified that he'll notice.

Swift pocketed the phone and sat silently. Gwyn pulled her knees up to her chin and circled her shins with her arms.

She sighed. 'I was so ashamed, I never told anyone, not even Caris, until that day I saw Guy at Tir Melys. We drove back here, and I broke down. It happened during the lunch break at school. That boy pushed me down beside the equipment store and did horrible things to me. I was crying when I told Guy Brinkworth. Do you know what he said? "*I'm sure he was just messing about. No need to make a fuss. You'll only cause a lot of trouble and you'll never live it down. You'll just get a terrible reputation.*" He couldn't be bothered. I had nightmares. Still have them sometimes.' She put her head down on her knees.

'You must have had a terrible shock when you saw Guy again.'

Her voice was muffled. 'He's disgusting. He shouldn't be allowed to go anywhere near a child. He thinks about himself and no one else.'

'I agree with you. Why did you go back to Tir Melys? Why attend Jasmine's concert, where you knew you'd see Guy?'

She shot back, 'Why shouldn't I? I wasn't going to let him limit what I did. I enjoyed looking at him. I had power over him, I was making money out of him and he didn't realise. That gave me a lot of satisfaction. He was making retribution for what he'd done.'

'You're not squeaky clean yourself, though. You've been pressurising Elinor and using your abuse to abuse her. Caris regretted getting involved in it.'

Gwyn said, 'Did she tell you that?'

'More or less. When did you realise that Caris had told Afan about it?'

Her eyes widened. 'I didn't. Oh God, why did she go and do that?'

He believed that she was telling the truth. He had to take a risk and hoped it would pay off. 'Because she was troubled, and they were good friends. He was already helping her and Morgan with their life in Cardiff, so she turned to him. Caris had an awful lot going on and the situation with Elinor got too much for her.'

'Why didn't she tell me?'

He saw that she was trying to absorb the information. 'Because you were part of the problem. You'd have tried to persuade her not to talk to Afan about it, wouldn't you?'

'I suppose that's why she'd been so elusive recently. She was avoiding me.'

'Have you been selling the jewellery on to fund the shop?'

'And my dad's care bills.'

'I wondered if that was the case. You've been hemmed in by money worries. Unlike the Merchants, you haven't got a large asset to sell.'

She responded to his understanding tone. 'I'd have gone under by now if it hadn't been for the jewellery.'

He debated how much more he should divulge but decided to carry on. Unless he was completely mistaken, Gwyn wasn't blameless, but she wasn't a murderer. 'In the recording, Elinor goes on to say that Afan spoke to her about what Caris had told him. He was shocked at your and Caris's behaviour and said it had to stop. He told Elinor it was an impossible situation, and it would be best if she and Guy were honest with their social worker. Elinor said she told you about that conversation on the Wednesday before Afan died and that you were furious. You were going to tackle him about it.'

Gwyn hugged her knees closer. 'No, that's not true! She didn't! Elinor didn't tell me that Afan knew all about it, not until . . .' She pressed her lips shut.

If DI Weber was still leading this investigation, she'd crucify him for what he was about to do. But she was in a hospital bed, and she had made him her informal deputy. He pulled his chair a little closer to Gwyn. He kept his voice understanding and quiet. 'Listen carefully now. You see where this is going, don't you? You see what Elinor is trying to do?'

Her shock was making her slow-witted. 'What do you mean?'

'Elinor's pointing a finger in your direction. She's desperate to adopt a child. She'll stop at nothing. I don't think you murdered Afan, but do you know who did? I believe you took crockery and a book to place by him in the cairn. That's the kindest thing you've done in a while, Gwyn.'

She seemed about to weep again but she fought for control.

'Elinor rang me, late that Monday afternoon. She sounded hysterical. She said she'd killed Afan because he'd found out what Guy had done to me and was insisting that she told the adoption people. She didn't say how Afan knew, and I was too stunned to ask.' She faltered. 'Elinor ranted on and on about the baby she needed. She said that Afan's body was in the cairn. I was so shocked I went cold all over. She said I had to swear not to tell anyone what she'd done, or about Guy and the school. I managed to calm her down, and I swore I wouldn't say anything. How could I? If I did, it would all come out, everyone would hear about what happened to me and what I'd been doing to Elinor. I thought I'd be charged with blackmail or extortion. A crime, anyway. Caris, too, and that would have broken her mam's heart. If I was in prison, there'd be no one to visit my dad. I'd already paid money I owed for his care and there was no way I could give it back.' She hit her fists repeatedly on her knees. 'What could I do? I had to agree to do what Elinor asked. I told her not to say anything to Caris about it. It was best to keep it between us. I'm so, so sorry. Afan was your friend.' She broke down in tears and hid her face in her arm.

Swift's back ached and his face was raw. He was tired of hearing people express their sadness and regret. He just wanted to move this investigation on, get it over with and escape the toxic confines of Tir Melys. 'Afan was your friend too. You discussed local history, shared an interest in the past, learned Welsh together. You wanted to honour him in a way he'd understand. On Monday evening, you took the crockery and put it by his body. Then you went to his cottage at Tir Melys. You weren't aware of my arrival. You took the beekeeping book and placed it with him. I wondered about someone running that risk, but it makes sense that it was you.'

She sat up. 'I'd ordered that book for him, it was new. He loved it. I wanted him to have it by him. I had to do something. Say sorry.'

His anger spilled out. 'A self-indulgent act, surely?'

Gwyn recoiled. 'I . . . I'm . . .'

'No, don't say sorry again. You didn't consider calling the police anonymously, instead of leaving his body where anyone, a child maybe, would find it?'

'I didn't dare . . . I couldn't . . . Can't you see?'

Swift ignored her pleadings. He was picking through a maze of information, going back over what Elinor had told him. Things about her marriage. He was still unsure. He spoke sternly to Gwyn. 'You realise that you've allowed a second murder to happen by not informing the police about what Elinor told you?'

She'd been too intent on Afan's death to consider the angles. Now it dawned on her. 'Did Elinor murder Caris?'

He didn't answer. Further on in the recording, Elinor said that after Afan's death, Caris had told her she was going to reveal the truth about Guy. If Elinor was the killer, she must have pretended that she'd found Caris's body because she could no longer stand the strain of waiting for someone else to discover the corpse. He had one last question for Gwyn. 'Did you go back to Afan's cottage last Sunday?'

Her voice was flat. 'No. I haven't been to Tir Melys since I took the book, apart from the concert.' She made a helpless gesture and sank back in the chair.

It was probably Elinor, then, snooping around to see if I'd found out anything. She must have taken a key at some point. Swift called the landline at Tir Melys, hoping to get hold of Spencer. It rang out.

He stood at the window and watched the world go by. Low, bruised clouds promised another storm. Tir Melys, this tightly woven community of people circling and watching each other in a labyrinth of secrets, including Afan. A pressure cooker waiting to explode. They were defeating him. He was bamboozled by the intricacies. He leaned wearily against the sash window frame. Scraps of conversation came back to him, comments about illness, confidences, controlling behaviour and the sense of belonging that Tir Melys inspired. He ran through who had chosen to confide in whom and why, and a picture came into focus. Once again, he'd been viewing Tir Melys from the wrong perspective.

He glanced at Gwyn. Her eyes were closed, and tears slid down her cheeks. She wasn't about to go anywhere. 'Gwyn, you need to listen. I have to go. I want you to lock your door until the police come here. Do you understand?'

She swallowed. 'Will they arrest me?'

'Yes. Then you'll be safe. You could be in danger. Let me out now, then lock up the shop and come back up here and lock your door. Hurry now.'

She did as he instructed, moving slowly. He rang Spencer as he drove out of Holybridge and left a message on his voicemail. Then he called the police station and informed them that they needed to go to Gwyn Bowen's address immediately.

CHAPTER 20

The storm broke when Swift was a couple of miles from Tir Melys. Bright flashes of lightning cracked the sky. Thunder crashed and the rain poured. The light faded to a shadowy gloom. A dull dread filled him. His phone rang and he pulled in. It was DS Spencer. The signal faded in and out. Swift could hardly hear him.

'. . . message but I'm . . .'

Swift said, 'Are you still at Tir Melys?'

'No . . . need to see . . .'

'Where are you?'

'Forensics . . .'

The signal faded and the call died. Swift swore and reversed back up the road. He saw that he had one bar on his phone and texted Spencer. To his relief, it ticked sent.

Urgent. Come back to Tir Melys.

He drove on fast through sheets of water, hunched over the wheel, barely able to see the road. At Tir Melys, he drove past the car park into the community. No one was out in the sweeping rain. The gardens were forlorn. Elinor was right, the fruit would rot. Yet even under this lowering sky, he could appreciate the remote beauty of the place and see why it could inspire a passion to cling to the land.

He slowed and parked outside the Merchants' house. He eased from the car, catching his breath as his back spasmed, and stood for a moment in the deluge. All was silent except for the rolling thunder.

He knocked on the door, waited and then knocked again. Jasmine opened it. She was in a man's tartan dressing gown with the belt drawn tight and she had the fuddled eyes of someone who's just woken. He was taken aback to see her without a hat. Her thin hair was white and cropped. She put a hand to her head in embarrassment.

'I'm sorry. Did I wake you?'

She leaned against the door. 'I've just got up. It's been exhausting, having the police here again. So many questions, so much upset. We're all deeply shocked at Caris's murder. And to think that it happened on our land, in a holy place! Elinor is in a dreadful state. It's as if we've all been hit by a steamroller with these two terrible deaths. If you don't mind, we're really not up to visitors.'

'I don't want to intrude, but it's important.'

She said with a pleading catch in her voice, 'Can't it wait?'

'I'm afraid not.'

She shrugged and waved him in. Peter was sitting in the willow armchair to one side of the fire in the kitchen, listening to Mozart and conducting with his hand. He wore another fusty fawn cardigan and backless slippers. A grey sort of man, the kind you'd hardly notice. He glanced over at Swift and carried on conducting. It was warm and snug in the room with the glowing fire. Condensation clouded the windows. An empty casserole dish stood on the table, still smelling savoury and delicious. It would be hard to give this house up.

Jasmine shifted the kettle onto the hot plate of the Aga and threw teabags into a pot. 'Well, what is it?' She had to raise her voice over the music.

Swift pulled a chair out and sat at the table. 'Afan knew about the plan to sell Tir Melys.'

He wasn't sure that Peter had heard him. Jasmine stood with her hand on the kettle.

'What do you mean? How?' Her regal manner had vanished, replaced with anxiety.

'Bruno told him the week before he died.'

Jasmine turned to her husband. 'Peter, did you hear that?'

He didn't respond. *The Marriage of Figaro* played on, and his hand swept from side to side. She switched off the music. Peter went on conducting. The kitchen was silent, apart from the hiss of the kettle.

Swift repeated himself. 'Afan knew about the plan to sell Tir Melys the week before he died.'

'Why did Bruno tell him?' Jasmine asked.

'Because he wanted to see if Afan would loan him some money to buy you out.'

Jasmine rubbed her forehead, moved the kettle off the hotplate and sat down opposite Swift. 'Well . . . so what? Why have you come here to tell us that?'

She had no inkling. He stared across at Peter Merchant's defeated expression and understood that he'd reached the right conclusion. 'Ask your husband.'

She turned in her chair. 'Peter? What does he mean?'

Peter got up slowly and threw another log on the fire. He watched the flames lick it and then straightened a cast iron skillet above his head. From the back, he could be mistaken for an old man, but beneath his fogeyish clothes, he was sinewy from his yoga practice. He started across to the table, his slippers flapping on the flagged floor, and then stopped. He swayed a little. Swift rose and pulled a chair out for him, gestured for him to sit. A small kindness never went amiss at a time like this.

Swift sat back down. 'I believe that Afan spoke to you, Peter, after Bruno had told him about your plan to sell, and the plot that he and Bryn were hatching. Afan disliked all the underhandedness, on both sides. He realised how much you genuinely loved Tir Melys and longed to stay here. I've seen you looking heartbroken over the prospect of losing it. Afan understood that you're more approachable than Jasmine and likely to listen, more open to negotiation. He said that you needed to be honest with your tenants so as to find a way forward. I'm not sure that you intended to kill him.'

Jasmine gazed at her husband. 'Don't be ridiculous. Peter could never harm anyone. Tell him, Peter. Tell him this is nonsense.' Her voice faltered and died as he shook his head. He reached out and patted her hand.

'Quiet, now, Jasmine. You've always done most of the talking but this isn't your show. I'm tired. Tired of listening to you and tired of all the subterfuge and worry. And for what? We're losing it all anyway. You see, Ty, I'm counting on the peace and quiet of a prison cell. Sounds odd, I know. Will they let me weave willow? It's the kind of thing inmates do, isn't it?'

Swift wasn't going down the road of empathising with a killer. 'No idea. Did you ask Afan to meet you on the coast path?'

'That's right. Away from the community, by Carreg Trefin. A place to talk and sort stuff out. I just wanted a bit of time to keep things under wraps, try and find a way out of selling up. I reckoned I could talk to Bruno and Bryn in confidence, find a resolution. But Afan was so bloody preachy and insistent. He said it wasn't fair on everyone, conducting negotiations behind their backs. He wanted to call a meeting of the whole community to discuss it.' He sighed.

'Afan and his bloody principles,' Swift nudged.

'Exactly. If he could just have backed off a bit . . . I'd been mending a planter and I had the screwdriver in my pocket. Suddenly, I was fed up of people telling me what to do. Nag, nag, nag. Voices all the time, badgering me. I *love* this place — I have done since the moment I set eyes on it. It called to me then and it still does. Bruno might have a blood connection to it, but I have a spiritual one. Jasmine takes front of house with her harp playing, but it's my heartstrings that are plucked when I contemplate leaving here. I had my wife calling the shots at home, Bryn and Bruno ganging up on us, Afan on his high horse, Giles forever contacting us and bleating on. He's an adult, why can't he get himself out of his own mess? Why should I be uprooted because he's made bad decisions? I was furious. This is my home, but it was as if I had no say, no importance. Something went pop in my skull. I went for Afan, shoved the screwdriver into him just to shut him up. We were near the cairn. I dragged him in there. And left him. He'd dropped his phone on the ground. I knew you were arriving, so I sent you the email. I'm not even sure why I did that, because I didn't really care what happened. Then I came home.'

Swift was trying to link events and people. 'Did you throw away the screwdriver and Afan's phone?'

'No. I chucked them on the ground. I thought of jumping into the sea at that point, but I couldn't do it.'

Swift had most of the pieces now, but not all of them. He said to Jasmine, 'You gave your husband an alibi for that time frame.'

She shivered and clutched the collar of the dressing gown. 'I was asleep. I usually am around that time. I had no reason to think that Peter wasn't here. Oh, Peter, what have you done?'

He said weakly, 'Plenty. But I didn't kill Caris. If I had, I'd confess.'

Peter had nothing to lose now, no reason to lie. Swift realised who Caris's killer must be. A sudden alarm seized him as he considered the consequences of her body being found. He didn't want to leave the Merchants, but he had no choice.

'The police will be back here very soon,' he said. 'I have to go. Stay here, in this room, until DS Spencer arrives.'

He dashed to his car, hoping that he was wrong about what might take place. If he was right, he prayed he wouldn't be too late.

* * *

Swift coasted the car quietly near to Cuddfan. There were no lights on in the house but as he stepped onto the path, he heard a faint yelp. Then silence again.

He edged forward to the studio, approaching it from one side, past an overflowing rain barrel. There was a strong smell of rotting vegetation and the ground squelched beneath his boots. He saw a dim light inside. A high scream and then another pierced the air and he moved quickly to the door, taking in the grim scene at a glance.

Guy Brinkworth had Elinor by the throat and was slamming her head against a wall. Blood streamed from her mouth onto his hands. He could just hear Guy yelling, 'You stupid, stupid bitch! Do you realise what you've done! Fucking poking your nose in! Why can't you just *shut up*?' Elinor tried to twist away but Guy leaned in, pinning her back against the wall. Swift saw a shadow to one side of the door. Frankie lay dead on the floor, a drill bit sticking from his throat. His eyes were open and glassy.

Swift tried the door handle, but it was locked. He hammered on the wood, shouting, 'Stop! The police are on their way! Guy, stop! Open the door!'

Guy glanced behind him for a second. His expression was feral and intent. He seemed to stare through Swift, and then turned back to attacking his wife. Swift took a few paces back and aimed a couple of kicks to the side of the door lock. The wood gave way, and he aimed another hard kick with his heel. The door burst open and Swift was inside. Guy released Elinor and she slumped forward. He spun round and faced Swift. His hair was loose, streaming around his face and he was pale, his eyes burning.

Swift panted, 'Stop, Guy. It's over. Stop now.'

'I'll say when it's over. *I'll* say!'

Guy launched himself forward. As Swift dodged, his wet foot slipped on the wooden floor and he went down, hitting his head on the side of a display cabinet. Guy was on top of him, hands around his throat, squeezing. Swift's vision blurred and the light grew dimmer. He went deliberately limp, but Guy tightened his grip and the blood pounded in Swift's head. He heard Elinor scream and as he passed out, he was aware of a bang. He imagined that thunder had rolled into the room.

* * *

Swift had never been so glad to see DS Spencer's pudgy, beetroot complexion. He sat in Spencer's car, rubbing his throat. A paramedic had checked him over and pronounced that his airways were bruised but not compromised.

Spencer handed him a bottle of water and he took a few sips. He croaked, 'Is Elinor okay?'

'She's on her way to hospital. She saved you. Hit Guy on the back of the head with a soldering block. He's been taken away unconscious.' He bit his lip. 'I thought you were as dead as the dog when we got here. The boss would never have forgiven me. She likes you — I can tell.'

'I like her too,' Swift said. *God, I sound like a soppy teenager, must be the oxygen deprivation.* 'Did you arrest Gwyn?'

'Yeah. She's at the station. My mam's always said that Gwyn's a warm-hearted girl. She'll be dead shocked.' He gave a huge yawn. 'Sorry, it's like I haven't slept for a week.'

'You won't get much sleep for a while yet, with four suspects to process.'

Spencer grimaced. 'Still, the boss will be thrilled. I can't get my head round it all. What led you to Peter Merchant?'

'I'm not sure.' This case had been like stirring a sauce that refused to come together. In Gwyn's flat he'd hit the moment when it mysteriously thickened. 'I reckoned that Afan might have approached Peter after Bruno told him about the Merchants' plan. Jasmine has thyroid problems which make her tired. Bruno mentioned that she slept most afternoons, so she could well have been asleep on that Monday when Afan died. I'd gathered that Peter has much more of an emotional investment in this place than Jasmine. She's tougher and sees it as a business, whereas he loves Tir

Melys and hated the threat of losing it. He resented his son and didn't see why he and Jasmine had to bail him out. I'd seen him doing yoga and although he seems feeble, he'd have the strength to kill and drag a man some distance. He's the quiet, slow-burn type who could flip and that led me to think that if Afan had cornered him, he could have lashed out.' Maybe it had been Elinor's comment that every worm turns that had led him to Peter. His brain was tired.

'Yeah, Peter's always seemed more of a mouse than a man.' Spencer gazed at Swift with the kind of devotion that Frankie used to bestow on Elinor. 'What about Guy? What made you suspect that he was going to harm Elinor?'

Swift sipped more water, holding it in his mouth and letting it ease down his throat. 'I wasn't sure, but once I'd spoken to Gwyn, I thought again about Elinor's smoke and mirrors technique. She was desperate, and she'd have done anything to preserve her marriage and the chance of adopting a child. Despite her confession to Gwyn, I just couldn't see her as a killer. I could only assume that she thought Guy had killed Afan, so she panicked and was covering up for him. That was the sole reason she'd make such a claim.' He coughed. 'I remembered Suki saying that Guy monitored Elinor and listened in on her conversations. He could well have overheard Afan talking to her about Caris and Gwyn, and the conversation when Caris said she was going to expose him. He could have decided to murder Caris to shut her up. He didn't care about the adoption — he's never really wanted a child. That was just a way of keeping Elinor busy and onside. He enjoyed needling the social worker too. It made him feel superior, which is when Guy's in his comfort zone. I'd bet money that he'd forgotten all about the miserable girl in the playground and her annoying little tale of woe. But when he overheard the details and recalled the incident, he wouldn't have wanted Gwyn's story to go public. Dr Brinkworth would have lost face and status, maybe even have become a pariah. Fingers would point.'

'Hurt pride,' Spencer said.

'Exactly.' Swift tried a gentle neck roll. It hurt, but it was bearable. He did another, anticlockwise. 'Guy must have concealed Caris's body in the hope that she wouldn't be found for a while. Maybe he wanted to buy time. She might have been in that cold chamber for weeks before anyone noticed a smell or stepped in there. I believe that Gwyn might have been his next victim if he'd believed there was a chance that she'd talk. Then the news broke about the Merchants wanting to sell up, and Elinor became even more distraught and as Guy would see it, emotionally incontinent. She told me that they'd been rowing and her attitude to him had become less sympathetic. They were both under enormous strain. He's a vindictive, callous bastard. I reckoned that once he found out that Elinor had stumbled on Caris's body, he might well feel trapped and see that as a betrayal. I worried that he'd turn his fury on her.' His throat throbbed. He slumped back in the car seat.

Spencer pursed his lips. 'I never liked him. He was well up himself.'

'Sometimes people are as rotten as they appear.'

'Well this is a right old kettle of fish and no mistake,' Spencer said, scratching his head.

Swift splashed water from the bottle on his face and massaged his neck. That was one way of putting it.

CHAPTER 21

Swift stood in Afan's shed, sticking labels on his friend's last batch of mead. When he'd finished the bottles, he crated them. They were now ready for the gathering after Afan's funeral. He stood over them for a moment. A final offering.

In the cottage, he took a couple of painkillers. His throat had improved but his back still ached. His beard had grown, and the constant rain and wind had whipped his hair into a knotted mess. If his cousin Mary could see him now, she'd ask him if he was going to audition for Captain Kidd.

He was going to clean and tidy the cottage before he left, but there was something he needed to do first. He drove to an address on the far side of Holybridge, near the warehouse where Caris had worked. He examined the car parked outside the rundown semi and noted the scrapes on the passenger side. He took out his Swiss Army knife and slashed the four tyres. When he rang the bell, a beefy man eating a chicken wing opened the door.

'Calvin Callender?'

'Yeah.'

Swift pushed through the door, barging Callender backwards. The chicken wing flew through the air. Callender stumbled and Swift moved in fast, pinning him, face against the wall, with an armlock. The force made his back throb but Callender was hurting more.

'You need to listen. If you say anything, I'll break your arm. I might break the other one too, just to give you a matching pair. Nod.'

Callender nodded. Swift wasn't an aggressive man but if he was pushed far enough, he didn't mind using the techniques he'd learned in Police College. Bullies were always cowards, which was just as well, as Callender was twice his size. He pressed on the arm just to cause some pain. Callender moaned.

'I didn't like you driving your car at me. You've damaged my handsome face. Who gave you my name and Morgan's number?'

'What's it to you?'

Another twist of the arm.

'S . . . Seth did.

'Seth who?'

'Ouch! Howard.'

'Who's he?'

'A cleaner at the cop shop.'

'How did he get them?' He forced the arm a bit higher.

'Christ! Don't! He was just earwigging. Why are you—?'

Swift leaned in. Callender smelled awful — sweat, chicken grease and something rancid. 'I've appointed myself Morgan's guardian angel. If you go anywhere near him, if you even turn his way, I'll send people to do you horrible damage. You're messing with London bad boys now, Calvin. Ever heard of the Krays?'

'Y . . . Yeah.'

'This lot makes them seem like teddy bears at a picnic. You've no idea who I do business with. Nod to tell me you understand.'

Callender nodded.

'Say, "I'm way out of my league." Nice and loud.'

'I'm w . . . way out of my league.'

'Good. Now go and have a shower. You stink.'

Back in his car, he took a breath. He doubted that Afan would have approved of the violence but on this occasion, he'd surely have turned a blind eye.

* * *

Afan's funeral was at the end of the second week of September, a day of blustery, intermittent showers. After the brief humanist service at the crematorium, about twenty people adjourned to Blasus. Sofia Weber wasn't at the service, but she was in the café, resting in a chair. She was pale and gaunt. She'd drawn her hair back in a tight pleat that emphasised the hollows of her face. Swift was shocked, she must have lost a stone in weight.

'I'm just making a guest appearance. Can't stay for long, too much to do,' she told him. She was still wearing her long coat and patterned DMs, but she'd made an effort to smarten up with black trousers and a navy shirt.

He could see that the stuffing had been knocked out of her. 'I'm not sure you should be here at all.'

'Well . . . on the plus side, my ankle's better, so I no longer need the stick. I suppose that's progress. I wanted to pay my respects. Spence was at the crem, wasn't he?'

'He was there. He has a good voice. He and Bryn belted out "Bread of Heaven". Can I get you a coffee?'

'Please, nice and strong. And a biscuit. Can't face much solid food but that would go down nicely.'

He helped himself to a glass of mead and fetched coffee and chocolate biscuits for Sofia. On the way back to her, he made a Motown selection on the jukebox: 'The Tracks of my Tears', 'Baby Love', 'It Takes Two' and 'My Girl'.

Sofia sniffed the coffee. 'Ta. Have you been at Tir Melys all the time?'

'No. I didn't want to stay around the community. I'd had enough of it. They needed space to absorb what had happened and I craved hot water, so I went back to London.' He'd been relieved to get away and put the miles between himself and the blighted place.

'Glad to see you've shaved, and your face has mended. Now you just look as if a cat scratched you. You resembled Myrddin the Wild when you came to see me in hospital. You alarmed one of the nurses.'

'And he is?'

'A medieval bard and prophet.'

'I'll take that as a compliment. I picked up Amira at Cardiff airport on my way back yesterday. She's staying at the Bridge Arms. I'm heading home tonight.'

Sofia glanced across at Amira, who'd been cornered by Kat. 'She's got a good face. Characterful. I've always envied that kind of bronze complexion. Truth is, I hate French women. They're always sleek and comfortable in their own skins.'

'You strike me as a woman who's content in herself.'

She wriggled her eyebrows. 'I will be, once I've got a functioning arm again. It was good of Amira to come. She and Afan must have parted amicably. She deserves better than Pippi Longstocking bending her ear.'

'Amira can hold her own.' In the car, she'd said little, taking in the scenery and asking a few questions about the funeral arrangements. He saw her put a hand on Kat's shoulder, a kind but deliberate parting gesture before she moved away to speak to Bruno. He said, 'Caris's funeral next.'

'Next week.'

'I won't be back for that. I need to stay in London to see my daughter.'

She smiled and said, 'I bet you're a fun dad.'

His spirits lowered at the tussles over Branna that lay ahead. 'I hope so.'

Sofia seemed to read his mood and hesitated, as if she was about to ask something further, but instead she said, 'I hear they're coping at Tir Melys.'

'They seem okay. Jasmine Merchant is lying low, she's rarely seen. I believe she sent a wreath for Afan but she decided not to attend today. Licking her wounds. Bryn and Bruno are forging ahead with the purchase. Kat and Suki are staying on. With the Brinkworths gone, there'll be an empty house. I talked to Bruno and he and Bryn have agreed to ask Morgan Callender if he'd like to move in and work there. Bruno would train him in beekeeping. I've advised them to put him on a sort of probation period if he accepts. He'd need to prove himself, up his game.'

'Spence's mum has been working on him. It might succeed. That lad needs a structure. But wouldn't Morgan worry that Calvin might seek him out?'

Swift hid behind his mead. 'That problem seems to have resolved itself. Can I get you another coffee?'

'No. I'm heading home in a min.' She circled an accusing finger at him. 'You should have told me about finding those sets of keys.'

'I know.'

'Hmm. The conversations you had with Elinor and Gwyn, not to mention the Merchants, were completely out of order.'

'It was a gamble, but what else could I do?'

She relented. 'You did right. Guy might have killed Elinor if you hadn't got to her when you did.'

'Don't forget Spencer. He didn't dawdle when he finally got my text and he did well in the end, getting Elinor to open up and talk. His puppy-dog eyes paid off. She always did prefer talking to Frankie. If you push Spence enough in the right direction, he gets there.'

'Most days, I'd like to push him off the bridge up the road.' Sofia sighed. 'I shouldn't be so hard on him. He sent me the biggest box of chocolates I've ever seen.' She leaned forward. 'Now, I've been disentangling the threads that were knotted around Tir Melys. I've interviewed Guy Brinkworth. That was an enjoyable chunk of my life. He corrected me on my use of "pertain", instructing me that I should have said "appertain", plus a wordy explanation of meanings and contexts that I won't bore you with.'

'Thank you for that.'

'He acknowledged that he overheard conversations that Elinor had with Caris and Afan about the incident with

Gwyn. That stressed him out. He commented that he might well have killed Afan himself, if Peter hadn't got there first.'

Swift loosened his tie and stretched his legs out. 'Yes, Peter did him a huge favour. Can you give me the details about what happened on the coastal path that day?'

'I expect that's allowed, and no one's listening. I've watched all the interviews with Elinor. She was used to reading Guy and interpreting his moods. He was jittery on that Monday before he went out — worrying about his past catching up with him. She went for a walk in the meadow late afternoon and decided to go along a little bit of the coastal path. She saw Guy in the distance, cycling fast towards her. That surprised her. He didn't usually cycle the coast path because of the stiles. He stopped and threw something into the sea. Then he air-pumped with his fist. She was alarmed, so she hid behind some gorse bushes and waited until he passed by. She saw that he appeared strange and very pale. When he'd cycled away, she walked along the path and saw Afan dead in the cairn. His eyes were open, and she slipped gloves on and closed them. She zipped up his cagoule too.'

Swift drank some mead. A flash of sun danced through the window on Sofia's freckles. 'Elinor and Gwyn were like those women who used to attend to the dead — making him ready and placing familiar things around him.'

Sofia wasn't impressed. 'So kind of them. As you know, Elinor can't keep things in. She believed that her husband had killed Afan because he always felt inferior to him, and it sent her into a panic. She'd no idea then that Guy had snooped on their conversations about Gwyn and Caris. Guy had seen the body as he cycled past the cairn and was overjoyed. He'd been wondering what to do about the growing problem of Afan, Gwyn and Caris. He'd been somewhat reassured when he'd heard that Gwyn didn't want anyone knowing about her assault at school, but he was vulnerable now that Afan wanted to expose his part in it. Because he's a nasty, malicious man he decided to collect the phone and weapon and throw them in the sea. Do the killer a big favour by way of thanks. His fist-pumping was sheer delight that someone had disposed of a man he hated, and who posed a threat to his comfy life.'

'Doesn't say much for the marriage, though, that Elinor immediately thought her husband was a murderer.'

'It certainly unravelled her. She needed to keep Guy safe at all costs, so that the adoption could proceed. She worried that once the police started to ask questions, Gwyn's school experience might come out and their plans would collapse. She walked around for some time, worrying at it. She knew that Gwyn didn't want the incident to become public knowledge. If she told Gwyn she'd killed Afan because he'd discovered what had happened at the school, that would ensure Gwyn kept quiet. Bind her in, make her part of the awful secret. She didn't weigh up what Caris might do or say in the aftermath. She was too muddled and confused, with her world crumbling. As soon as she found Caris's body, she must have suspected that Guy had killed her. She's on suicide watch at present. The loss of the dog seems to be affecting her as much as anything. She's got his ashes, apparently. Sleeps with them under her pillow.'

There was a crash. Spencer had dropped a plate of sandwiches on the floor. Sofia shook her head. 'He's a *pendafad*, but he's my *pendafad*. Well . . . I have to get back to the station. I can't leave this complex case to the tender mercies of Spence. It's been good to work with you.'

'You too. Maybe we can meet when you're in better health.'

'Maybe we can.' She put her good hand out and smiled. 'Take care, Lone Ranger. It's been interesting.'

He saw her out to her cab. The fleeting sun struck her hair and gleamed on dark gold strands as she climbed in carefully. Her coat snagged in the door and she had to yank it in. Her eyebrows danced. He waved as the cab departed. He was caught by a pang, a sensation of loss.

The day grew gloomy as the afternoon wore on. A sharp breeze whipped the trees. Swift walked Amira to the Bridge

Arms. She was wearing a thin wool coat over a linen dress and shivered.

'This must be a shock after the warmth of Lyon,' Swift said.

'Certainly is. But sadness chills you too, doesn't it?'

'It does.'

'I haven't had a drink yet,' she said at the pub door. 'Will you have one with me before you go, to toast Afan?'

The pub was quiet, the fire glowing warmly. They sat beside it with their glasses of Malbec. Swift could see how Amira had matured in the years since he'd last seen her. She was more composed, but she still had the open, frank expression that he remembered.

'This is good wine. I needed it. Afan loved absinthe but I've never developed a taste for it,' she said.

'I haven't drunk it in years. Probably not since I last sat in a bar with Afan.'

They sat quietly for a while. 'I've been going over everything,' she said, regarding him with her almost black, cat-shaped eyes. 'Afan was beset by other people's problems. They all came to him for help: Morgan and Caris, Bruno, Kat, Elinor with her marital woes and then Caris again, with her story about Guy and Gwyn. It demonstrates what a good, kind man he was but my goodness! He was just trying to live a simple life, but they wouldn't let him.'

Swift agreed. 'He was too kind, too willing to listen. If he could have concentrated on his bees and mead, he'd still be with us. But unless you're a hermit, hiding out in the chapel, there's no such thing as a simple life. Wherever there are groups of people, there are problems. Jealousy, cruelty, rancour, betrayal — Tir Melys had its fair share.'

'More than its fair share, I'd say. Oh, Ty, you came here expecting to have a pleasant break with an old friend and see what you stepped into!'

'Hmm.' *Typical of you*, Ruth had said. *Nothing can ever be straightforward. Have you ever thought that trouble seems to follow you around?* Not that he expected any sympathy from that quarter these days. Although, to be fair to her, she had accepted his wish to discuss the wedding with Branna.

'How did Guy get Caris alone so that he could stab her?' she asked.

'I've heard the outline. He decided that she posed too much of a risk after he heard her saying that she couldn't keep quiet about Gwyn.' He paused. 'Although Caris carried a lot of angst and guilt about that, I'm not sure that she would have gone public. She had too much to lose, just as Gwyn had, and her overriding instinct was to protect Morgan and her mother.'

'So she died needlessly.'

'Quite possibly. Guy phoned Caris while she was on the train back from Cardiff, sounding guilty and remorseful. He told her that he needed to make amends and was trying to work out the best way forward. He said he was desperate not to do anything to impede the adoption, because it meant everything to Elinor. He begged Caris to meet him and talk it over. She agreed. He picked her up on the edge of town and said he'd like to speak to her in the chapel, where it would be private and quiet. He promised to have her home in time to cook lunch. He must have put on a good show of appearing genuine and repentant. In the chapel, he stood near the hermit's chamber and then pushed Caris in and stabbed her.'

Pain crossed Amira's face. She took a drink of wine. 'How ironic, that Elinor found her body.'

'That was a traumatic time for Elinor. Bryn had just announced that the Merchants were planning to sell Tir Melys. Despite all her efforts and sacrifices, her covering up for Guy, she saw the chances of adopting a child slipping away. Then, after a row with Guy, she found Caris. Even then, she tried to protect him and make Gwyn a suspect.'

'Will Peter and Guy get long sentences?' Amira asked.

'Hard to predict. The minimum for murder is fifteen years. Elinor's mental health will be taken into account. She told me that I must find her "unhinged". She was driven to the edge and I'm not sure she'll come back from there.'

'And Gwyn Bowen?'

'She's on bail. Who can tell how things will go for her? Guy failed her when he had a duty of care so that will be considered. But in the end, she was a criminal.'

'Such a sad young woman.'

'I'm sad for her, but sadder for the victims. I'm sorry for the loss of Caris but it's Afan I grieve for.' It hardly seemed to matter now, but he'd wondered which of the many problems Afan had wanted to talk to him about. Given the timing, he'd decided that it must have been the situation with Kat. That was personal and would have made his friend uneasy. Afan would have been unable to see any end to the constant pressure. He told Amira.

She bit her lip. 'What would you have said to Afan about that?'

'The only thing I could have said — stop paying her, stop the manipulation. Forgive yourself for what happened at Ogmore.'

'You were a good friend.'

Not in the end. 'I'd have tried to be when I was here, if I'd had the chance.'

Amira raised her glass. 'Here's to Afan. *Adieu*.'

'*Adieu*.' Swift clinked his glass to hers.

The fire crackled. Raindrops blew against the window beside them. Swift watched the sprays of water and drank deeply. *Fountain rain*.

THE END

ALSO BY GRETTA MULROONEY

THE TYRONE SWIFT SERIES
Book 1: THE LADY VANISHED
Book 2: BLOOD SECRETS
Book 3: TWO LOVERS, SIX DEATHS
Book 4: WATCHING YOU
Book 5: LOW LAKE
Book 6: YOUR LAST LIE
Book 7: HER LOST SISTER
Book 8: MURDER IN PEMBROKESHIRE

DETECTIVE SIV DRUMMOND SERIES
Book 1: THESE LITTLE LIES
Book 2: NEVER CAME HOME

Thank you for reading this book.

If you enjoyed it please leave feedback on Amazon or Goodreads, and if there is anything we missed or you have a question about, then please get in touch. We appreciate you choosing our book.

Founded in 2014 in Shoreditch, London, we at Joffe Books pride ourselves on our history of innovative publishing. We were thrilled to be shortlisted for Independent Publisher of the Year at the British Book Awards.

www.joffebooks.com

We're very grateful to eagle-eyed readers who take the time to contact us. Please send any errors you find to corrections@joffebooks.com. We'll get them fixed ASAP.

Printed in Great Britain
by Amazon

13946663R00155